HE SEES YOU
YOU
WHEN YOU'RE SLEEPING

HE SEES YOU
WHEN YOU'RE SLEEPING

A Novel

ALTA HENSLEY

An Imprint of HarperCollins*Publishers*

HE SEES YOU WHEN YOU'RE SLEEPING. Copyright © 2024 by HarperCollins. Excerpt from HE KNOWS WHEN YOU'RE AWAKE © 2025 by HarperCollins. All rights reserved. Printed in the United States of America. No part of this book may be used or reproduced in any manner whatsoever without written permission except in the case of brief quotations embodied in critical articles and reviews. For information, address HarperCollins Publishers, 195 Broadway, New York, NY 10007. In Europe, HarperCollins Publishers, Macken House, 39/40 Mayor Street Upper, Dublin 1, D01 C9W8, Ireland.

HarperCollins books may be purchased for educational, business, or sales promotional use. For information, please email the Special Markets Department at SPsales@harpercollins.com.

hc.com

FIRST AVON A TRADE PAPERBACK PUBLISHED 2025.

Designed by Diahann Sturge-Campbell

Holly illustration © Federico Panzano/Stock.Adobe.com

Library of Congress Cataloging-in-Publication Data has been applied for.

ISBN 978-0-06-343395-3

25 26 27 28 29 LBC 5 4 3 2 1

To Ava & Kenna. I told you . . . Flowers & Rainbows

CONTENT WARNING

This book contains some dark elements:

Stalking
Nonconsensual snow shoveling
Dominance & submission
Impact play
Voyeurism
Forced Christmas Joy
Exhibitionism
Hidden cameras
Possessive love
Graphic sex
Wearing of ugly Christmas sweaters

Proceed with caution . . .

Fa la la fucking la.

I can't lie in bed all morning avoiding the day, and yet here I am.

The Christmas lights strung on the large snow-covered hedge outside my window do little to get me in the spirit of what needs to happen for the day. The reflections of the twinkling lights dance on the frosted windowpane, creating a myriad of colors. But it all feels hollow.

I draw in a deep breath, tasting pine and cinnamon from the scented candle I've kept lit since first waking in a failed attempt to get me in the mood for work.

Chloe Hallman, social media influencer, can't exactly be a Scrooge during the holidays. Especially when you're the brand ambassador for Moth to the Flame Designs, a jewelry company that makes a huge portion of their annual profits this time of year.

But right now, I'm a stark contrast to the polished, always cheerful Chloe Hallman who adorns Instagram feeds and social media timelines. The festive cheer, the joyful banter, and the lively pictures of me draping costume jewelry on with cherry cheeks are all part of the job. Chloe Hallman is a brand, an icon of merriment in the wintry days of December. But that's not me, not today. Today, I'm just Chloe.

With a sigh, I throw back the cozy quilt and swing my legs over the edge of the bed. My feet touch the icy wooden floor as I rummage through my closet for a suitable outfit—something green and red perhaps, with a touch of gold. A laugh that should feel natural surfaces as I pull out a rather ostentatious Christmas jumper.

Remind me again why people love these things?

My phone rings, and I know there are only a few people in my life that would call me rather than text. Glancing at the screen, I see it's Aunt Sue. Of course it's her.

I hesitate for a moment before answering, the gaudy jumper still dangling from my other hand.

"Hi, Aunt Sue," I say, trying to inject some cheer into my voice.

"Oh, sweetie! I'm so glad I caught you. I know you couldn't make it to Thanksgiving this year, but we'd really love to have you for Christmas. I know flights are atrociously expensive right now, but I saw Southwest was running a deal to Phoenix and they really have improved their customer service, and . . . yeah, anyway, I thought I'd give you a call." Her voice is as warm and syrupy as ever.

I grimace, glad she can't see my face. "I really appreciate the invite, but—"

"I know you said you're allergic to cats, but they have great medicine for that now and—"

"Aunt Sue," I interrupt, pinching the bridge of my nose. "It's not just about the cats."

There's a pause on the other end of the line, and I can almost hear the gears turning in her head. "Oh," she says, her voice dropping an octave.

"It's a really busy time of year for me with work."

There's an awkward silence. "I know your mother wouldn't want you to be alone during the holidays," she begins. "And—"

"Aunt Sue, please." I cut her off, my voice sharper than I intend. I take a deep breath, softening my tone. "I know you mean well, but I'm not alone. I have friends here, and plans."

It's not entirely a lie. I have friends, even if our plans are more of the "maybe we'll grab a drink" variety than anything concrete.

"Well, if you change your mind . . ." She trails off, hope still lingering in her voice.

"I'll let you know," I say, knowing I won't.

We spend the next ten minutes catching up and having small talk, but I can still sense her disappointment.

As I hang up the phone, a wave of guilt washes over me. I'm not allergic to cats, for one. And I could easily make the trip to Phoenix. My excuses are weak. I know Aunt Sue means well, but the thought of spending Christmas with my extended family, surrounded by reminders of my parents and how much we all loved the holiday season, is more than I can bear.

I toss the gaudy jumper onto the bed and sink down next to it, running my fingers over the scratchy fabric. Mom would have loved this monstrosity. She always had a flair for the dramatic when it came to holiday attire.

A sudden shout from outside interrupts my thoughts. I quickly make my way to the window, pressing my face against the frosted glass to get a better look. Outside, my eighty-two-year-old neighbor is lying in a heap of snow with a shovel next to him.

I watch as Mr. Haven groans, attempting to pull himself off his snow-lined walkway. His elderly body disagrees with his effort, and I wince in sympathy.

"Stay there, Mr. Haven!" I shout. "I'm coming out to help."

Shoving my feet into the nearest pair of boots, I barely pause to grab a coat before rushing out the door. The frigid New York winter air hits me like a punch in the stomach, but I push through it, trudging through the thick layer of snow from last night's storm.

"Are you hurt? You should have asked me for help," I chide as I look his body over for any visible injury. "What are you doing shoveling your walk by yourself?"

"Was trying to get the path cleared before the mailman comes. Didn't think I'd be taking a tumble."

I glance over at my shoveled walkway. There is hardly a speck of snow on mine courtesy of the landlord. Why in the hell he'd shovel my side in our row of connected town houses and not Mr. Haven's makes no sense.

"You should have knocked on my door, Mr. Haven," I scold as I attempt to get him off the ground. His hand trembles in mine, frail and cold, making me feel guilty for having been sulking indoors, cocooned in my flannel blanket by the warmth of the cinnamon-scented candle.

"Let me help," a man who is walking his dog calls out from the other side of the street. His bulky figure is almost hidden beneath layers of thermal clothing, cheeks reddening in the cold, and a beanie pulled down low over his ears. The dog is a large husky, its tail wagging excitedly at us. "Are you hurt?" he asks as he ties the dog to the porch railing and kneels down beside Mr. Haven.

"I don't think so," Mr. Haven responds, his voice shaky from the cold, or perhaps from the fall.

"I'm a firefighter. If you'd allow me, I'd like to check you over to be sure nothing is broken before we get you standing?" he offers, his own breath frosting in the air as he speaks.

His eyes are kind, a bright green that stands out against the white winter wonderland. They flicker toward me, offering a small smile as he continues his examination of Mr. Haven, whose color seems to be returning.

"I'm Jack," the stranger introduces himself after ensuring Mr. Haven is not seriously injured, extending a gloved hand toward me. His name slips from his lips with an air of familiarity as if it's been etched into the corner of my mind.

"Chloe," I reply, shaking his hand and trying not to shiver from something other than the snow-laden breeze. "And this is Mr. Haven. Someone who should not be out here shoveling his own walkway."

Jack's eyes crinkle at the corners as he smiles, or maybe grimaces— hard to tell. "Right, then, Mr. Haven," he says, helping the man to his feet once again. "How about you take it easy for the rest of today?" He picks up the shovel and adds, "You let Chloe help you inside, and I can finish up what you started."

Mr. Haven tries to protest, but he's clearly outmatched by both of our determined expressions. With a bemused shake of his head, he concedes, leaning heavily on my shoulder as we make our way slowly toward his front door.

The husky, evidently finished with its bout of curious sniffing, darts forward to meet us at the entrance. Blue eyes glinting, it nuzzles into Mr. Haven's unsteady grip, drawing a genuine smile from the old man.

I glance over my shoulder at Jack, who is now industriously shoveling, his broad back moving with the effort. The snow seems to have picked up again, fat flakes falling steadily and muffling the sounds of the city.

"Thank you, Jack," I say, my voice carrying over the wind. He pauses to acknowledge my appreciation with a nod and a wave of the hand before continuing on.

Inside, Mr. Haven's home is warm and comforting, smelling of old books and coffee. I help him take off his heavy coat and hat, guide him to his recliner by the fireplace where his calico cat, Miss Patches, is curled up. She raises her head at our entrance, letting out an indignant meow as if scolding us for disturbing her peace. As Mr. Haven settles into the cushions, I notice a faint sigh of relief escape his lips.

"I'm going to make you some tea to warm you up," I tell him, heading toward the kitchen. I fill up the kettle with water and set it on the stove, the gas flame dancing under the cold metal. "So why didn't you wait for the landlord to shovel your path?"

"That old coot?" he says from the other room. "He's good for one thing only and that's cashing our checks at the beginning of the month."

"That's not true," I argue. "He shoveled mine. In fact, he always does." Not only has he been shoveling my walkway after every storm, but he also hung the Christmas lights outside my window. Granted, it was a single and simple strand of lights on my tall shrub, but I appreciated the effort.

"Ha! Not that lazy fool. I've known Lionel for years, and that man hasn't stepped a foot on this property since . . . who knows?"

I reenter the living room with the steaming mugs. "But if he didn't, then who did?" I ask, handing Mr. Haven his tea.

He chuckles, cradling the mug between his gnarled hands. "Maybe Santa's elves. Or you have yourself a helpful stalker."

CHAPTER TWO
JACK

How many nights have I done this now? Lurking, watching, waiting. It's become an addiction I can't control.

I crouch low beneath the window, careful not to disturb the freshly fallen snow since the last time I secretly shoveled. Can't leave any trace that I was here.

I can't stop myself from coming back, night after night. The thrill of observing unseen, of peering into a life not my own, has sunk its hooks deep into me. I tell myself each time will be the last, that I'll break free of this compulsion.

But I can't.

For some reason, I can't stop.

My breath forms small clouds in the frigid air as I slowly raise my head, enough to peer over the windowsill. The warm glow from inside spills out, a stark contrast to the darkness enveloping me. There she is. . . .

Noticing the snow around me, my thoughts return to this morning. To seeing Chloe face-to-face. I had touched her. Barely, but our hands had touched. I can still feel the warmth of her skin, the softness of her fingers as they brushed against mine when I helped her with her neighbor. Seeing Mr. Haven splayed out on his snow-covered walkway this morning made me feel like a real dick. Over the past few years, I've been shoveling Chloe's walkway after a snowstorm for three reasons.

The first is because snow means footsteps. Footsteps mean evidence. And the last thing I need is my boot prints leading a trail to right outside her window.

The second reason is it gives me comfort. It reminds me of when I was a kid, when my mother was still alive and we were a small family. I would shovel walkways to earn extra cash so I could buy my mom chocolate-covered cherries and a perfume called Charlie Blue at the neighborhood drugstore.

The third reason is . . . well . . . I don't want Chloe to slip.

And yet, I let that poor man suffer that exact fate.

I made a commitment right then and there as I was lifting the man off the ground that I'd keep his walkway as clean as I keep Chloe's.

The neighbor's calico cat brushes against my legs, her furry body a sudden warmth in the night air. I reach down to shoo her away, hands trembling slightly from the adrenaline pumping through my veins.

"Shoo," I hiss under my breath. "You're going to give me away."

The cat merely blinks up at me with luminous eyes before slinking off into the shadows cast by the tall hedges lining the property. I press back against the prickly branches, heart still hammering in my chest as I try to collect myself.

Even though I'd consider myself a pro at this stalking game, I'm never truly at ease. The fear of getting caught always remains.

These hedges are the only thing keeping me concealed from prying eyes—the only barrier between myself and discovery. Even so, I know I'm taking a huge risk every time I stand outside Chloe's bedroom window.

A car drives by on the street, headlights sweeping across the yard. I duck down instinctively, heart racing. The neighbor's porch light flicks on suddenly. I freeze, scarcely daring to breathe. Has someone seen me? But no, it's the motion sensor. Still, it's a stark reminder of how precarious my position is.

I should go. I know I should go. But I can't tear myself away, not yet. Just a few more minutes, I tell myself. Always just a few more minutes.

I glance at my watch, the glowing hands telling me I have one hour until eleven thirty—before the lights come on. I need to make the most of my time. The last thing I want is to be lit up with red and green and give Chloe a heart attack as she sees me staring back at her from the other side of the glass pane. But at least for now, I'm in the dark, and she's distracted by her work.

The old windows and building work to my advantage, amplifying the noises within.

Her voice is clear and bright. Sitting in front of her phone, set up on a stand, her face lit up with enthusiasm, she describes her latest piece.

"You guys, look at this one," she says as she caresses the red jeweled necklace resting on her perfect collarbone. "It's chunky, but perfect for a holiday party. Has a sort of retro vibe but is also modern. It's the right blend to be a great conversation piece. And the red color is spot on for all the holiday colors we're wearing this time of year. And the price is right on budget. I'd give this a ten out of ten for sure."

Because of my nightly visits, I know more about jewelry than any man in my profession should know. Firefighters know fires and smoke, not gold and silver. But Chloe's passion is infectious, and I found myself drawn to her more and more as each addicting night took hold.

I know every detail of her curvy frame, the way she sits upright when showing off a particularly dazzling piece, or how she tucks a loose strand of dark brown hair behind her ear when pondering about some jewelry design.

I've memorized her schedule, her mannerisms, the way her eyes light up when she's truly excited about a piece. It's become an obsession, watching her jewelry videos late into the night, my phone screen illuminating my face in the darkness of my apartment.

Except for the times, like now, that I stand outside her window in the cold. Watching. Obsessing. Stalking.

I've viewed her videos so many times that I can practically lip-sync along with her enthusiastic descriptions. My breath fogs the air as I inch closer, careful to stay hidden. I should leave. I know I should. But I can't tear myself away from the warm glow of her room, the sight of her biting her lower lip in concentration. Just a few more minutes, I tell myself. Just a little longer.

"Next up," I hear her say. "I have something from my personal collection."

She reaches for a small, velvet box and cradles it carefully in her hands.

"My mother's," she murmurs to the camera with a softness in her voice that makes my heart clench. "I guess I'm sharing this with you guys because . . . well, it's the holiday season. And she always loved the holidays. She wasn't one to dress up or get extra fancy, but the holidays were the one time when she would. Jewelry was always part of it."

She opens the box slowly, careful not to disrupt the contents within. I strain my eyes to see from my vantage point.

Inside is a ring, a gemstone brilliantly catching and refracting the light from her lamp. A blue sapphire, cut in the shape of an oval surrounded by little diamonds, glints back at me.

"It's not the most valuable piece in the world," Chloe says softly, almost reverently. She lifts it out of its velvet confines to show it off to her followers. "But it was hers. And now it's mine."

A pang of guilt hits me like a punch to the gut as I realize the depth of my intrusion. Despite the physical distance, despite the hidden nature of my presence, I'm invading one of her most intimate moments—sharing something personal about her family.

Yes, she's telling all her viewers, but she isn't telling me.

Yet, I can't tear away from this scene as she gingerly puts her mother's ring on her finger. Even from my distance, I can see her eyes well up with tears even as she tries to keep her composure.

"But that's enough about me." She suddenly blinks away the wetness in her eyes and forces a smile for her audience. "Let's move on to something brighter."

She reaches for another item from her table, but I find myself unable to concentrate on what she's saying next.

My thoughts are mired in guilt, confusion, a longing I've been trying to suppress. In the anonymity of the shadows, I fight a silent battle with myself as Chloe continues her show. She isn't aware of my presence, but here I am privy to every word she speaks, every emotion she displays. But it's not about me being a silent spectator; it's also about how these stolen moments are affecting me. How they're making me feel things I'd never considered before.

"All right, here we go. This one is a bit more fun and traditional for the holidays." She holds up a pair of reindeer-shaped silver earrings, their antlers adorned with tiny multicolored gems.

Suddenly, my phone vibrates in my pocket, providing an unwelcome distraction. A text from my chief—a structure fire alert. All hands needed. Duty calls. It's my night off, but it's not uncommon for me to get the call-ins, or my buddies asking if I can cover a shift for them. I'm single, have no kids or family needs, have no real life to speak of, and frankly, I love my job. Other than watching Chloe, I have little else on my plate. Pathetic yes, but the facts.

Good ol' Jack can bail you out.

Being a workaholic does pay off, however. I get a sweet deal to park my truck at the station a few blocks away from my apartment, which saves me a fortune.

I take one last look at Chloe, etching this moment into the corners of my memory. She's laughing now, her sorrow from a few moments ago replaced with unbridled joy as she talks about the next piece of jewelry.

As I get into my truck and drive off, I glance back at Chloe's house. The single strand of Christmas lights is about to turn on, like they are every night when I leave. And like always, I promise myself that this will be the last time I come around to watch her from afar.

But deep down inside, I know that's a lie.

Chloe Hallman is my drug.

CHAPTER THREE
CHLOE

Taking the ferry from St. George to Manhattan, I lean against the railing as the salty breeze whips through my hair. I should go inside as it's butt cold, but there's something about the view of the wall of glass and steel ahead of me that mentally prepares me for my meetings at Moth to the Flame Designs. I have to go through the steps of my hype game one more time. Deep breath in, deep breath out.

I am a creative powerhouse.

My ideas are fresh and innovative.

I wouldn't have been asked to be their brand ambassador if I didn't have the something something.

I've got this.

I only come into the office a couple times a week to pick up the jewelry they want me to showcase and attend a few meetings. You'd think I'd get used to it, but I always feel so out of my league when I walk into the building and face the sleek, polished interior and the impeccably dressed employees. But this is where I'll be expected to dazzle them with my social media prowess and convince them I'm worth every penny of my admittedly generous contract.

I straighten my secondhand blazer—although vintage and, in my opinion, trendy—and try to channel the confidence I mustered on the ferry. The elevator ride to the fourteenth floor feels endless, my stomach doing somersaults as I ascend.

As the doors open, I'm greeted by the familiar scent of leather and expensive perfume. I paste on my best influencer smile and strut toward the reception desk, my knockoff heels clacking on the marble floor.

"Good morning, Chloe," the receptionist chirps, her perfect teeth gleaming. "Sloane is waiting for you in the showroom."

"Thanks, Marissa," I reply, trying to match her enthusiasm.

The showroom door looms before me, and I take one last deep breath before pushing it open. The room is bathed in soft, flattering light that makes every piece of jewelry sparkle like stars.

Sloane, one of the designers, and someone I truly consider a friend, stands in the center of the room, her red hair swept into an elegant updo. She turns to me with a smile. "We have such great new pieces for the holidays. Wait until you see these."

As I approach Sloane, my eyes are immediately drawn to the dazzling array of jewelry spread out on the velvet-lined trays before her. Delicate gold chains adorned with shimmering crystals, bold statement pieces in vibrant gemstones, and intricately designed rings that catch the light from every angle. Though Moth to the Flame is known for affordable "costume jewelry," the pieces are always elegant and have a level of class that blows me away. It's a treasure trove of beauty, and for a moment, I forget my insecurities.

"Oh my god, Sloane," I breathe, my eyes widening as I take in the stunning collection. "These are absolutely gorgeous."

Sloane beams, her pride evident in her sparkling eyes. "I knew you'd love them. This season, we're really focusing on versatility and timeless elegance with a modern twist."

She picks up a delicate necklace, a teardrop-shaped moonstone pendant suspended from a fine gold chain. "This piece, for example, can be worn as a simple pendant or—" she deftly manipulates the chain "—converted into a lariat style for a more dramatic look."

I nod, envisioning the perfect way to showcase this adaptable piece. "That's brilliant. My followers will go crazy for the two-in-one aspect."

As Sloane continues to show me the collection, my initial nervousness fades away, replaced by genuine excitement. This is why I love what I do—the buzz of discovering new, beautiful things and sharing them with the world. My mind is already racing with ideas for photoshoots and video concepts to showcase these pieces.

"And here's the pièce de résistance," Sloane says, a mischievous glint in her eye. She reaches behind her and produces a velvet box, opening it with a flourish.

Inside lies a pair of earrings that take my breath away. They're chandelier-style, cascading with tiny, iridescent opals that catch the light and throw rainbows across the room. The design is intricate yet modern, a perfect balance of elegance and edge.

Opals were my mother's birthstone and her favorite.

"My mom would have adored these," I say, more to myself than to Sloane.

"I remember your mom always loved opals," Sloane says, her voice gentle. "That's part of why I chose this stone when I designed this piece. In memory of her great taste."

"Sloane . . ." I swallow back my emotion. "These are definitely going to be the star of the holiday collection," I say, my voice stronger now, infused with newfound confidence. "I have so many ideas for how to showcase them."

Sloane grins, clearly pleased with my reaction. "I can't wait to see what you come up with. Your creativity never ceases to amaze me."

As we continue to discuss the collection and brainstorm ideas for the upcoming social media campaign, my earlier doubts melt away. Yes, I may not fit the mold of the typical high-fashion influencer, but that's precisely what makes me valuable. My unique perspective and ability to connect with a diverse audience are why Moth to the Flame chose me.

By the time we wrap up our meeting, my mind is buzzing with excitement and inspiration. I carefully pack up the samples I'll be using for my content creation.

"We need to get drinks soon," she says. "I've been so busy, but I've missed seeing you outside of work."

"Absolutely," I agree, feeling a warmth spread through me at the invitation. "Maybe next week? I'll text you."

As I make my way back to the elevator, there's a newfound spring in my step. The insecurity that plagued me earlier has been replaced by a sense of purpose and belonging.

"Chloe!" I hear call from behind me.

Sigh . . . Tyler . . .

I turn reluctantly, plastering on a polite smile as Tyler, the marketing VP, hurries toward me. His perfectly coiffed hair doesn't move an inch as he jogs up, flashing me a toothy grin that doesn't quite reach his eyes.

"Glad I caught you," he says, slightly out of breath. "I wanted to chat about your last Instagram post. The engagement was good, but I think we could push it even further."

I resist the urge to roll my eyes. Tyler, with his business degree and penchant for corporate jargon, always seems to think he knows better than me when it comes to social media strategy.

"Oh?" I say, keeping my tone neutral. "What did you have in mind?"

He launches into a convoluted explanation about hashtag strategies and optimal posting times, peppering his speech with phrases like "synergistic approach" and "vertical integration." I nod along, mentally counting down the seconds until I can escape.

". . . and if we leverage your personal brand more aggressively, we could see a significant uptick in conversions," he finishes, looking at me expectantly.

I take a deep breath, reminding myself that Tyler, despite his annoying demeanor, is technically my superior. "Those are some interesting ideas, Tyler. I'll definitely take them into consideration for my next post."

He beams, clearly pleased with himself. "Great! I knew you'd see it my way. Oh, and one more thing, on a personal note—"

But before he can continue, the elevator doors open with a soft ding. I've never been so grateful for an interruption in my life.

"Sorry, Tyler, I've got to run. I have a shoot scheduled this afternoon," I say, backing into the elevator. "I'll email you my content plan for next week, okay?"

He opens his mouth to protest, but I'm already jabbing the close-door button. As the doors slide shut, cutting off his disappointed expression, I let out a sigh of relief.

The elevator descends, and I lean against the wall, closing my eyes for a moment. The contrast between my interactions with Sloane and Tyler couldn't be starker.

I hail a cab to head to my next appointment—a photoshoot for a small, up-and-coming jewelry designer. As we crawl through the midday traffic, I find myself comparing the two brands in my mind.

Moth to the Flame, with its sleek offices and corporate structure, offers stability and prestige. But there's something thrilling about working with smaller, independent designers for my other . . . side project. I have another account that is very much . . . well . . . me. It's a delicate balance, maintaining relationships for both accounts while staying true to my own style and values.

The cab drops me off in front of a converted warehouse in Bushwick. The brick exterior is covered in vibrant murals, a complete opposite to the polished marble of Moth to the Flame's headquarters. I take a deep breath, centering myself before I step inside.

The interior is a creative chaos of workbenches, tools, and half-finished pieces. The air is thick with the scent of metal and resin. I spot Hailey, the sole designer, hunched over a workbench, her dark curls wild and untamed.

"Chloe!" she exclaims when she sees me, her face lighting up. "I'm so glad you're here. I've finished the final pieces for the collection."

As I approach, I marvel at the intricate designs spread out before her. Where Moth to the Flame's jewelry is rich and decadent, Hailey's work is darker and edgier. Each piece tells a story, from the rough-hewn silver cuffs embedded with uncut gemstones to the delicate wire sculptures that look like they might take flight at any moment.

"These are incredible, Hail," I gasp, running my fingers over a necklace that looks like it was woven from moonbeams and stardust. "Your work keeps getting better and better."

I hate to admit it, because I truly do love Sloane and her designs, but Hailey's jewelry is much more my style. It's gothic in nature.

Collars, chokers, metal and raw. It's a blend of BDSM club and Victorian elegance that speaks to my soul in a way Moth to the Flame's more mainstream pieces never quite manage. Her jewelry feeds the alter ego inside of me. It fuels the "Chlo" as I like to call her.

"Thanks. I really poured my heart into this collection. It's inspired by ancient myths and legends—you know, the dark, twisted ones that nobody talks about anymore."

I nod, understanding completely. Hailey has always been drawn to the shadows, finding beauty in the things most people overlook or shy away from. It's one of the reasons we clicked when we first met at an underground art show two years ago.

"So, are you ready to channel your inner dark goddess for the shoot?" Hailey asks, wiggling her eyebrows mischievously. "Dark, gothic Christmas?"

I grin, feeling a surge of excitement. "You know I am. Let's bring out Chlo."

Hailey claps her hands together. "Yes! I've got the perfect backdrop set up in the back room. It's all black velvet and twinkling lights—like a starry night sky."

As we move to the makeshift studio, I start to shed my professional persona. I change into my favorite little black dress, fishnets, and sexy black pumps. Gone is the polished influencer in her secondhand blazer and knockoff heels. In her place emerges Chlo—edgy, daring, and unapologetically herself.

Hailey helps me into the first piece—an intricate silver collar adorned with black opals and razor-thin chains that drape across my collarbone. It's heavy and cold against my skin, but it feels right. Like armor.

"You look fierce," Hailey says, stepping back to admire her handiwork. "Like some kind of warrior queen from another dimension."

I turn to the full-length mirror and barely recognize myself. My eyes seem darker, my cheekbones sharper. The collar transforms me, bringing out a side of myself I usually keep hidden.

"All right, Chlo," I whisper to my reflection. "Time to shine."

The photoshoot flies by in a blur of flashing lights and costume changes. Each piece Hailey puts on me feels like it's unlocking a different facet of my personality. The moonbeam necklace makes me feel ethereal and mysterious. The rough-hewn cuffs make me feel powerful and untamed.

As we wrap up the final shots, I feel a twinge of regret. I don't want to take off these pieces and go back to being regular Chloe.

"You know," Hailey says, as if reading my thoughts, "you could keep that look if you wanted. The world could use a little more Chlo."

I laugh, but there's a part of me that's tempted. "Maybe someday. For now, I think Chloe needs to stay in charge."

As I change back into my work clothes, I wonder what Tyler or Sloane would think if they saw me dressed like a dark vixen rather than the sweet girl next door. Would they even recognize me? Would they understand this part of me?

I say goodbye to Hailey with a promise to have the edited photos to her by the end of the week. As I step out into the fading afternoon light, it's like I'm straddling two worlds—the sleek, corporate world of Moth to the Flame Designs, and the raw, creative chaos of independent designers like Hailey.

For now, I need to find a way to balance both. But someday, I think, Chlo might be ready to step into the spotlight.

As I walk toward the subway station, my mind is still reeling from the contrast of my day. The weight of Moth to the Flame's elegant pieces in my bag seems to pull me in one direction, while the lingering sensation of Hailey's edgy creations tugs me in another. I'm split, torn between two versions of myself.

The subway car is crowded, and I find myself wedged between a suited businessman and a tattooed artist type. It feels oddly fitting, given my current state of mind. As the train lurches forward, I close my eyes and let the rhythmic rumbling settle my thoughts.

When I finally reach my stop in Manhattan and emerge onto the street, I fish out my phone with one more task for the day while I wait for the next ferry home. I call my landlord to complain about him shoveling my walkway but failing to shovel Mr. Haven's.

I dial the familiar number, steeling myself for the conversation ahead. My landlord, Mr. Grayson, picks up on the third ring.

"Hello?" His gruff voice comes through the speaker.

"Hi, Mr. Grayson. It's Chloe Hallman from 1004 Brennan," I say, trying to keep my tone light and friendly. I also am not sure if he'll remember who I am. It was my parents who were longtime tenants of his, and I merely took over the lease—the very expensive lease—when they passed.

"Ah, Chloe. What can I do for you?"

I take a deep breath. "I wanted to talk to you about the snow-shoveling situation. I noticed that you cleared my walkway, which I appreciate, but Mr. Haven's wasn't done. I'm a bit concerned about him."

There's a pause on the other end of the line. "Shoveling?"

"Yes, that's right. He's in his eighties, and I worry about him trying to navigate an unshoveled path. He fell and—"

"Look, Chloe, I can't be responsible for every tenant's walkway. Nowhere does it say in your lease that I provide snow removal."

I feel a flicker of annoyance. The Chloe from this morning might have backed down, but I can feel a bit of Chlo's fire in my veins.

"I understand that, but Mr. Haven is elderly. It's a safety issue. And since you did mine—"

"I don't know what you're talking about. I don't provide snow removal. At all."

I pause, confused. "But . . . my walkway was cleared. In fact, it's rarely not cleared. I assumed you had done it."

Mr. Grayson sighs heavily on the other end of the line. "Listen, kid. I don't know who cleared your walkway, but it wasn't me or any of my people. Maybe you've got a secret admirer or something."

Mr. Haven had already said as much, and yet my mind races, trying to make sense of this new information.

"I . . . I see," I stammer. "Well, I apologize for the misunderstanding. But is there any chance you could arrange for Mr. Haven's walkway to be cleared? I'm really worried about him."

"Not my problem," Mr. Grayson grunts. "If you're so concerned, why don't you do it yourself?"

Before I can respond, he hangs up. I stand there for a moment, phone still pressed to my ear, feeling a mix of frustration and bewilderment.

As I lower my phone, a chill runs through me that has nothing to do with the cold. Who has been shoveling my walkway all this time? And why?

CHAPTER FOUR
JACK

Pete's Café isn't the type of place I'd normally visit. Not until Chloe that is. I've always been the type of guy who would make my coffee at home and avoid the overpriced, pretentious coffee shops in my neighborhood that seemed to be popping up on every corner. Even if I do pass it every day on my way to the fire station.

Jesus, I'm beginning to sound like my grandpop, god rest his soul.

But Chloe visits this location every Tuesday without fail, often Wednesday, and even Fridays on occasion when she goes to the Moth to the Flame office. So here I am. The guy who has spent a majority of his adult life as a loner unless you count work, suddenly daydreaming about holding hands over steaming mugs of coffee.

I even caught myself defending Pete's to my fire captain the other day when I entered with the telltale cup that proved I overspent on something waiting for me in a pot at the station. "It's not just about the coffee," I found myself saying. "It's about the experience, the atmosphere."

As I push open the heavy wooden door, the rich aroma of freshly ground beans greets me. The café is bustling with the morning crowd, a mix of suited professionals and artsy types hunched over their laptops.

I scan the room, my heart rate quickening as I search for Chloe's familiar face. She's already in line, and no one is behind her. Not until I take the spot, that is.

She doesn't know I'm here.

She never does.

But I am. I always am.

I take my place behind her, close enough to catch a whiff of her jasmine perfume. My palms are sweaty, and I wipe them on my pants, rehearsing the words I've practiced a hundred times in my head.

"Hey there," I want to say. "Fancy seeing you here." But the words catch in my throat. Thank god, because who the hell says the word *fancy*?

I've memorized her order by now. A large soy latte with an extra shot of espresso and a sprinkle of cinnamon on top. She'll treat herself to one of Pete's famous blueberry scones, which have now become a favorite of mine as well. Those little fuckers are addictive.

Today, she's all business, tapping away at her phone as she waits her turn. It's out of her normal, however. She's not one of those girls who lives on their phones twenty-four seven. Shocking considering what she does for a living. But something I've always liked about Chloe is she seems to be an observer—like me. She watches people—like me.

Although she doesn't stand outside someone's windows in the dark—like me.

"Next!" calls the barista, and Chloe steps up to place her order.

I listen intently, hoping to catch some detail I might have missed, some clue to who she really is.

"Large soy latte, extra shot, cinnamon on top," she says, her voice melodic and confident. "And . . . you know what? I'll take a blueberry scone too. It's been a long week."

I smile to myself. Even her small indulgences are endearing.

As she moves to the side to wait for her order, I step up to the counter. The barista, a young guy with thick-rimmed glasses and an ironic mustache, raises an eyebrow at me.

"Let me guess," he says with a knowing smirk. "Large black coffee?"

I clear my throat, suddenly aware of how transparent I've become. "Actually," I say, surprising myself, "I'll have what she's having."

The barista's eyebrows shoot up, but he shrugs and punches in the order. I fumble with my wallet, acutely aware of Chloe standing just a few feet away. As I wait for my change, I steal a glance at her. She's leaning against the counter, still absorbed in her phone, a slight frown creasing her forehead.

I want to ask her what's wrong, to be the one to smooth away that worry line. But I'm just another stranger in a coffee shop, not the confidant I long to be.

"Order for Chloe!" the barista calls out, and she steps forward to claim her drink and scone. As she turns to leave, our eyes meet for a brief moment. My heart skips a beat as she flashes a polite smile, the kind you give to someone you pass on the street. It's nothing special, but to me, it's everything.

But then she pauses, studies me for a moment, and realization dawns in her facial expression. "Hey, I know you. You're the man who helped my neighbor. Jack, right?"

"Uh, yeah," I stammer, caught off guard by her recognition. "That's me."

"I didn't know you came here."

My pits begin to sweat, and my mouth goes dry. "Yeah . . . I work at the station down the street."

"Oh." She pauses as if absorbing the information and then smiles.

"I never got to thank you properly," Chloe says, her eyes warm with genuine appreciation. "You were so helpful, and then the fact that you shoveled his walkway was really nice."

My face heats, unsure how to handle the praise—especially from her. "Just being neighborly," I mumble, rubbing the back of my neck.

She glances down at the T-shirt I'm wearing. It has the fire department's logo. Although I rarely wear my full uniform to work, preferring to change when I get there, I do often wear one of the T-shirts since the blue cotton with the FDNY logo seems to make up most of my attire after ten years of working. Ever since I was eighteen when I was brought on as a seasonal, it's all I've ever known.

She takes a sip of her latte. "You must have an exciting job. Dangerous too, I imagine."

I shrug, not wanting to come across as boastful. "It has its moments. But mostly, it's just about being there for people when they need help."

She nods thoughtfully, and I can see a glimmer of genuine interest in her eyes.

"Order for Jack!" the barista calls out.

I turn to grab my drink, and when I look back, I notice Chloe eyeing my cup curiously.

"Soy latte with cinnamon?" she asks, a hint of amusement in her voice. "That's . . . unexpected."

My face heats up again. "Uh, yeah. Trying something new," I lie, knowing full well I've ordered her exact drink. I reach for my scone, knowing how guilty I look. What does it tell her about me that I copied her exact order?

Chloe's lips curve into a knowing smile, and for a moment, I wonder if she's seen through my flimsy excuse. But then she just nods, taking another sip of her own latte.

"Well, Jack the firefighter," she says, her tone playful, "since we're both here and you're trying new things, why don't you join me? I was just about to sit down and go over some work, but I could use a break."

My heart leaps into my throat. This is the moment I've been waiting for, dreaming about for . . . years?

Jesus. Has it been that long? Jesus Christ.

And now that it's here, I'm paralyzed with fear and desire to finally connect with this woman.

"I . . . uh . . . sure," I manage to stammer out. "That'd be great."

We make our way to a small table by the window. Sunlight streams in, catching the reddish highlights in Chloe's dark hair. She sets down her phone and takes a bite of her scone, closing her eyes briefly in enjoyment.

"God, these really are addictive, aren't they?" she says, echoing my earlier thoughts.

I nod, trying to appear casual as I sip my latte. The taste is unfamiliar—sweeter and smoother than my usual black coffee. But I find I like it, or maybe I just like sharing this moment with her.

"So, Jack," Chloe says, leaning forward slightly. "Tell me more about being a firefighter. How long have you been doing it?"

As I start to answer, I feel a mix of elation and guilt. This is everything I've wanted—a chance to talk to Chloe, to get to know her. But there's a voice in the back of my mind reminding me that this isn't how it's supposed to happen. That I shouldn't be here, shouldn't know so much about her already.

I push the thoughts aside, focusing instead on the way her eyes light up as I tell her about my first big fire, the adrenaline rush of racing to a call. For now, I let myself believe that this is normal, that I'm just a guy having coffee with a beautiful woman he's interested in.

I'm not the stalker outside her window memorizing every curve of her body.

But as Chloe laughs at one of my jokes, her phone buzzes on the table. She glances at it, and that worried frown returns.

"Everything okay?" I ask, unable to stop myself.

She sighs, running a hand through her hair. "It's just work stuff. Nothing major."

I nod, wanting to press further but knowing I shouldn't. I shouldn't care this much about a stranger's problems. But Chloe isn't a stranger to me, even if I am to her.

"So what do you do?" I ask, knowing that I shouldn't know this information even though I do.

"I'm an influencer. Sales, I guess you could say. For jewelry brands."

"That sounds interesting."

She shrugs, a wry smile playing at her lips. "It has its moments. Not as exciting as running into burning buildings, I'm sure."

I chuckle, trying to downplay my job. "Trust me, it's not all excitement. There's a lot of waiting around, cleaning equipment, and paperwork too."

"Well, I win there. I don't have paperwork." Chloe leans in, her eyes sparkling with curiosity. "But still, you must have some incredible stories. What's the craziest thing you've ever seen on the job?"

I pause, considering. There are so many stories I could tell, but I'm wary of coming across as an arrogant jackass, as some firefighters love to do. I've never been one to do so just to get in some girl's pants, and yet here I am now. But this is my chance to impress her, to keep her interested.

"Well," I begin, "there was this one time we got called to a house fire. When we arrived, we found out it wasn't just any house—it was a hoarder's home."

Chloe's eyes widen. "Oh no, that must have been awful."

I nod, remembering the chaos of that night. "It was like navigating a maze of junk, with smoke licking at our heels. We had to create pathways just to move through the house. Junk everywhere. Everywhere. And the smell . . . I can't possibly describe the smell of burnt hoarder house."

As I continue the story, I watch Chloe's reactions closely. She gasps at the tense moments, laughs at the absurd details, and nods sympathetically when I describe the homeowner's distress. It's intoxicating, having her full attention like this.

"Wow," she says when I finish. "That's incredible. You guys really are heroes."

My face heats once again at her praise. "We're just doing our job," I mumble, suddenly self-conscious that my face keeps changing colors from white to red to white to red.

Chloe shakes her head. "Don't downplay it. What you do is amazing." She pauses, then adds with a grin, "Although I have to say, I'm a little disappointed there weren't any cats stuck in trees in that story."

I laugh, grateful for the moment of levity. "Oh, we wouldn't be true firefighters if we didn't rescue a cat in our day."

"I knew it!"

"Well, if it's cats you want, I've got a doozy for you," I say, leaning in conspiratorially. "Picture this: a three a.m. call about a 'large animal' stuck in a tree. We show up, expecting maybe a raccoon or a possum. But no—it's a full-grown mountain lion."

Chloe's jaw drops. "You're kidding!"

"I wish I was," I chuckle. "This beast, who actually was some eccentric guy's pet, had escaped and gotten itself stuck about thirty feet up an oak tree. And let me tell you, it was not happy to see us."

"What did you do?" Chloe asks, completely enthralled.

"Well, first we had to call animal control. But they were short-staffed and couldn't get there for hours. Meanwhile, this cat is getting more agitated by the minute. We couldn't leave it there—someone's pet could've wandered by and become lunch. Hell . . . *we* could have become lunch."

I pause for dramatic effect, enjoying the way Chloe leans in closer, hanging on my every word.

"So, there I am, inching up this ladder with a tranquilizer gun borrowed from a local vet. Heart crashing against my chest, palms sweating—because one wrong move and I'm cat food. I get within range, take aim, and . . ."

"And?" Chloe prompts, eyes wide.

"I sneeze. Loudly. The mountain lion, startled, loses its footing and starts to fall. I manage to get off a shot, but now I've got a hundred and fifty pounds of semiconscious, very angry cat plummeting toward me."

Chloe gasps, her hand flying to her mouth. "Oh my god, what happened?"

I grin, savoring the moment. "Let's just say I gained a newfound appreciation for airbags that day. My team had set up a jump cushion, just in case. The cat and I both landed on it—thankfully, on opposite ends."

Chloe bursts out laughing, a warm, genuine sound that makes my heart skip a beat. "That's insane! I can't believe you actually experienced that."

"That's because I didn't. I'm kidding," I admit, laughing loudly. "But it makes for a great story at parties."

Chloe's laughter dies down, replaced by a mock scowl. "You had me going there for a minute," she says, playfully swatting my arm. "I can't believe I fell for that."

I grin, enjoying the easy banter between us. "Sorry, I couldn't resist."

We fall into an easy conversation, swapping stories about our jobs and lives. I'm careful not to reveal too much, to only share what a casual acquaintance might reveal. But it's hard when I want to tell her everything, when I want her to know me as well as I know her.

As we continue to talk, I find myself relaxing, forgetting for moments at a time about the circumstances that brought me here. It feels so natural, so right, to be sitting across from her, sharing stories and laughter.

But then I catch sight of my reflection in the window, and reality comes crashing back. I see myself as I truly am—a man living a lie, pretending to be something I'm not. The guilt rises in my throat like bile.

Chloe must sense the shift in my mood. "Everything okay?"

I force a smile. "Yeah, just remembered I have my shift I need to get to. I should probably get going."

She nods, looking slightly disappointed. "Of course. Well, it was really nice talking to you. Maybe we'll run into each other here again sometime?"

"Yeah, maybe," I say, knowing full well I'll be here every Tuesday, Wednesday, and occasional Friday, like always. "I come here a lot," I add to make it not so obvious how obsessed I am.

As I stand to leave, Chloe reaches out and touches my arm lightly. "Thanks again for helping Mr. Haven. It's good to know there are still people like you in the world."

Her words are like a knife to my heart. If only she knew the truth about me, about why I was really there that day. I mumble a goodbye and hurry out of the café, the bell above the door jingling cheerfully behind me.

Outside, I lean against the brick wall, taking deep breaths of the cool morning air. What am I doing? This isn't me. I'm not this creepy stalker, this liar. I'm a firefighter, for Christ's sake. Chloe's right. I am a good person. I am.

But as I start walking to work, I can't shake the image of Chloe's smile, the sound of her laugh. I tell myself this is the last time, that I'll stop coming to the café, stop following her.

Okay . . . I'm a liar.

I miss her already.

CHAPTER FIVE

CHLOE

It takes me a minute to recognize him. It's not like I wouldn't be able to spot him in the office setting, but at my house? Standing on my porch? "Tyler?"

He nods, shifting awkwardly from foot to foot. "Hey, Chloe. I, uh . . . I hope you don't mind me dropping by unannounced like this."

I blink, still processing the sight of the VP of marketing on my doorstep. "How did you know where I lived?"

St. George is nowhere near the office in Manhattan, so there is no way this is a "just in the neighborhood" type of situation.

Tyler's gaze darts away, and he rubs the back of his neck. "I, uh . . . I may have looked up the address in your contract. I know that's probably crossing a line, but I really wanted to talk to you the last time you were in the office, but you rushed out and . . ."

A mixture of curiosity and unease floods in. Tyler and I have always been friendly at work, but we've never hung out outside the office. What could be so urgent that he'd track down my home address?

"Is everything okay?" I ask, my brow furrowing with concern.

"Oh yes, everything is fine. It's just that—" He swallows hard.

"Well . . . the company holiday party is coming up and I was thinking."

My stomach tightens. Is he about to ask me out? To the company party, of all places?

"Tyler," I start, ready to let him down gently, but he holds up a hand.

"I know you don't really do Christmas and all. Sloane told me why and . . . I'm sorry for that. But well . . ." His face is so red that I can't tell if it's from embarrassment or the cold. "I was wondering if you'd like to come with me?" Tyler blurts out, his words tumbling over each other.

The chilly December air nips at my exposed skin, but I barely notice it. My mind is reeling, trying to process Tyler's unexpected invitation.

"I . . . I don't know what to say," I stammer, genuinely caught off guard. It's true that I've avoided the company holiday party ever since my parents—well, ever since. The idea of facing all those festive decorations, the forced cheer, makes my chest tighten.

But Tyler's earnest expression and the hint of hope in his eyes makes me hesitate.

He must sense my reluctance because he quickly adds, "It doesn't have to be a date or anything. I just thought . . . maybe if you had someone to go with, it might be easier. And I promise, no mistletoe or cheesy Christmas carols."

"Look," I say, softening my tone, "I appreciate the offer, I really do. But I'm not sure I'm ready for that yet."

Tyler nods, his shoulders slumping slightly. I feel bad. He seems like a nice guy, I suppose. I mean . . . I wouldn't really know. I've only seen him at work, but I do feel bad considering he came all the way to my house. He's not bad looking. In fact, he's quite handsome in a smart accountant sort of way, with his tousled brown hair and warm hazel eyes. I find myself reconsidering, almost against my will. But then I remind myself that guys like Tyler simply don't do it for me.

Too nice. Too straitlaced.

I'm not exactly looking for the bad boy. In fact, I don't want that either. But I do want someone who can challenge me, someone with a bit of an edge. Someone who doesn't follow all the rules.

Someone who has the same sexual interests as me.

And something about Tyler tells me that the man likes his coffee very vanilla.

"I appreciate you coming all this way, Tyler," I say, trying to soften the rejection. "But I don't think it's a good idea."

Tyler nods, his disappointment evident but not surprising. "I understand. I'm sorry for bothering you at home like this."

As he turns to leave, a gust of wind whips down the street, rustling the bare branches of the trees lining my sidewalk. The cold air bites at my exposed skin, and I find myself calling out before I can stop myself.

"Wait, Tyler. Do you . . . do you want to come in for a cup of coffee? It's freezing out here."

His eyes light up, and for a moment, I regret the invitation. But it's too late now, and besides, it's just coffee. What harm could it do?

As I lead him into my small living room, I notice how out of place he looks. His crisp button-down shirt and pressed slacks seem at odds with my eclectic decor and the general lived-in feel of my space.

"Nice place," he says, his eyes roaming over the abstract art on my walls and the collection of vintage vinyl records that belonged to my father stacked in the corner.

"Thanks," I reply, heading to the kitchen. "How do you take your coffee?"

"Black is fine," he calls back.

I pause, my hand hovering over the coffee maker. Black coffee? Maybe there's more to Tyler than I thought.

When I return with two steaming mugs, I find him examining my bookshelf. He turns to me with a raised eyebrow. "The Marquis de Sade? I wouldn't have pegged you for a fan of eighteenth-century erotic literature."

I nearly drop the mugs. "Oh, that's . . . that's for research," I stammer, feeling my face flush.

Tyler's lips quirk into a small smile. "Research, huh? What kind of research requires the works of the man who gave us the word *sadism*?"

As I struggle to form a response, I realize that maybe, just maybe, I've underestimated Tyler. The fact that he even knows this is—

I set the mugs down on the coffee table, trying to regain my composure. "I like to read a bunch of things," I say, aiming for nonchalance but hearing the defensiveness in my voice. "I'm interested in all kinds of literature."

Tyler nods as he drinks his coffee, but there's something in his eyes that unsettles me. A glint of . . . curiosity? Excitement? I can't quite place it, but it makes me acutely aware that we're alone in my house.

We drink our coffee in silence. Awkward, painful silence.

Tyler's gaze jerks to the bookshelf, then back to me.

He's harmless. Right?

"So," Tyler says, breaking the silence. His voice is low, almost a purr. "What other interesting literature are you hiding on those shelves?"

I swallow hard, my throat suddenly dry despite the coffee. "Nothing special," I manage. "Just your typical bestsellers and classics."

Tyler sets his mug down and stands up, returning to the bookshelf. I remain frozen in my seat, watching as his fingers trail along the spines of my books.

"Typical bestsellers and classics, huh?" he says, pulling out a worn paperback. "Like this copy of *Story of O*? Another research project?"

My heart hammers in my chest. I'd forgotten that was there, nestled innocently between my Dickens and Austen.

"I . . . I . . ." I stutter, unable to form a coherent thought.

Had I known I'd have a surprise guest from work stopping by, I might have done a sweep of my house. The thought of what is or isn't in my bookcase has never been an issue. The hermit in me has never been faced with this uncomfortable situation before.

Tyler turns to face me, the book dangling from his fingers. His eyes lock on to mine, and I see that glint again—definitely excitement now, mixed with something darker.

"You know," he says, his voice low and husky, "I've always found that the most interesting people are the ones with the most interesting bookshelves."

Tyler is weird. Plain and simple.

I should be able to discuss this book. I'm an adult, for fuck's sake, but I can't seem to find my voice. The room feels too small, too warm, and Tyler's presence is suddenly overwhelming.

"I . . . I'm not that interesting," I finally manage to say, my voice cracking as I do.

Tyler takes a step closer, still holding the book. "I beg to differ," he says softly. "I think you're very interesting. And I think there's a lot more to you than meets the eye."

My heart is thumping so hard I'm sure he can hear it. I should ask him to leave. I should stand up, take the book from his hand, and show him the door. But I can't move. I'm transfixed by his gaze, by the way he's looking at me like he can see right through me. Plus, I don't want to upset him. I have to work with this guy.

Tyler stares at me—innocent but not—and I find myself sinking deeper into the couch, as if trying to disappear into the cushions. He's still holding *Story of O*, his thumb absently caressing the worn cover.

"You know," he says, his voice barely above a whisper, "I've always believed that our deepest desires, our darkest fantasies, they're nothing to be ashamed of. They're what make us human."

Ewww stop. He's going to ruin this book for me.

A bead of sweat trickles down my back. The room seems to shrink around us, the air thick and heavy. I should say something, anything, to break this tension, but my mouth is dry, my tongue leaden.

"So," I say, desperate to change the vibe of the room, "the recent designs lately are amazing. I'm excited to show them off. In fact, I'm going to go live as soon as you leave."

The intensity in his gaze makes me squirm, so I stand and head toward the door. This is not the same Tyler from the office, the one who blushes when someone tells a slightly off-color joke. This Tyler is . . . different. But not different in a good way. Different in a way that tells me I need to gracefully get him out my door.

Tyler takes a step closer, his eyes never leaving mine. "Going live? That sounds interesting. Maybe I could stick around and watch?"

The air in the room suddenly feels thick, oppressive. I take an involuntary step back, bumping into the bookshelf behind me.

"I don't think that's a good idea," I say, trying to keep my voice steady. "I'll get too nervous knowing someone is watching."

He doesn't move.

"Thanks for stopping by though."

For a long moment, he stares at me, his expression unreadable. Then, just as suddenly as his demeanor changed, the mask of the affable executive slips back into place.

"Of course," he says, forcing a laugh that doesn't reach his eyes. "I'm sure you have a lot to do."

I nod, relief washing over me as Tyler sets down his coffee mug and moves toward the door. But as he reaches for the handle, he pauses and turns back to me.

"If you change your mind about the party . . ."

As he finally exits, I close the door behind him and lean against it. Why was that so weird?

I shake off the unsettling feeling and double-check that I've locked the door. Something about that interaction has left me rattled, but I can't quite put my finger on why. Maybe I'm just paranoid after recent years of living alone.

Trying to push Tyler out of my mind, I focus on setting up for my live stream. I arrange the latest Moth to the Flame designs on my desk, adjusting the lighting to showcase them perfectly.

I take a deep breath, centering myself before going live. This is my element. This is where I shine.

"Hey, everyone!" I say brightly as the red light blinks on. "Thanks for joining me tonight. I've got some exciting new pieces to show you . . ."

CHAPTER SIX
JACK

Obsession has a flavor.

I can taste it on my lips.

Before I "met" Chloe, I would have never known this little disturbing fact. It's a bitter tang, like copper pennies and unripe persimmons. Sometimes I catch myself running my tongue over my teeth, chasing that elusive taste as I stand outside her window.

Chloe barely knows I exist, of course. Our brief meetings don't count because she's only met my outer shell. Nice Jack. Gentleman Jack. Fireman Jack, who is always there to help. She hasn't met the real Jack. The Jack who is creeping outside her window.

But I know everything about her. The way she takes her coffee at home (one sugar, splash of soy milk, a sprinkle of cinnamon). Her favorite song ("Psycho Killer" by Talking Heads). She dances around her room with her eyes closed with the song blasting as a way to hype herself up before she goes online. I know the exact shade of her eyes (amber flecked with gold). I know that she likes to wear fluffy socks but can never sleep with them on. Each day that passes, I'm learning more and more. It's endless but I'm determined to discover everything I possibly can.

I watch her from afar, collecting these precious details like a fucked-up psycho hoarding shiny trinkets. Each new discovery about Chloe feeds my obsession, intensifying that metallic flavor in my mouth.

Tonight it's snowing around me as I lurk outside her bedroom window. Delicate flakes settle on my eyelashes as I peer through the frosted glass. Chloe is curled up on her bed, bathed in the soft glow of her bedside lamp. She's reading, her brow furrowed in concentration. I imagine I can hear the whisper of pages turning.

My breath fogs the window, and I wipe it away impatiently. Can't let anything obstruct my view. My fingers leave smudges on the glass, and I realize with a start that I've forgotten my gloves. Sloppy. I can't afford to be sloppy.

Chloe shifts, stretching languidly like a cat. Her oversize T-shirt rides up, exposing a strip of pale skin above her pajama bottoms. My mouth goes dry, that familiar taste intensifying. I swallow hard.

I press closer to the window, my fingertips leaving ghostly imprints on the glass. The cold bites into my skin, but I barely notice. All of my attention is focused on Chloe as she sets her book aside and reaches for her phone.

A faint blue glow illuminates her face as she scrolls, her lips curving into a small smile. Who is she texting? A friend? A lover?

I can't see.

I hate not being able to see.

Jealousy flares hot in my chest, and I have to force myself to take deep, calming breaths. The vapor from my exhales creates a misty veil between me and my obsession.

Suddenly, Chloe looks up, her gaze seeming to pierce right through the window. For a heart-stopping moment, I'm certain she's seen me. I freeze, not daring to move a muscle. But her eyes slide past, unseeing, as she gets up and pads over to her computer.

Her shirt is short and my eyes lock on how the fabric barely covers the curve of her ass. She glances over her shoulder toward the window as if—

I drop to the ground, my heart pounding so loudly I'm sure she must hear it. Pressed against the cold earth, I hardly dare to breathe.

That copper-penny taste floods my mouth again. It's both thrilling and nauseating. Part of me wants to spit, to rid myself of this physical manifestation of my obsession. But another part, a darker part, savors it.

I should leave. I've already stayed too long, taken too many risks. But I can't tear myself away.

Just one more minute, I tell myself. One more glimpse.

I lie there for several more minutes, snow melting beneath me, soaking through my clothes. When I'm certain it's safe, I slowly raise my head.

Chloe sits at her desk, the glow of the computer screen casting eerie shadows across her face. Her fingers fly over the keyboard, and I strain to see what she's typing. Is it a message to someone? An email? A diary entry?

The thought of Chloe keeping a diary sends a charge through me. What secrets might she confide to those pages? What hidden desires and fears might she reveal?

I lean closer, my nose nearly touching the glass. If I could get a better angle, maybe I could—

A chirp from her ceiling startles me, and I jerk back instinctively. It's the smoke detector, its little light blinking in the darkness. The smoke detector's chirp reminds me of my day job, and for a moment, I'm disoriented. Fireman Jack seems so far removed from this version of me, crouched in the snow outside Chloe's window.

Chloe looks up at the detector, frowning slightly. She stands, stretching again, and I drink in the sight of her lithe body silhouetted against the warm light of her room. She walks to her closet, rummaging around until she emerges with a step stool.

My heart races as she sets up the stool beneath the smoke detector. Is she going to change the battery? That's my job. I should be the one up there, keeping her safe.

She climbs up, reaching for the device, and her shirt rides up even further. I can see the edge of her panties against her creamy thighs, the delicate curve of her legs. My fingers twitch, aching to trace those lines.

Suddenly, Chloe wobbles on the stool. For a split second, I forget myself entirely. I'm halfway to my feet, ready to burst through the window and catch her before she falls. But she steadies herself, letting out a soft laugh that I can hear through the glass.

I sink back down, shaking. That was close. Too close. What if I had given myself away? What if she had seen me?

But another part of me, that dark, hungry part, whispers: *What if she had fallen? What if you had saved her?*

The fantasy unfolds in my mind. Chloe, falling. Me, crashing through the window in a shower of glass. Catching her in my arms, feeling her warm body against mine. Her looking up at me with those amber eyes, full of gratitude and awe.

And then, as if in slow motion, she'd lean in closer. I'd feel my heart pounding, my breath catching in my throat. Her lips would brush against mine, soft and sweet, tasting faintly of strawberry lip balm. The kiss would deepen, and I'd lose myself in the moment, forgetting about anything else but Chloe.

All I'd think about is Chloe. Only her. Always.

I shake my head, dispelling the image. It's a dangerous line of thinking. Not to mention batshit crazy. I can't afford to get lost in such fantasies. I need to stay focused, stay hidden.

The detector chirps again. Taunting her.

She struggles to open up the detector but is unable to do so. She pounds on it with her fist and is rewarded with another chirp.

"Fuck this," she says as she disappears into the other room. She returns a moment later with a broom. "Take this, you dirty bastard."

I literally feel a part of my soul die a slow death as I watch Chloe raise the broom, preparing to strike the smoke detector.

No, no, no! God no. That's not safe. She could damage it, leave herself unprotected. She could burn alive in her sleep. She could— just no. You don't do this. The scenarios play out in my mind, each more horrifying than the last.

The urge to intervene is overwhelming.

Chloe swings the broom, connecting with the smoke detector with a crack. She lets out a triumphant "Ha!" that I can hear even through the ringing of my ears. The girl is going to cause me to stroke out.

The smoke detector and its incessant chirping now silenced. She looks pleased with herself, a mischievous grin playing on her lips.

Bad, bad girl!

I want to burst through that window and explain the dangers, lecture her on fire safety, spank her naughty and perfect ass, and then beg her to let me fix it properly.

She yawns, stretching her arms above her head. The movement causes her shirt to ride up again, exposing a tantalizing strip of skin. I force myself to look away, focusing instead on the broken smoke detector.

I need to fix this. I need to keep her safe.

An idea forms in my mind. It's risky, but I can't bear the thought of leaving her unprotected. I'll come back tomorrow, in my firefighter uniform.

I'll knock on her neighbor's door, flash my most charming smile. I'll be Nice Jack, Gentleman Jack, Fireman Jack.

And then I'll be inside her house. In her space. Surrounded by her scent, her belongings, her life.

The thought sends a shiver down my spine, that copper-penny taste flooding my mouth once more.

I watch as she turns off her computer and pads back to her bed. She slides under the covers, reaching for her book once more. The bedside lamp casts a warm glow over her features, softening them. She looks angelic, peaceful. Completely unaware of the fact that hives are practically forming on my skin.

She broke the firefighter code. Never. Disable. An. Alarm.

Thinking of punishing her again for her naughty acts has my cock twitching in my pants. I force those thoughts away, disgusted with myself. I'm here to protect her, not . . . not have an inconvenient boner.

I watch as Chloe's eyelids grow heavy. She marks her place in the book and sets it on the nightstand, then clicks off the lamp. The room plunges into darkness. I need to go now. I'm no longer looking into a lit room where I can see her, but she can't see me. If she looks out her window, there is a chance she'll see me once her eyes adjust to the darkness.

But I still wait. It's as if I'm cemented in place.

I watch the rise and fall of her chest, counting her breaths, waiting for them to slow and deepen. One, two, three . . . By twenty, I'm certain she's asleep. Only then do I allow myself to move, my joints stiff from standing for so long in the cold.

As I leave, a twig snaps beneath my foot. The sound seems impossibly loud in the silent night. I freeze, but there's no movement from inside. Chloe sleeps on, oblivious.

I exhale slowly, my breath a white plume in the air. It's time to go. I've pushed my luck far enough tonight. But I'll be back . . .

CHAPTER SEVEN
JACK

I know her routine. She rarely deviates. Every Tuesday at seven thirty, she emerges from her inherited house that doesn't quite fit her personality and walks briskly down the street, her heels clicking against the uneven sidewalk. She carries a worn leather purse that's seen better days, but it's large enough to carry a laptop which she often does but not always. Today, she's carrying the laptop. I can tell by the slight tilt of her shoulder, compensating for the extra weight. Her hair is pulled back in a tight bun, not a strand out of place. She's wearing that navy blue jacket again, the one with the slightly frayed cuff that she thinks no one notices.

As she rounds the corner heading to catch the morning ferry to Manhattan and Pete's Café, I slip out of my hiding spot, knowing this is my time to act. Her home will be empty. Now all I have to do is get inside.

I already know she doesn't have a key under a flowerpot or beneath a rock. I have one chance. I'm hoping her neighbor is my ticket in. I've observed their interactions: friendly waves, occasional cups of sugar borrowed, conversations as they collect their mail. If anyone has a spare key, it's him.

"Mr. Haven," I say as the elderly man opens the door. He's wearing a faded flannel robe and fuzzy slippers, his wispy white hair sticking out in all directions. His rheumy eyes squint at me in confusion. "I don't know if you remember me but—"

"Oh yes, you're the nice gentleman who helped me the other day when I fell on the ice." He glances over my shoulder to the scene of the incident.

I nod, relieved he remembers. "That's right. I wanted to check in and see how you're doing today."

Mr. Haven's eyes crinkle as he smiles. "Oh, I'm right as rain, thanks to you. Just a few bruises, nothing serious." He pauses, then adds sheepishly, "Though I must admit, I'm a bit embarrassed about the whole thing. Slipping like a newborn colt at my age." Mr. Haven's gaze lingers on my uniform. "You're in uniform today."

I chuckle softly, looking down at my uniform. "Ah, yes. I was off duty when I helped you. Today I'm on my way to the station for my shift."

Mr. Haven's eyes light up with interest. "I always wanted to be a fireman when I was a kid. I bet you have some great stories."

I smile, nodding. "It certainly keeps life interesting. But listen, I was hoping you could help me out. Chloe mentioned that her fire detectors were beeping and driving her crazy. I said I'd swing by and replace the batteries for her and check them. I knocked on her door and she's not home. But since I'm here, I was hoping you'd have a key so I could run in really quick before I head off to work."

Mr. Haven hesitates, then smiles. "Of course. That's so nice of you. People these days don't seem to look out for each other like they used to. It's refreshing to see someone so willing to help." He shuffles back into his house, returning a moment later with a small key. "Here you go. It's the spare Chloe gave me for emergencies."

I take the key, feeling its weight in my palm. "Thank you, Mr. Haven. I really appreciate this. I'll pop in, change those batteries, and be on my way."

"Take your time, young man. I'm sure Chloe will be grateful." Mr. Haven's eyes twinkle. "And maybe next time you're off duty, you can stop by and share some of those firefighter stories. I'd love to hear them."

"Of course." As I turn toward Chloe's apartment, I notice that the snowflakes that were falling lightly have picked up intensity, swirling in the air and accumulating on the ground. "Actually, when I'm done with her alarms, I'm going to shovel your walkway and put salt down if you have any. Let's get you ready for the storm coming this afternoon."

"Oh, that's very kind of you," Mr. Haven says, his voice warm with gratitude. "The salt's in the garage, but don't trouble yourself too much. I know you're on your way to work."

I wave off his concern. "It's no trouble at all. I've got plenty of time before my shift."

With a final nod to Mr. Haven, I make my way to Chloe's door. The key slides smoothly into the lock, and I step inside. The house is quiet and dark, with a faint scent of cinnamon in the air. I pause for a moment, letting my eyes adjust to the dimness. The living room is tidy, with a plush couch and a bookshelf filled with colorful spines. I look around, taking in the part of her house I've never seen. I've committed every inch of her bedroom to memory from all my time standing outside her window, but this is all new territory for me. The space is exactly as I imagined it would be—cozy and inviting, just like Chloe herself. I resist the urge to explore further and remind myself why I'm here. Focus on the task at hand.

I spot the smoke detector on the ceiling near the kitchen and head toward it. It's not the one that she bashed, but I'm going to check it anyway since I'm here. I pull over a kitchen chair to stand on, wishing I had taken my boots off before entering her home. But I'm on a time limit since I don't know exactly how long I have before Chloe returns.

The battery compartment opens easily, and I replace the old batteries with new ones from my backpack that I brought. The detector gives a reassuring chirp as it comes back to life.

I move to the one in her bedroom, the one that I watched her crush into pieces to silence. I brought a spare detector, pretty sure her other one is beyond repair. The scent of cinnamon is stronger here, emanating from a small diffuser on her nightstand. Her bed is unmade, the comforter twisted as if she'd left in a hurry.

The broken smoke detector taunts from the ceiling. I carefully remove it, my fingers brushing against the jagged edges where Chloe's frustration had taken its toll. As I work to install the new one, my eyes wander around her bedroom, drinking in every detail. The framed photos on her dresser, the half-empty mug of coffee on her nightstand, the pile of clothes draped over a chair—each item feels like a precious clue, another piece of the puzzle that is Chloe.

I finish installing the new detector and reach for my backpack once again. My hands shake. My mind screams no. I shouldn't do it. I should stop. But I don't. Instead, I pull out a nanny camera. It would fit so perfectly next to this alarm and Chloe would never be the wiser.

My heart races as I position the tiny camera, angling it just so. It blends seamlessly with the new smoke detector, practically invisible unless you know exactly what to look for. I take a deep breath, trying to calm my nerves. This is wrong, I know it's wrong, but I can't help myself. I need to see her, to know her, to keep an eye on her at all times.

Last night when I came up with this plan, I justified it by telling myself it's so I don't have to stalk outside her window anymore. I'd be taking one step closer to not being the creeper. I'd wean myself off. I'd . . . I'd be able to protect her better. That's what I tell myself as I secure the camera in place, my fingers clumsily moving.

As I step back to admire my handiwork, a wave of guilt makes me want to vomit. What am I doing? This isn't protection; it's invasion. I'm violating Chloe's trust, her privacy, her very sense of security in her own home. The weight of my actions suddenly feels crushing.

I reach up, ready to tear down the camera, to undo this terrible mistake. But as my fingers brush against it, the creeper stalker in me returns. And he's so much stronger than the good angel on my shoulder telling me how fucked up this is.

I leave the camera in place, my upper lip sweating. The guilt is still there, but it's overshadowed by a sick sense of anticipation. I'll be able to see Chloe whenever I want now, in her most private moments. The thought both thrills and disgusts me.

Quickly, I gather my tools and make my way out of the bedroom. I need to leave before I do anything else I might regret—or worse, before Chloe returns home. I lock up and head back to Mr. Haven's house, my mind racing with thoughts of Chloe and the camera I've just installed.

Mr. Haven greets me with a warm smile, oblivious to what I've done. "All fixed up?" he asks.

I nod, plastering on a fake smile. "Yes, sir. Batteries changed and everything's in working order. She'll be safe now."

As I shovel Mr. Haven's walkway and spread salt, my mind races. What have I done? What will I do next? The line between protector and predator has never felt so blurry.

CHAPTER EIGHT
CHLOE

I don't know why I was hoping to see Jack today at the café—maybe on his way to work, but I was. Disappointment sinks in as I scan the familiar faces, none of them his. I stir my latte absently, watching the foam swirl into intricate patterns. The chatter and clinking of cups fade into background noise as my mind wanders.

I find an empty table by the window, pulling out my own computer to edit some new videos. But I can't focus. My gaze keeps darting to the door every time the bell chimes, hoping it will be him walking in.

Thirty minutes pass, then an hour. The latte grows cold beside me, barely touched. I scold myself for wasting so much time pining over someone who clearly isn't interested. Jack and I had barely spoken, mostly small talk and mostly about work. Yet something about his easy smile and the way his eyes crinkled when he laughed has wormed its way into my heart.

But is he really my type? After my last boyfriend, I swore to myself that I'd steer clear of vanilla, and something about Mr. Fireman screams vanilla. For the same reasons I had zero interest in Tyler, I should feel the same about Jack. I'm ready for something . . . spicier.

As if on cue, my phone rings and I see it's Tyler calling me. Why not text? At least I'd have time to think of ways to politely reject his advances. I don't want to answer, but he is technically one of my bosses so I reluctantly answer the call, steeling myself. "Hello, Tyler."

"How's my favorite influencer?" His voice is jovial, but there's an undercurrent of something else. Expectation, maybe.

I know the only way I can move forward with Tyler is by acting like our last exchange wasn't as awkward and unsettling as it was. I need to work with this man.

I force a light tone. "Oh, you know, trying to get some work done in my favorite café. What's up?"

"Yeah, I see you."

I scan the room quickly. Huh? How does he see me?

"Well, I was hoping to catch you in person, and I remembered how you often come into the office with your coffee and I remembered it was Pete's Café. I'm actually right outside. Mind if I join you?"

My stomach drops. This is . . . weird. I glance out the window and spot him on the sidewalk, phone to his ear, waving at me with a grin.

"Um, sure," I manage, ending the call as he pushes through the door.

Tyler saunters over, all confidence and cologne. He slides into the chair across from me, his eyes roving over my face in a way that makes me want to squirm.

"Fancy meeting you here," he says with a wink.

I muster a weak smile. "Yeah, what a coincidence."

He leans in, lowering his voice. "Listen, Chloe. I've been thinking. Why don't we grab dinner tonight? Just the two of us. I know this great little Italian place."

I open my mouth, scrambling for an excuse. "I don't think that's a good idea. Mixing work with—"

"Since you're a contractor and not an employee, I seriously doubt—"

"It's not a good idea," I cut in. "Sloane gave me a bunch of jewelry to show when we met this morning, and I haven't done any recording lately. I'm super behind, and with the holidays . . ." I lie as I take a deep breath. "Timing isn't right."

Tyler's smile falters for a moment, but he quickly recovers. "But that's just it. It's the holidays and we shouldn't be all about work."

I feel trapped, cornered by Tyler's persistence. His eyes bore into mine, expectant and hungry. I quickly gather my stuff. "In fact, I really need to get going. I'm doing a Zoom with Sloane later today that I need to get ready for."

As I stand up, Tyler's hand shoots out, gripping my wrist. "Chloe, wait—"

The bell above the door chimes, and I look up reflexively. My heart skips a beat as Jack walks in, his firefighter uniform crisp and neat. His eyes scan the café, landing on me. Our eyes meet, and for a moment, the rest of the café fades away. A smile starts to form on his face, but it quickly fades as he takes in the scene—Tyler's hand on my wrist, my obvious discomfort.

Jack's brow furrows, and he starts walking toward us. Tyler, oblivious to Jack's approach, leans in closer. "Come on, Chloe. One dinner. What are you afraid of?"

I seize the opportunity. "Oh, Jack! I'm so glad you could make it. I was getting ready to leave because I thought you weren't coming," I call out, waving him over.

Tyler's head whips around, his eyes narrowing as he takes in Jack's uniform.

Jack looks confused for a split second before catching on. "Sorry I'm late," he says smoothly, coming to stand by our table.

I stand up quickly, gathering my things. "Tyler, I'm so sorry, but I have plans with Jack that we are now late to. We'll have to catch up another time."

Tyler's jaw tightens, but he forces a smile. "Of course. No problem at all. We'll talk soon."

I nod, relief soothing the anxiety inside as Jack and I make our way to the door. Once outside, I let out a long breath. "Thank you so much. You have no idea how much you just saved me."

Jack's eyes crinkle as he smiles, and my heart does a little flip. "Happy to help. Care to tell me what I just walked into?"

I hesitate, weighing the situation. Part of me wants to brush it off, act like nothing happened. Another part of me, the loud warning bells in my head, wants to admit that something with Tyler is off. Either way, it's not Jack's problem, and I don't want to play the damsel in distress. He deals enough with that at his job.

I settle for a half-truth. "A coworker who doesn't quite understand boundaries. Nothing I can't handle."

Jack's eyebrows raise slightly, but he doesn't push. "Well, I'm glad I could help, even if it was unintentional."

We stand there for a moment, the crisp winter air nips at my cheeks, and it's brought a flush to Jack's cheeks, and . . . Jesus . . . his uniform fits him perfectly. I try to push away the thoughts of how good he looks, reminding myself of my earlier reservations.

But I realize I don't want this moment to end, don't want to say goodbye to Jack just yet.

"Can I buy you a coffee?" I blurt out. "You know, as a thank-you." I glance at the front door. "Not here, of course. And I should probably leave before he comes out." I notice his uniform again. "Unless you're on your way to work."

"I have the day off today," he says, then pauses. "I mean, I had something I had to do today that required me to be in uniform. But I'm done and free."

"So coffee?" I ask.

"I have a better idea."

Jack's eyes twinkle with boyish charm as he says, "How about we grab some hot chocolate instead? I know this amazing little place a few blocks from here. They make it from scratch with real melted chocolate."

My heart flutters at his suggestion. It feels intimate somehow, more special than just grabbing coffee. "That sounds perfect," I reply, unable to keep the smile from my face.

Walking the streets of downtown Manhattan, near the water, in the winter, next to a fireman, and on our way to get hot chocolate. What could get more Christmas than that?

As we walk, our breath misting in the cold air, I find myself stealing glances at Jack. His profile is strong, jawline defined, and there's a quiet confidence in the way he carries himself. It's genuine and grounded.

"So, day off, huh?" I say, breaking the comfortable silence. "What do firefighters usually do on their days off?"

Jack chuckles, the sound warm and rich. "Walk next to pretty girls to get hot cocoa." We round a corner, and Jack points to a small, cozy-looking shop with steamed-up windows. "Here we are. Best hot chocolate in the city, I promise."

The scent of chocolate and cinnamon envelops us as we step inside. It's warm and inviting, with mismatched chairs and tables, and shelves lined with old books.

As we wait in line, Jack turns to me. "Listen, about what happened back there . . ." He hesitates, his brow furrowing slightly. "If you ever need help or someone to be nearby . . . No pressure, of course."

"Thank you," I manage to say. I shrug. "No big deal really. I just have a stalker."

Jack's eyes widen, his expression turning serious.

I immediately regret my flippant comment. "No, no, it's not like that. I was joking. No stalker for me."

Jack's face relaxes slightly, but something I can't quite make out still lingers in his eyes.

We reach the counter, and Jack insists on paying for our hot chocolates despite my protests. As we wait for our drinks, I notice how at ease I feel with him. There's something about Jack that seems so familiar, but I can't quite put my finger on it.

"I know we've just met," I begin. "But it feels like I know you from someplace."

Jack smiles warmly. "Maybe we knew each other in a past life," he jokes.

Our drinks arrive, steaming mugs topped with a swirl of whipped cream and a dusting of cocoa powder. We find a small table by the window, and I wrap my hands around the warm mug, inhaling the rich scent.

"I think I've fallen in love just from the smell," I say, taking a sip. The chocolate is thick and velvety, with a hint of cinnamon. "Oh wow, you weren't kidding about this place."

Jack grins with a wicked glimmer in his eyes, clearly pleased by my reaction. "Told you. It's my little secret."

I take another sip, savoring the rich flavor. "Well, consider me impressed. I might have to make this my new spot. And I like secrets."

Jack grins, oblivious to the bit of whipped cream on his upper lip

I laugh and gesture to my own lip. "You've got a little . . ."

He wipes it away, his cheeks flushing slightly. "So I told you one of my secrets. Now it's your turn to tell me one of yours."

I hesitate, my fingers tightening around the warm mug. God, if only I could tell him my darkest and most desired secret. What if I told him that nothing would turn me on more than having him knock our hot chocolates to the floor with one swoop of his arm and throw me across the table instead? He'd tear off my clothes and fuck me without a second thought to the people around us. Nothing could get in the way of his hunger for me and—

Jesus . . . I don't want to risk chasing the man out of the building.

"Well," I begin, lowering my voice and searching for a safe answer, "I have a secret addiction to trashy reality TV shows. The more drama, the better."

Jack's eyes light up with amusement. "Really? Which ones?"

"All of them," I admit, feeling my cheeks warm. "But my absolute favorite is *Love Island*. It's so ridiculous and over-the-top, but I can't stop watching. I call it Cringe Island and yet I watch every episode."

He leans in, a conspiratorial grin on his face. "Want to know a secret? I may have binged a season or two of that myself."

I gasp in mock horror. "No! And here I thought you were this tough, macho firefighter."

"Hey, even tough, macho firefighters need a guilty pleasure," he laughs.

Our conversation flows easily after that, jumping from topic to topic. We discuss our favorite books (he loves historical fiction, I'm more into psychological thrillers), our go-to comfort foods (mac and cheese for him, ice cream for me), and our most embarrassing moments (his involves a high school talent show and a failed magic trick).

As we talk, I find myself drawn to the way his eyes crinkle when he laughs, and yes, *crinkle* is the perfect word to describe it. I'm also drawn to the passion in his voice when he talks about his job, the gentle way he listens when I speak. It's refreshing, especially compared to the men I've dated in the past.

Before I know it, hours have passed. The sky outside has darkened with the next predicted snowstorm coming, and the café is starting to empty out.

"I can't believe how late it's gotten," I say, glancing at my watch. "I should probably head home."

Jack nods, looking a bit disappointed. "Yeah, I guess we should call it. I should stop by the station anyway and see if they need any help prepping for tonight's snow."

We gather our things and step out into the chilly air. The street is busy with people hurrying past, bundled up against the cold.

"I can go to work later if you'd like me to escort you home instead?" Jack says, his breath visible in the afternoon air.

I hesitate for a moment, loving the idea of prolonging this day. But I don't want to come off as needy or too clingy. "That's sweet of you to offer, but I think I'll grab a cab."

Okay, so this is where he needs to ask me for my number. Come on, Jack. Ask me for my number.

Jack nods, his expression a mix of understanding and something else—disappointment, maybe? He shoves his hands in his pockets, rocking back on his heels slightly.

"Well, I had a great time today," he says, a soft smile playing on his lips. "It was nice getting to know you better."

My heart sinks a little. Is this it? Are we just going to part ways without any promise of seeing each other again?

Ask me for my number!

As I'm about to say goodbye, Jack clears his throat. "Listen, I was wondering . . ." he starts, then pauses, seeming to gather his courage. "Would it be okay if I got your number? Maybe we could do this again sometime?"

Relief and excitement flood through me. "Yes, absolutely," I reply, perhaps a bit too eagerly. I fumble for my phone, nearly dropping it in my haste.

We exchange numbers, our gloved fingers brushing as we hand our phones back and forth.

We stand there for a moment, neither of us quite ready to leave. Snowflakes begin to fall softly around us, catching in Jack's dark hair and eyelashes. The urge to reach out and brush them away is overwhelming.

Instead, I take a step back. "I should go. Thanks again for today, Jack. For everything."

"Anytime," he says softly. "Get home safe, Chloe."

I turn and start walking away, my heart light despite the heavy snow beginning to fall. I've only gone a few steps when Jack calls out.

"Hey, Chloe?"

I turn back, eyebrows raised in question.

Jack is standing there, snowflakes swirling around him, a hesitant smile on his face. "I was thinking . . . there's this Christmas market opening up tomorrow night in Bryant Park. They've got ice skating, hot cider, the works. Would you maybe want to check it out with me sometime this week, if you're going to be back in the city?"

My heart skips a beat. I can already picture us strolling through twinkling lights, sipping warm drinks, maybe even holding hands as we glide across the ice. It sounds magical, perfect even.

But a nagging voice in the back of my mind reminds me of my earlier reservations. Is Jack really my type? Am I setting myself up for disappointment by pursuing something with someone who might be too . . . safe?

I bite my lip, weighing my options. The hopeful look in Jack's eyes makes my decision for me.

"That sounds wonderful," I say, unable to keep the smile from my face. "I'd love to."

Jack's face lights up, his grin wide and genuine. "Great! I'll take a look at my work schedule, and I'll text you the details later?"

I nod, my own smile mirroring his. "Sounds perfect. I'm looking forward to it."

I finally turn to leave, hailing a cab with a wave.

CHAPTER NINE

JACK

I blame Tyler for the fact that I am once again standing outside her window in the fucking cold. I swore to myself the stalking would stop but old habits die hard.

My jaw clenches involuntarily. My fingers are numb inside my pockets, but I barely notice.

I had to make sure she was safe. Something about seeing Tyler in the coffee shop touching Chloe didn't sit well with me. Could it be because I wanted to tie him to a coffee shop chair and slowly chop his hand off with a butter knife? Maybe. But regardless, I couldn't resist the urge to return to her house to see she got home okay.

So here I am again, breath coming out in puffs, watching her once again.

The soft glow from her bedroom window casts a faint halo on the frost-covered lawn. I can see her moving around, probably getting ready for bed. My heart races as I imagine her slipping out of her clothes, her smooth skin bathed in the warm lamplight. It's later than I normally come to watch her, so late that I had to unplug her Christmas lights so I'm not lit up. I hope she doesn't notice. I hope that I can simply watch her in peace. Watch her slide into bed and—

I shake my head, trying to clear those thoughts. I'm here to protect her, not . . . whatever this is. But deep down, I know it's more than that. It always has been.

A car door slams nearby, startling me. I duck behind a hedge, my pulse vibrating in my ears. Footsteps crunch on the icy sidewalk, coming closer. I peer through the branches as I wait for everyone to settle for the night. Settle so I can watch Chloe.

Chloe appears in my view again, and I hold my breath as I notice something different about her. She's not in pajamas as I expected. Quite the opposite. She's wearing a raven-black wig, bright red lipstick and a tight, revealing black dress I've never seen before. *What the fuck?*

Where is she going at this hour?

I watch as she applies more makeup, her movements hurried and nervous. She keeps glancing at her phone, as if waiting for a message. My stomach churns with a mix of jealousy and concern. Is she meeting someone?

She applies jewelry I've never seen before either. It's a choker . . . no . . . it's a collar. It's gothic in style, with a small silver ring dangling from the front.

She then stands in front of her mirror in all her mysterious beauty, and I barely recognize her. In fact, if I didn't know it was Chloe, I'm not sure I'd be able to pick her in a lineup.

She's fucking stunning.

My fingers twitch with the urge to grab my phone and snap a picture, but I resist.

She then moves to her computer and sits down. With a couple of clicks, a website is pulled up. I squint to get a better look, and I instantly recognize it.

Holy fucking hell . . .

My heart nearly stops.

I can't believe what I'm seeing. Chloe, my sweet, innocent Chloe, is logging in to a Dark Secrets account.

I have a Dark Secrets account. But Chloe? My sweet angel Chloe?

I watch in stunned silence as she adjusts her webcam and begins to type something. A chat window pops up, filling with messages from eager viewers.

Unlike when she does her influencer jewelry videos, she doesn't turn on her ring light. She's shadowed by a flickering candle nearby.

Chloe takes a deep breath, visibly steeling herself. She applies a lace mask over her thick eyelashes to hide her identity even more. Then she smiles at the camera—a sultry, confident smile I've never seen before. It's like she's transformed into a different person entirely.

She starts to move sensuously, running her hands over her body, cupping her breasts, caressing her pussy, and spreading her legs as she speaks to her audience. I can't hear what she's saying as she has put sexy music on in the background, but I can see her lips moving, forming words I never thought I'd see coming from her mouth.

I'm frozen in place, unable to look away as she slowly starts to unzip her dress. Part of me wants to rush in there and stop this, to protect her from the prying eyes of strangers. But another part, a darker part I try to ignore, is utterly captivated.

How have I missed this? *Years* of sitting outside her window, and this is the first time I've seen this? It's obvious this is not her first time on this site. Clearly, she does so much more once I leave her for the night.

As I watch, transfixed, a flurry of emotions courses through me. Shock, arousal, jealousy, and a twisted sense of pride all war for dominance. My sweet Chloe, the object of my obsession for so long, has depths I never imagined.

The chat window explodes with activity as Chloe—no, her alter ego—begins her performance. I can almost feel the heat of the laptop against her skin, the hungry eyes of faceless strangers drinking in every curve and gesture. My fists clench in my pockets, nails digging into my palms.

She moves with practiced grace, each motion calculated to tease and entice. The dress slips lower, revealing a tantalizing glimpse of lace underneath. I'm torn between averting my eyes and drinking in every detail, committing it to memory.

A car engine rumbles to life down the street, snapping me back to reality. I glance around nervously, suddenly aware of how exposed I am. If anyone were to see me now, lurking in the shadows, watching this private show . . .

When I look back, Chloe is holding something up to the camera. It takes me a moment to recognize it: a hot-pink dildo, thick and large. My mouth goes dry as she runs it along her thigh, her lips curving into a wicked smile.

Holy shit, this escalated quickly!

Is this what some melted chocolate does to a girl?

This is too much. I need to leave, to process what I've seen. But my feet feel rooted to the ground, my eyes locked on the window. I've watched Chloe for years, thinking I knew everything about her. Now I realize I know nothing at all.

I took the girl out for hot cocoa like she was a virginal eighteen-year-old. Jesus, she must think I'm a goddamn Boy Scout. Had I known . . .

She leans back further so I can get a better view of exactly where she plans to put that dildo. My legs go weak, and I have to grip the hedge to stay upright. I thought I was protecting her, keeping her safe from the darkness of the world. But she was already deep in it, reveling in it even.

I watch as she positions herself, ready to give her audience what they're clamoring for. My fingers twitch toward my phone again, this time to open the Dark Secrets app. I could join the stream right now, be one of those faceless usernames cheering her on.

Will she see the light from my phone if I do?

I hesitate, my thumb hovering over the app icon. The temptation is overwhelming. But something stops me. Maybe it's the last shred of decency I have left, or maybe it's the fear of being caught. Either way, I force my hand back into my pocket.

The music changes into something lower. Enough so that I can actually hear her speak now as she inserts the dildo past her silky folds.

Holy shit! I'm staring at Chloe's bare, and absolutely perfect pussy.

"Something happened today," she says. "Something that got me in the mood to fuck myself for all of you to see."

I press my face to the glass, straining to hear every word. My curiosity is piqued, overriding even my arousal.

"I saw someone today," Chloe continues, her voice husky and breathless as she works the toy inside herself. "I had the most perfect day. Something right out of a Hallmark movie." She giggles and then moans. "But it was very G-rated."

Fuuuuuuck me. She's talking about me. About out meeting over cocoa and whip cream!

I lean in, my heart constricting as I strain to catch every word. Chloe's voice is low and sultry, punctuated by soft moans as she pleasures herself.

"It was so innocent," she continues, her breath catching. "We had hot chocolate and walked in the snow. He was such a gentleman." She laughs, a sound caught between amusement and arousal. "If only he knew what I really wanted. You all know exactly what I want, don't you?"

My mind reels. I struggle with a surge of conflicting emotions—shock, jealousy, arousal, and yes . . . embarrassment. How did I not pick up on this? My Chloe. My Chloe is . . .

"I wanted him to push me up against a wall," Chloe gasps, her movements becoming more frantic. "To rip my clothes off and fuck me right there in the snow."

Part of me wants to burst through her door, to be the man she's describing. But I'm rooted to the spot, a voyeur to her darkest fantasies.

"But instead," she pants, "I'm here with you. My faithful viewers. You know what I really need, don't you?"

The chat explodes with comments. I can only imagine what they're saying, what they're asking her to do. Chloe reads a few aloud, each one filthier than the last. She complies with their requests, her body writhing on her black leather office chair.

I'm trembling now, from both the cold and the intensity of what I'm witnessing. This is Chloe stripped bare—not just physically, but emotionally. The sweet, pure girl I thought I knew is gone, replaced by this seductive creature who knows exactly what she wants.

As she nears her climax, Chloe locks eyes with the window. For a heart-stopping moment, I feel like she's looking right at me. Like she knows I'm here, watching her most intimate moment. It's as if she knows she should have pulled the curtains shut to give herself privacy, but she never does. Never. It tells me one thing. She likes to leave them open . . . tempting the universe. Inviting . . .

"Oh god," she moans, her back arching, eyes closing. She thrusts the dildo in all the way and cries out.

I fixate on the sexiest thing I've ever seen, mesmerized, as she shudders through her orgasm.

My legs nearly give out as I watch Chloe climax, her body quivering with pleasure. The intensity of her orgasm seems to radiate through the window, electrifying the cold night air around me.

As Chloe comes down from her high, she slumps back in her chair, a satisfied smile playing on her lips. She reaches for a towel off-screen and begins to clean herself up, still engaging with her audience.

"Thank you all for joining me tonight," she purrs, her voice slightly hoarse. "You know how to make a girl feel special."

She leans in close to the camera, her eyes sparkling with mischief. "Same time next week? I might have a special surprise for you all."

With a wink and a blown kiss, she ends the stream. The window goes dark as she shuts off her computer, leaving me standing in the shadows, my mind reeling from what I've just observed.

I stand here, frozen. The silence of the night seems deafening. My breath comes in short, ragged gasps.

What do I do with this information? The Chloe I thought I knew is gone, replaced by this sultry, confident woman who bares her soul (and body) to strangers online.

I shake my head, trying to clear my thoughts. I need to leave before someone spots me. As I turn to go, my foot kicks a rock, the sound seeming to echo in the quiet night.

Suddenly, Chloe's bedroom light flicks back on. I freeze, my heart tightens. Did she hear me? I press myself against the side of the house, praying she doesn't look out the window.

I hear the soft creak of her window opening. "Hello?" Chloe's voice, tentative and slightly fearful, cuts through the night air. "Is someone there?"

I hold my breath, not daring to move a muscle. Seconds stretch into an eternity as I wait, praying she'll give up and go back inside. When I don't hear anything, I quickly leave, running down the street to where my truck is waiting.

I slide into my truck, hands shaking as I fumble with the keys. My mind is racing, replaying every moment of what I watched. The image of Chloe, transformed into her vixen alter ego, is burned into my retinas. I can't shake the sound of her voice, husky with desire, as she described what she really wanted from our innocent cocoa date.

I know I shouldn't, but before I can stop myself, I'm opening the Dark Secrets app.

My fingers hover over the search bar. What name would she use? Something mysterious, sexy as fuck . . . I search through the most recently uploaded videos and streams, my heart racing with each attempt. Finally, I see her.

The profile picture is a close-up of red lips and a hint of that lace mask.

Username: BlackAsChlo.

I click on her profile, scrolling through the content she offers. My mouth goes dry as I see thumbnails of her previous shows, each one sexier than the last. There's a button to subscribe to her channel, to gain access to exclusive content. There's no fee attached, which tells me one thing: Chloe does this by choice. Not for monetary gain.

My thumb hovers over it, trembling slightly. This is a line I never thought I'd cross. If I do this, there's no going back. I'll be one of them, one of the faceless usernames cheering her on, asking for more.

But isn't that what I've always been? A faceless observer, watching from the shadows?

Before I can change my mind, I hit Subscribe. The screen loads, and suddenly I'm in, privy to Chloe's secret world. I scroll through her posts, each one revealing a side of her I never knew existed.

She likes toys. I like toys.

She likes kink . . . so much kink. I fucking adore kink.

One video catches my eye. The thumbnail shows Chloe—no, BlackAsChlo—in a dimly lit room, her wrists bound above her head. The title reads, "Punish me, Daddy."

My finger hovers over the play button. This is wrong. I shouldn't be seeing this. But I've already crossed so many lines tonight. What's one more?

I press Play.

The video starts with Chloe struggling against her restraints, her eyes wide behind her mask.

"I've been a bad girl," she says.

Her latest video is there, the one I saw in person. I hit Play, my breath catching as I watch the scene unfold from a new angle.

Chloe's voice fills my truck, erotic and alluring. "I saw someone today," she purrs, and I shiver, knowing she's talking about me. I watch, transfixed, as she pleasures herself, describing in vivid detail what she wished I had done to her.

My hand drifts to my lap, almost of its own accord. I know this is wrong—

I can't do this. Not yet. Not yet . . .

I shut off my phone, my hands shaking. The night's revelations swirl in my mind. As I sit there in my truck, I realize that everything has changed. The game has shifted, the rules rewritten. And I'm not sure if I'm the protector anymore, or just another moth drawn to Chloe's flame.

I start the engine again, my mind made up. I need to see her again, to look into her eyes knowing what I know now. To see if I can spot a glimmer of BlackAsChlo behind Chloe's innocent facade.

CHAPTER TEN
CHLOE

"Hello?" I call out as I walk toward the window.

Why am I saying hello to a potential serial killer standing outside my window? And why in the hell am I walking toward him?

My heart pounds as I take another step. The rational part of my brain tells me it was the wind. I didn't hear anything more than a tree branch falling. My chance meeting with Tyler today is making me paranoid. But the irrational part, the part that's been on high alert since I saw his face at the café, insists there's someone out here. And when I came home today, my walkway had been shoveled *again*.

I take another hesitant step, my bare feet silent on the hardwood floor. I strain my ears, listening for any sound that might confirm my fears.

Silence.

Then, a soft scraping noise. My breath catches in my throat. That was definitely not the wind.

I should run. I should turn around, grab my phone, and lock myself in the bathroom. But my body isn't listening to reason. I'm moving forward again, my hand outstretched toward the window to crack it open so I can hear better.

Still silence.

It's nothing. I'm just acting crazy.

But not crazier than coming home almost immediately after my date . . . not date . . . maybe date . . . with Jack and obsessing over every little detail of our conversation. Not crazier than going on Dark Secrets tonight and getting my rocks off for all my subscribers.

Giving up and closing the window, I return to my computer, my heart rate slowly returning to normal. I settle into my chair, the soft glow of the screen illuminating my face in the dimly lit room. My fingers hover over the keyboard, ready to do mindless scrolling through Dark Secrets and seeing what fun pics and videos I can find.

But I can't shake the unease. My eyes keep darting to the window, half expecting to see a face pressed against the glass. I will myself to focus on my feed, but the images blur together, failing to capture my attention or arouse me like they usually do.

A soft ping from my phone makes me jump. I grab it, heart racing again, but it's a notification from Dark Secrets. A new message. Probably from one of my regular subscribers, asking for a custom video or a private chat.

I open the app, my finger hovering over the message icon. But something catches my eye in the notifications tab. A new follower. I tap on it, curiosity overriding my lingering fear.

The username makes my blood run cold: WinterWatcher.

It can't be. It's a coincidence, right? But as I click on the profile, the bio reads: "I like to watch from afar. Always from afar."

My hands shake as I scroll through WinterWatcher's activity. He's liked every single one of my posts from the past month already.

He's studying me.

My mind races, trying to connect the dots. Tyler at the café. The shoveled walkway. The noise outside my window. And now this . . . WinterWatcher.

I close the app, my breath coming in short, sharp gasps. It's too much of a coincidence.

Tyler?

No, this is ridiculous.

I'm in my head. I know I can get like this once I get worked up. It's not easy being a single woman living alone in New York.

Tyler is nice. Too nice.

That's the problem. That's why I'm not interested in him. I want a man who can dominate me. Someone who can make me cry out as he spanks me, who can tie me up and make me beg for release.

But now my thoughts return to Jack. Jack is nice. Is he too nice?

I shake my head, trying to clear my muddled thoughts. Jack is different. There's an undercurrent of intensity beneath his polite exterior that I can't quite put my finger on. But Tyler . . . Tyler's niceness always feels forced, like he is trying too hard to be the perfect gentleman.

Taking a deep breath, I turn off my computer. I'm done for the night.

As I change into my pajamas, I can't shake the feeling of being watched. I double-check the locks on my windows and look outside one last time. My Christmas lights are off. Were they always off?

Sliding into bed, I pull the covers up to my chin, feeling like a child afraid of the monsters in the closet.

Sleep eludes me. I toss and turn, my thoughts a jumbled mess of Tyler, Jack, and WinterWatcher. Every creak of the house makes me start, my heart leaping into my throat.

Around 3 a.m., I give up on sleep. I reach for my phone, telling myself I'll just scroll through social media to distract myself. But my fingers betray me, opening the Dark Secrets app instead.

WinterWatcher has been active. He's left comments on my older posts now, innocuous things like "Beautiful" and "Stunning." But there's one comment that makes my heart stop: "I wonder what other dark secrets you have."

Something inside of me wants to respond. But I never speak to any subscribers. I never interact. I never comment. I'm not going to start now . . .

My thumb hovers over the reply button, twitching in suspense. I've never broken my rule of nonengagement before, but something about this situation feels different. Dangerous. Maybe if I respond, I can get more information, figure out if this really is Tyler or just some random guy.

It can't be Tyler. Why am I thinking it's Tyler? In fact, why do I think I know WinterWatcher at all? He could be anyone. He could even be a she. Why am I overreacting?

I turn off my phone and roll over. I toss and turn for another hour, my mind racing with possibilities. Every shadow seems to move, every noise amplified in the stillness of the night. Finally, as the first hints of dawn start to creep through my curtains, I drift into a fitful sleep.

My dreams are a confusing jumble of images: Tyler's too-wide smile, Jack's intense gaze, and a shadowy figure standing outside my window, watching. Always watching.

I wake with a start, my alarm blaring. For a moment, I'm disoriented, the events of last night feeling like a distant nightmare. But as I reach for my phone to silence the alarm, reality comes crashing back. It's time to be Chloe. Cute, bubbly, admired by many Chloe Hallman, jewelry influencer.

BlackAsChlo needs to go back into the shadows where she belongs.

CHAPTER ELEVEN
CHLOE

How many days is normal to wait for a text after a date? Not that Jack and I had an actual date. It was just a coincidental meetup. But he said he'd text, so I stare at my phone for what feels like the hundredth time today, willing it to light up with a notification.

It wasn't a real date, I keep reminding myself. Just a chance encounter. But the way his eyes crinkled when he smiled, how attentively he listened to every word I said . . . it felt like more.

I sigh and toss my phone onto the desk, determined to stop obsessing. But as I turn away, a faint buzz makes my heart leap. I snatch it up, fumbling in my haste.

It's just an Insta notification. Disappointment crashes over me.

"Get a grip," I mutter to myself.

Deciding to obsess over something else, I decide to look at my views and engagement on my most recent post for Moth to the Flame. I wasn't feeling it while filming, and I have a pretty good feeling that my video is going to prove to me that my viewers felt the same way.

As I scroll through the analytics, my suspicions are confirmed. The view count is dismal, likes are sparse, and the comments are . . . well, there aren't many. I groan, slumping back in my chair. This is exactly what I needed—another blow to my already fragile ego. If I want to remain the brand ambassador for Moth to the Flame Designs, I'm going to have to get my shit together. I need this job if I want to remain in this house. This is not even up for debate. I need to pull myself together and focus on creating content that will resonate with my audience.

In desperate need of a pick-me-up, I close out that app and move to the one I actually love being part of. I try really hard not to log in to Dark Secrets until the late hours as my reward for staying focused and on task, but right now, I need the dopamine hit from the comments I know are waiting for me from my live last night.

This is my true escape, my secret world where I can be anyone I want. The persona I've crafted here is confident, mysterious, and alluring—everything I wish I could be in real life.

The notification icon is lit up, and I tap it eagerly. Comments and messages flood in, each one a little burst of validation. You were amazing last night! Can't wait for your next stream! You're the highlight of my evening!

I bask in the praise, feeling my mood lift with each message. Here, in this digital realm, I'm adored. Desired. Important. It's potent, and for a moment, I forget about my real-world troubles—the lackluster content, spending another holiday without my parents, living in their house which is far above my means, and the lingering disappointment of Jack's silence, wondering if I read more into our hot chocolate date—not date—than he did.

But as I scroll through the comments, one causes my heart to race.

I loved how you finally showed more of your face. I wish you had shown even more.

Wait! What?

I pull up my replay to see for myself. Panic sets in. My heart races as I frantically scan through the video, praying it's a misunderstanding. But there it is—a moment where the camera slipped, and the lighting is just right, revealing more of my features than I ever intended. It's only a few seconds, but it feels like an eternity as I watch my carefully crafted anonymity crumble.

I slam my laptop shut, breathing heavily. This can't be happening. My mind whirls with potential consequences. What if someone recognizes me? What if this gets back to Moth to the Flame, to the brand I represent? I signed a morality clause! No way does masturbating with a dildo on a live stream classify as moral. Fuck me. Fuck me and not in the fun dildo-fuck-me kind of way.

The life I've built could come crashing down around me.

What will Moth to the Flame do if they know that rather than promoting their jewelry next to gingerbread and mistletoe, I'm instead using their delicate chains and pendants as sensual props in my late-night streams? The thought makes me nauseous. I've worked so hard to keep these two worlds separate, and now they're threatening to collide in the most catastrophic way possible.

I know better than this. I've always been so careful. But Jack . . . he got me so . . . fuck . . .

With trembling fingers, I reopen the laptop and start damage control. I delete the video, hoping it hasn't been screen-recorded or shared elsewhere. But the internet is forever, and I know deep down that I can't undo what's been done.

My stomach grumbles and I'm not sure if it's from fear or hunger, but because I haven't eaten since breakfast and I've been cooped up inside all day working, I decide to venture out for some food . . .

and a stiff cocktail. Maybe a change of scenery will help clear my head and give me some perspective on this mess.

I grab my coat and keys, hurrying out the door before I can change my mind. The crisp evening air hits my face, and I take a deep breath, trying to calm my nerves. I take a look around and I'm struck by how quiet the neighborhood is.

Almost too quiet.

And I get this eerie feeling that eyes are on me.

I shake off the paranoia, chalking it up to my frayed nerves. Still, I glance over my shoulder as I walk down the sidewalk. The street-lights cast long shadows, and every rustle of leaves makes me jump.

The local pub is a few blocks away, and I set off at a brisk pace, my mind still racing.

As I walk down the street, I try to take in the holiday decorations adorning the storefronts and lampposts. Twinkling lights and garlands of evergreen should lift my spirits, but they only serve as a stark reminder of how alone I feel.

Alone and lost.

As I push open the heavy wooden door of The Rusty Nail, the familiar scent of beer and fried food greet me. It's busy for a weeknight, the low hum of conversation punctuated by occasional bursts of laughter. I make my way to the bar, squeezing into an empty spot.

"What'll it be?" the bartender asks, wiping down the counter.

"Whiskey, neat," I reply, surprising myself. I'm usually more of a fruity cocktail kind of girl, but I can't exactly order a piña colada and sound cool, and tonight calls for something stronger. "And a side of fries, please." Not the healthiest dinner, but it will hit the spot.

The bartender nods and pours me a generous measure. I take a sip, wincing at the burn. As the warmth spreads through my chest and kills every single germ I may or may not have had in my body, I scan the room, half hoping to see a familiar face and half dreading it.

No one is here. Just me. Alone.

But that is when the door opens and snow comes flurrying in, followed by a tall figure in a dark coat. My heart skips a beat as I recognize the silhouette. Jack.

He stamps his feet, shaking off the snow, and looks around the pub. Our eyes meet, and for a moment, I'm frozen. Should I wave? Pretend I didn't see him? Before I can decide, he's making his way over to me, a hesitant smile on his face.

"Hey," he says, sliding onto the stool next to me. "Fancy meeting you here."

I try to keep my voice casual, despite the butterflies in my stomach. "I, uh . . . do you come here often?"

He shakes his head, signaling the bartender. "I'd like to tell you this was a coincidence," he begins with a smile, "but I actually saw you walking in here from across the street," Jack admits, a sheepish grin on his face. "I was on my way to salt Mr. Haven's walkway. I hope you don't mind me joining you."

My heart races at his confession. He saw me and decided to follow? Part of me is thrilled, but another part is wary. After all, I barely know this man.

"No, I don't mind," I say, trying to sound nonchalant. "It's nice to see a familiar face."

Jack orders a beer and turns to face me fully. "Cheers," he says as he raises the glass.

I clink mine against his, the whiskey sloshing dangerously close to the rim. "Cheers," I echo, taking another sip. The alcohol is already starting to dull the edges of my anxiety, but Jack's presence brings a new kind of nervousness.

"So," he says, his eyes gleaming in the dim pub light, "what brings you out on a night like this? Escaping the holiday madness?"

I laugh, but it comes out more like a nervous titter. "Something like that," I reply vaguely. How can I explain that I'm here drowning my sorrows over a potential career-ending mistake in my secret online life? "Needed a change of scenery, I guess. What about you? Isn't it a bit late to be shoveling snow?" I pause and decide to ask something that has been bothering me ever since I came home and saw the snow removed again. "You didn't by chance shovel my walkway yesterday?"

Jack's eyes widen slightly as he lowers his beer. "Ah, you caught me," he admits with a sheepish grin. "I hope you don't mind. I was already helping Mr. Haven and decided to do yours too."

My heart flutters at his thoughtfulness. "That was really sweet of you," I say, feeling a warmth that isn't just from the whiskey. "Thank you."

He shrugs, looking almost embarrassed. "It was nothing, really. I like helping out where I can."

There's a pause as we both sip our drinks, the noise of the pub swirling around us. I'm hyperaware of how close we're sitting, our knees almost touching. I'm grateful when the bartender arrives with my fries, simply because it breaks this odd tension between us.

"Funny story," I add. "When I came home yesterday and saw it done, I started to really feel I may have a stalker. A snow-shoveling stalker."

CHAPTER TWELVE
JACK

Trying to act cool and collected while your palms sweat isn't easy. I wipe my hands on my jeans for the third time, hoping Chloe doesn't notice. She's mentioned having a stalker more than once. She's noticed her walkway being cleaned. And me entering the same bar she entered was pushing things too far. And after watching her last night . . . everything has changed. Everything.

I saw her videos. I can see what she's favorited. I can see everything and all her hidden kinks. And fuck me . . . they are the same as mine. If Dark Secrets were a dating app, we'd be a match.

But I'm fucking up. I'm getting too close.

Am I hoping to get caught? Because I'm acting really fucking careless right now.

"A stalker to shovel your snow, huh?" I say as I chase my question with my beer. "Most people would consider that a good thing."

"I've been getting this feeling lately. And I heard noises . . ." she says. "Last night I freaked myself out and—" She shakes her head. "Clearly I was overreacting since you just admitted to doing my walkway."

"You live in a safe neighborhood," I add. "And it was windy last night. But make sure you lock up and keep your eyes open just in case." I feel like an absolute creep. I'm the cause of her distress, and I'm trying to play it down like it's nothing.

The tension in her shoulders relaxes a bit, but I can still see doubt lingering in her eyes. "Yeah, you're probably right," she says, but her voice lacks conviction.

I need to change the subject, and fast. "So, tell me about your Christmas plans. Anything fun planned? A trip?"

She sighs, taking a sip of her whiskey and grimacing.

"Not really," Chloe says, setting down her glass. "Holidays aren't really my thing."

"No family to visit?" I ask, trying to keep my tone casual.

Yes, I already know the answer to this question, and I feel like an asshole bringing up a painful topic, but I need to take a huge step away from familiar. I feel as if I'm getting too close to being caught. I need to play the perfect stranger role. I need to ask all the "normal" questions a man who knows nothing about a woman would ask.

Chloe shakes her head, a glimmer of sadness crossing her face. "Not anymore. It's just me."

Guilt stabs at my gut as I see the pain present. As much as I want to tell her that I know more about her family situation than I should, I can't let on.

"I'm sorry to hear that," I say, reaching out to touch her hand briefly before pulling back. "The holidays can be tough when you're on your own."

She nods, her eyes distant. "Yeah, it's . . . it's not easy. But I manage. What about you? Big family celebration planned?"

I chuckle, trying to lighten the mood. "Nah, I'm a bit of a lone wolf myself. Probably order some Chinese food and watch terrible Christmas movies." Wanting to give her a little more, I add, "My mother loved the holidays when she was alive, but now that it's just me . . ." I shrug. "You know."

"Was she your only family?"

"Yeah, and when she died, I bounced around as a kid does in that situation, but Christmas was never the same."

Chloe's eyes soften, and for a moment, I see a look of genuine empathy. "I'm sorry about your mom," she says quietly. "It's hard, isn't it? Trying to celebrate when the people who made it special are gone."

I nod, surprised by the sudden lump in my throat. I hadn't meant to bring up my mother, but something about Chloe makes me want to open up. "Yeah, it is. Sometimes I think about trying to re-create those old traditions, but it feels . . . empty."

She reaches out, her fingers lightly brushing against mine. The touch sends a jolt through me, and I have to resist the urge to pull away. I'm not used to this kind of gentle contact, especially not from her. As if she senses my discomfort, she pulls away and reaches for her drink again.

"I lost my parents a little over two years ago," she admits. "Car accident we were all in. Things haven't been the same since."

I know, I want to say. I want to admit that I was the one working the scene that night. That I was the firefighter who pulled her parents' bodies from the wreckage. That I held her shaking hand as I got her into the ambulance. That I went to the hospital after my shift to check on her and have watched over her ever since.

I swallow hard, forcing myself to maintain eye contact. "I'm so sorry. That must have been devastating." The words feel hollow, inadequate. I want to tell her everything, to confess that I was there, that I've known her pain intimately since that night. But I can't. It would ruin everything.

She nods, blinking rapidly. "It was. Still is, sometimes. But life goes on, right?" She attempts a smile, but it doesn't reach her eyes.

I nod sympathetically, keeping my expression neutral despite the turmoil inside me.

Chloe takes another sip of her whiskey, this time not grimacing at the taste. "You know, it's funny. I haven't talked about them in . . . I can't even remember how long. My therapist would probably say this is progress."

I chuckle, trying to keep the mood light. "Well, I'm honored to be part of your progress, then."

She laughs, a genuine sound that makes my heart skip. "You should be. I don't open up to just anyone, you know."

The irony of her statement isn't lost on me. If only she knew how close we really are.

"I'm glad you feel comfortable with me," I say, meaning every word. "Sometimes it's easier to talk to a stranger, isn't it?"

"But you aren't a stranger, are you?"

Her words hang in the air, and for a moment, my heart seizes. Does she know? Has she figured it out? Has she been playing a game of cat and mouse with me? Toying with me to see me squirm? I had tested the limits, and maybe it's time for the truth to be revealed.

I force myself to stay calm, however. Waiting to see.

"What do you mean?" I ask, trying to keep my voice steady.

Chloe smiles, and a wave of relief washes over me. "I mean, we've shared hot chocolate together now. That means something." She giggles. "But yeah, something about you has always felt . . . familiar. You don't feel like a stranger. At least not anymore." She leans in, her eyes searching mine. "There's something about you, Jack. I can't quite put my finger on it, but . . . I feel like I can trust you. Is that crazy?"

I swallow against the guilt and desire warring inside me. "No, not crazy at all. I feel the same way about you."

And it's true. Despite everything, despite the lies and the secrets, I do feel a connection with Chloe. One that goes beyond my initial fascination with her. One that scares me more than I'd like to admit. And after what I discovered about her last night . . . Well, it's fair to say that my obsession has grown to a completely new level of insanity.

This woman is my dream girl, and she doesn't even know it.

"Another drink?" I ask, desperate to break the tension.

She nods, and I signal the bartender. As he pours our drinks, I steal glances at Chloe. She's playing with a strand of her hair, lost in thought. I wonder what she's thinking about. Is she still worried about her stalker . . . aka me? Is she thinking about her parents? Or is she thinking about me?

The bartender sets down our drinks, and Chloe raises her glass. "To new friends," she says with a smile.

I clink my glass against hers, ignoring the voice in my head that screams I'm anything but a new friend. "To new friends," I echo.

"I'm sure you see a lot of car accidents in your job," she says.

My mind races, trying to figure out how to respond without revealing too much.

"Yeah, unfortunately, it's a big part of the job," I say carefully. "Every accident is different, but they're all tough to deal with."

Chloe nods, her eyes distant. "I can't imagine what it must be like, being the first on the scene, seeing people . . . broken." She looks at me then, her eyes searching mine. "Have you ever . . . lost anyone? On the job, I mean."

The question hits me like a punch to the gut. Images flash through my mind: her parents' mangled car, the smell of gasoline and blood, the way her mother's hand had gone limp in mine as I tried to pull her from the wreckage. Chloe had been so lucky to have survived that night. No one should have walked away from an accident like that and yet she had.

I take a long swig of my drink, buying time. "Yeah," I say finally, my voice rough. "It happens. More often than I'd like."

"I'm sorry," she says in a way that could melt the most heartless of hearts. "That must be so hard."

I nod, not trusting myself to speak. The irony of her comforting me about her own parents' death is almost too much to bear.

"You know," she continues, her voice thoughtful, "I never got to thank the firefighters who were there that night. When my parents . . ." She trails off, shaking her head. "It's all a blur."

My heart pounds so loudly I'm sure she must be able to hear it. I want to tell her. I want to confess everything. But I can't. Not now, not like this.

Chloe shakes her head, her eyes misty. "This night is becoming a bummer." She finishes her drink in one gulp, then stands up abruptly. "Why don't we go for a walk and take in the Christmas lights."

I hesitate for a moment, caught off guard by her sudden change in mood. But I can't deny the appeal of spending more time with her, even if it means prolonging this dangerous game.

"Sure," I say, standing up and reaching for my coat. "Some fresh air might do us both good."

CHAPTER THIRTEEN
CHLOE

Shoveling snow, hot chocolate, and now walking beneath the snowflakes of New York. How much more Hallmark movie can you get?

Oh and Jack. He's a freaking fireman, for Christ's sake.

I shake my head, laughing at the absurdity of it all. Jack catches my eye and grins, his perfect teeth gleaming against the glow of the Christmas lights.

"What's so funny?" he asks. "Care to share?"

"Nothing," I reply, trying to suppress my smile. "Just thinking about how perfectly Christmassy this is. And I'm not exactly the most in-the-spirit person. I'm two steps away from being a Scrooge."

Jack chuckles, his breath visible in the frosty air. "Well, we can't have that, can we? I'll make it my personal mission to turn you into a regular Cindy-Lou Who by Christmas Eve."

I roll my eyes but can't help the warmth spreading through my chest. "Good luck with that, Fireman Jack. I'm a tough nut to crack."

"I love a challenge," he says, winking at me. "Besides, I have a few tricks up my sleeve."

As if on cue, I slip on a patch of ice and Jack reaches out and catches me by the arm. I legit slipped, but you couldn't ask for a better setup.

I steady myself, my hand lingering on Jack's arm a moment longer than necessary. "Smooth move," I mutter, both to myself and him. "Is this one of your tricks?"

Jack's eyes twinkle with mischief. "Nah, that was all you. But I'll take credit for the save." He takes hold of my hand. "But I will keep a hold of this. Just in case."

"Just in case," I parrot as our fingers lace together.

We continue walking, our footsteps stomping in the fresh snow. The city feels quieter than usual, muffled by the blanket of white.

"So, Ms. Scrooge," Jack says, breaking the comfortable silence. "What's your usual Christmas tradition? Sitting alone in a dark room, plotting against holiday cheer?"

I snort. "Close. It usually involves a bottle of wine, Chinese takeout, and binge-watching true crime documentaries."

Jack's eyebrows shoot up. "Wow, you weren't kidding about the Scrooge thing. That's . . . intense."

I shrug. "Hey, don't knock it till you've tried it. Nothing says happy holidays like learning about serial killers while stuffing your face with lo mein."

Jack laughs, squeezing my hand. "All right, all right. No judgment here. But maybe you can find a middle ground between murder docs and *Miracle on 34th Street*?"

I groan dramatically. "Next thing you know, you'll be asking me to hang stockings and sing carols."

"Don't tempt me." He grins. "I've got a great singing voice. I could serenade you with 'Baby, It's Cold Outside' right here on the street."

"Please don't," I laugh, bumping his shoulder with mine. "I'd hate for you to become the next victim of one of my true crimes."

Jack feigns a hurt expression. "Ouch. And here I thought I was making progress with you."

I roll my eyes again but can't help smiling. "You're doing all right, I guess. But don't push your luck."

We round a corner, and suddenly we're face-to-face with a massive Christmas tree in the center of a small park. It's decked out in thousands of holiday lights, ornaments of all sizes, and a giant star on top. The sight is breathtaking, even to my Grinch-like heart.

"Wow," I breathe, unable to hide my awe. "I haven't seen this lit up before. I'm not usually out at night much."

Jack's grin widens. "See? Even the toughest nut can crack a little."

I try to scowl at him but fail miserably. "Fine, it's pretty. Happy now?"

"Ecstatic," he replies, tugging me closer to the tree. "Come on, let's get a closer look."

As we approach, I notice a small group of carolers gathered near the base of the tree. Their harmonies float through the crisp air, and I find myself humming along despite my best efforts not to.

Jack notices, of course. "Is that 'Silent Night' I hear you humming?"

"Absolutely not," I deny quickly. "I was just . . . clearing my throat."

"Right," he says, clearly not buying it. "Well, since you're 'clearing your throat,' why don't we join them?"

I shoot him a look of mock horror. "Join the carolers? Me? I thought you were trying to spread Christmas cheer, not traumatize innocent bystanders."

Jack laughs, the sound warm and rich. "Come on, it'll be fun.

And I promise to sing extra loud to cover up any, uh, throat clearing you might do."

Before I can protest further, he's leading me toward the group. They welcome us with bright smiles and nods, barely missing a beat in their rendition of "Deck the Halls." Jack jumps right in, his voice surprisingly melodic. I stand there awkwardly for a moment, mouth firmly shut.

But then Jack gives my hand a gentle squeeze, his eyes encouraging. And something in me softens. Maybe it's the magical lights, or the infectious joy of the carolers, or just Jack's unwavering enthusiasm. Whatever it is, I find myself opening my mouth and joining in, quietly at first, then with growing confidence.

We stay with the carolers for a few more songs, and I hate to admit it, but it's . . . nice. There's something magical about our voices blending together in the cold night air, with the magnificent tree towering above us.

As we finish "We Wish You a Merry Christmas," Jack leans in close, his breath warm against my ear. "See? I knew you had it in you, Cindy-Lou."

I elbow him playfully. "Don't get cocky, Fireman Jack. This doesn't mean I'm going to start watching Hallmark movies or anything."

"Baby steps." He gives me a toothy grin. "But I'd say this is definitely progress."

We bid farewell to the carolers and continue our walk toward my home, our joined hands swinging between us. The neighborhood seems different now, softer somehow. Or maybe it's me that's softening.

"So," Jack says after a while. "Chinese food and true crime, huh? You know, that doesn't sound half-bad. Maybe we could do that together sometime before Christmas to get us in the spirit. It might be a better date than ice skating and more Christmas cheer in Bryant Park. What do you think?"

I nearly trip over my own feet at his suggestion. He used the word *date*. A date? With Jack? The idea sends a flutter through my stomach that I'm not entirely sure how to interpret.

"A date?" I echo, trying to keep my voice casual. "I thought your mission was to make me more festive, not corrupt you with my Grinch-like ways."

Jack shrugs, a lopsided grin on his face. "Who says we can't do both? We'll eat Chinese food, watch true crime, and then follow it up with *It's a Wonderful Life*. Best of both worlds."

I laugh at the image. "That sounds . . . surprisingly appealing, actually." I pretend to consider it for a moment, tapping my chin thoughtfully. "Well, I suppose I could pencil you in. But fair warning: my commentary during true crime docs can get pretty dark."

"Wanna know a secret? I happen to like dark," he says, his eyes connecting with mine.

Jesus. I swallow hard, trying to ignore the sudden spark of electricity between us. "Dark, huh? Be careful what you wish for, Jack."

He holds my gaze, his expression turning serious. "I'm not afraid of the dark. Or of you."

My thoughts return to my video on Dark Secrets and how close I came to revealing my true self. The intensity of the moment throws me off balance. I look away, focusing on the snow-covered sidewalk. "Maybe you should be," I mutter, more to myself than to him.

Jack's hand tightens around mine, but he doesn't say anything. We walk in silence for a few moments. I'm not sure why I said that, why I let that little hint of darkness slip out. Maybe it's the magic of the night getting to me, making me feel more open than usual.

Jack clears his throat. "You know . . . I'm not all rescuing kittens from trees and running into burning buildings."

I glance at him, surprised by the seriousness in his tone. "Oh? Secrets too?"

Jack's expression is unreadable in the dim light. "More than I'd like to admit."

We've stopped walking now as we reach my front porch, standing in a pool of light from the nearby Christmas colors on my hedge. Snowflakes dance around us, but I barely notice them. I'm captivated by this new, mysterious side of Jack.

I study his face, trying to decipher the meaning behind his words. "Care to elaborate on that, Fireman Jack?"

He steps closer, his eyes intense. "I'm not sure you're ready for that side of me."

My heart races at his proximity. "And here I thought you were a walking Hallmark movie," I tease, but my voice comes out breathier than I intended.

Jack's lips quirk into a half smile. "There's a lot you don't know about me yet. Just like I'm sure there's a lot I don't know about you."

"Careful," I warn, but I'm not sure if I'm talking to him or myself. "You might not like what you find out."

"Try me," he challenges, his voice low.

We stand there, the tension between us suffocating. I'm acutely aware of how close we are, how easy it would be to close the distance between us. Part of me wants to run, to retreat back into my safe, cynical world. But another part, a part that's growing stronger by the second, wants to take the risk.

Kiss me, Jack.

Come on . . . do it.

Kiss me.

Nothing . . . damn it.

"Maybe . . ." I pause, gathering my courage. "Maybe we could start with that date. Chinese food, true crime, and all the dark commentary you can handle."

Jack's face breaks into a genuine smile. "I'd like that. A lot."

He leans in, and for a moment I think he's going to finally kiss me. Instead, he brushes a snowflake from my cheek, his touch sending a jolt of heat straight to my pussy.

"Good night, Ms. Scrooge," he murmurs. "Sweet dreams of sugarplums and serial killers."

I laugh softly, trying to ignore the disappointment at the lack of a kiss. "Good night, Fireman Jack. Try not to save too many kittens before our date."

As I watch him walk away, his broad shoulders dusted with snow, I try to suppress the little schoolgirl inside of me that wants to squeal. Jack is charming, handsome, and surprisingly intriguing. But I have dated enough vanilla men to know how this ends. And Jack may be sexy as fuck, but no way is he the type of man that would pull my hair, choke me out, and fuck me as I plead for mercy.

I unlock my front door, still feeling the ghost of Jack's touch on my cheek. As I step inside, I'm hit with the silence of my empty house. The contrast between the magical night outside and the stark reality of my solitary life is jarring.

Shrugging off my coat, I head straight for the kitchen and pour myself a generous glass of wine. I need to clear my head, to shake off this ridiculous Hallmark movie feeling that's threatening to overtake me.

I settle onto my couch, laptop open, ready to dive back into editing my latest video. But my mind keeps wandering back to Jack. His smile, his laugh, the way his hand felt in mine . . .

"Get it together," I mutter to myself, taking a long sip of wine. "He's just a guy. A hot, charming guy who probably has no idea what he's getting himself into."

I try to focus on my work, but the words on the screen blur together. Instead, I find myself imagining what our date might be like. Would Jack be shocked by my dark humor? Would he be disgusted if he knew the things I think about, the things I crave?

My hand unconsciously drifts to my neck, fantasizing about the feeling of being choked, controlled. God, I crave that in someone . . . someone like Jack. The thrill, the danger, the exquisite balance of pain and pleasure.

I shake my head, trying to dispel the thoughts. There's no way Jack, with his boy-next-door charm and heroic job, would be into anything like that. He'd probably run screaming if he knew the truth about me. But then I remember the intensity in his eyes when he said he wasn't afraid of the dark. The way his voice dropped when he hinted at his own secrets.

I close my laptop, giving up on getting any work done tonight. My mind is too full of Jack and possibilities. I lean back on the couch, letting my imagination run wild.

I picture his strong firefighter's hands gripping my throat, his eyes dark with desire. In my mind, he pins me against the wall, his body hard against mine. "Is this what you want?" Fantasy Jack growls in my ear. "Is this dark enough for you?"

My breath quickens as the fantasy takes hold. I slip a hand beneath my waistband, finding myself already wet. As I touch myself, I imagine it's Jack's fingers, rough and demanding. In my mind, he takes control, pushing me to my knees, fisting his hand in my hair.

"Oh god," I moan softly, my fingers working faster. The fantasy is so vivid I can almost feel Jack's presence, smell his scent—a mix of smoke and pine and pure masculinity.

I circle my clit with my fingers, imagining they're his thumb. I pulse harder, the sensation intensifying, my body responding to the fantasy with a growing urgency.

In my mind, he speaks again, his voice low and demanding. "Do you want it rough, or sweet? Do you want to submit or take control?"

And I choose both. I imagine him tying me up, restraining me, forcing me to be vulnerable and powerless. In the same breath, I also envision his tender touch, his lips tracing delicate patterns on my skin, whispering promises of pleasure and pain intertwined.

My hips buck involuntarily as the fantasy intensifies. I'm so close now, teetering on the edge of release. In my mind, Jack's hands roam my body, alternating between gentle caresses and forceful grips. His mouth claims mine in a searing kiss, then travels down my neck, leaving a trail of fire in its wake.

"Please," I whimper, both to the Jack in my mind and to the empty room around me.

Fantasy Jack smirks, a wicked glint in his eyes. "Please what? Use your words."

I arch my back, my fingers working faster, mimicking what I imagine his touch would feel like. "Please . . . I need . . ."

"What do you need?" His voice is a low growl that sends shivers down my spine.

"You," I gasp. "I need you. All of you. The darkness, the light, everything."

In my mind, he rewards my honesty with a bruising kiss, his hands everywhere at once. I'm lost in the sensations, real and imagined blurring together. The tension builds, a coiling spring ready to snap.

"Come for me," fantasy Jack commands.

I'm close to the edge when suddenly, my phone buzzes. I jump, startled out of my reverie. It's a text from Jack.

Sweet dreams, it reads. Looking forward to our date. P.S. I like my lo mein extra spicy. Hope you can handle the heat.

I stare at the message, my heart racing. Is he flirting? Or am I reading too much into it, seeing innuendo where there is none?

I type out several responses, deleting each one. Finally, I settle on, I can handle more heat than you'd expect, Fireman Jack. Sweet dreams to you too.

As I hit Send, I wonder if I've said too much, revealed too much of my true self. But then I remember the look in Jack's eyes, the hint of something deeper, darker. Maybe, just maybe, there's more to Jack than meets the eye.

And maybe, just maybe, I'm ready to find out.

CHAPTER FOURTEEN
CHLOE

"Your last post was epic!" Sloane says the minute I answer the phone. She never wastes time with a "hello" or "how are you?" It's straight to business with Sloane.

"You think?" I ask, fishing for the compliment. I've been feeling down lately due to lower views, and her praise really does mean the world. Not just as a friend but as someone who actually works for the company.

Maybe I still have a job at Moth to the Flame . . . at least for a bit longer.

"Seriously, Chloe. The way you explained how to layer necklaces without them getting tangled up. How have I lived this long and not known all you have to do is link them together and then treat them as one big necklace? Pure gold."

I smile at the praise and greedily want to hear more. "Really?"

"Really. The higher-ups are buzzing about the reach. I wouldn't be surprised if you get a call from Jasmine herself today."

Jasmine. The CEO of Moth to the Flame. My palms start to sweat at the mere thought of it.

"Anyway, that's not why I'm calling," she says. "I'm heading to Montauk for Christmas. My family is getting together, and I need a wingman. I need someone by my side to help me navigate the chaos. You in?"

I hesitate. Christmas in Montauk sounds amazing, but spending it with Sloane's family? That's a whole different story. I've heard tales of their wild holiday gatherings—the competitive gift exchanges, the heated political debates, the infamous eggnog incident of 2018.

"I don't know, Sloane," I say, biting my lip.

"Oh come on!" she pleads. "It'll be fun. Plus, you can use it as material for your next post. 'How to Survive a Family Christmas Without Losing Your Mind.' Or 'What Necklace to Wear to Hang Yourself.' It'll be a hit!"

She's not wrong—it would make for great content.

But I'm not ready to be cheery and in the spirit. Not yet. I wasn't kidding when I told Jack that I'm a Scrooge. I just can't . . .

"Sloane, I appreciate the offer, but I don't think I'm up for it this year," I say, trying to let her down gently. "Christmas isn't really my thing, you know? Not since—"

"I know. But you can't grieve them forever."

A lump forms in my throat. Sloane's words hit me hard, even though I know she means well.

"I'm not grieving forever," I say, my voice barely above a whisper. "I just . . . need more time."

There's a pause on the other end of the line. I can almost see Sloane's face softening, her usual bravado giving way to concern.

"I didn't mean to push," she says gently. "But maybe . . . maybe this is exactly what you need. A change of scenery, some chaos to distract you. My family may be nuts, but they're also warm and welcoming. You won't have to be alone with your thoughts."

I close my eyes, picturing the empty family home that awaits me for the holidays. The thought of spending another Christmas surrounded by memories and ghosts of Christmases past makes my chest tighten. I'm starting to question staying in this house. Taking on a lease that is far too expensive for me. But I can't say goodbye. It still smells like them. I can still hear their voices. This house is still them.

I take a deep breath, feeling the weight of the decision pressing down on me. Sloane's offer is tempting, a lifeline thrown into the sea of my grief. But can I really face a bustling family Christmas when my own family is so painfully absent?

"Ask me again next year. I promise I'll stop acting like a lump of coal. But I need this year to figure out my shit. Face my shit," I finally say, my voice cracking slightly. "I need to face the memories head-on, you know? Maybe it's time I stop running from them."

Sloane sighs, but I can hear the understanding in her voice. "I get it. But promise me you won't spend the whole time moping around in your pajamas, eating old Chinese food and watching terrible crime docs."

I laugh. "I make no such promises." My thoughts go to Jack and how I may have a partner in crime with my acts.

"At least mix in some action movies or something. *Die Hard* is technically a Christmas movie, you know."

"I'll consider it," I say, smiling despite myself.

"Fine. I'll accept this answer for now. But then you owe me. Let's get drinks tonight. We haven't had our traditional ugly sweater cocktail hour yet this year. It's time," she suggests.

I glance at my calendar, already knowing it's empty. "Sure, I'm free. Where should we meet?"

"The usual spot. Tonic at eight. Don't forget your ugliest sweater!"

I laugh, picturing the gaudy reindeer-covered monstrosity I'd picked up at a thrift store last year. "Oh, don't worry. I've got just the thing."

We chat for a few more minutes before hanging up. I don't have long to get ready if I want to catch the ferry to Manhattan and considering that I've been working on admin all day wearing nothing but sweats and a messy bun, I have some work to do if I'm going to have a chance of measuring up to Sloane's effortless beauty.

I rummage through my closet, tossing clothes left and right. Finally, I unearth the sweater—a garish green thing with a stuffed reindeer head protruding from the front, its red nose flashing with tiny LED lights.

As I pull it on, I grin at my reflection in the mirror and think of Jack. What would he think if he saw me? Not exactly a Scrooge right now.

After spending entirely too long applying makeup and trying to turn my unwashed hair into something presentable, I grab my bag and head out the door.

I slam into what feels like a brick wall but is only a man's chest.

"Whoa there!" a familiar voice chuckles as hands steady me. "Where's the fire?"

"Tyler?" I step back. Why is he at my house? Again.

His eyes travel down to my sweater, and his lips twitch into a grin. "Nice reindeer. Very . . . festive."

"Uh, yeah." I don't like the feeling I'm starting to get. Another unannounced visit is just . . . weird.

"Wanted to congratulate you on your latest post. It's causing quite a stir at the office. We thought we should increase the number of pieces you show off this week since engagement is high," Tyler says, his smile not quite reaching his eyes. He lifts a black velvet bag. "So I volunteered to bring you some more jewelry so you don't have to come all the way to the office."

"Oh . . . okay," I say as I take the bag and place it inside next to the door, not entering the house. "I'll get on that first thing tomorrow."

I shift uncomfortably, acutely aware of how close he's standing. "But I'm actually heading out right now. I'm meeting Sloane for drinks."

"Oh, Sloane," Tyler says, his tone shifting slightly. "You two are pretty close, aren't you?"

I nod, trying to edge past him. "Yeah, we've been friends for a while. Listen, Tyler, I really need to go. I don't want to miss the ferry."

He doesn't move. "You know, I've been thinking. Maybe we should grab a drink sometime, just the two of us. Professional, of course. Discuss some ideas for future posts."

Alarm bells.

"That's . . . nice of you to offer," I say, trying to keep my voice steady. "Maybe we can discuss it at the office sometime?"

Tyler's smile falters for a moment before returning, a bit too wide. "Sure, sure. No pressure. Just thought it might be good to collaborate more closely. You know, given the fact that your posts have had low engagement before the most recent . . . and I'd hate to see you lose your seat with the company."

The implication hangs in the air between us. Is he threatening me? Suggesting he has some sway over my job security?

"Right," I say, finally managing to step around him. "Well, I really do need to go. Thanks for stopping by."

I hurry down the steps, my heart racing. As I reach the sidewalk, I can't resist glancing back. Tyler is still standing there, watching me with an unreadable expression.

The entire ferry ride to Manhattan, I can't shake the uneasy feeling that I'm being watched, but I know it's impossible. I left

Tyler on my porch, and he wouldn't have been able to catch up to me without me noticing. But something is definitely off about him. I can't quite put my finger on it, but off. I debate whether to tell Sloane about Tyler's visit but decide against it. No need to ruin our night out with work drama.

As I approach Tonic, I spot Sloane through the window. She's wearing a sweater that appears to be made entirely of tinsel and Christmas ornaments. I laugh louder than normal, my earlier discomfort fading away.

"There you are!" Sloane exclaims as I enter. "I was beginning to think you'd gotten tangled up in that reindeer."

I settle onto the barstool next to her, grateful for the warmth and cheer of the bar. "Sorry I'm late. I had an . . . unexpected visitor."

Sloane raises an eyebrow. "Oh? Do tell."

I hesitate, then shake my head. "It's nothing. Let's focus on more important things—like how many candy canes are actually attached to your sweater?"

Sloane grins and launches into a detailed explanation of her sweater's construction. As we laugh and sip our festive cocktails, I push thoughts of Tyler and work stress to the back of my mind. For now, at least, I can just enjoy this moment with my friend.

"So, I have a confession," Sloane says as she orders us two more drinks.

"Oh?" I raise an eyebrow, taking a sip of my peppermint martini. "This should be good."

"Actually . . . it's you who should be confessing. You're holding out on me. I thought we were close enough to not keep secrets."

I nearly choke on my drink. "What are you talking about?"

Secrets would be an understatement. The question is, which one?

Sloane crosses her leg, flips her hair and narrows her eyes. "A little birdie told me you've been spending time with a certain someone."

My face is suddenly very hot, and I'm grateful for the dim lighting in the bar. "It's not what you think. We're just—"

"It's fine," she interrupts. "You didn't sign an exclusivity contract or anything. You can show off other jewelry besides Moth to the Flame. And Hailey has some amazing pieces. She's far more . . . edgy . . . gothic. I'm surprised you like it so much. I didn't peg it as your style."

I blink in confusion, my mind racing to catch up with Sloane's words. Hailey? Jewelry?

"Oh," I say, trying to hide my relief that we aren't speaking about Jack or even Dark Secrets. "Yeah, Hailey's jewelry is . . . different, but in a good way."

"You don't have to hide it from me. I mean . . . my designs are still far superior," she teases.

I laugh, grateful for the misunderstanding. "Of course they are. No one can top your designs."

She preens at the compliment, tossing her tinsel-adorned hair. "Damn straight. But seriously, it's okay to branch out a bit. Just don't let Jasmine catch wind of it. You know how possessive she can be about her brand ambassadors."

I nod, remembering the stern talking-to another influencer had received for wearing a competitor's bracelet in an Instagram post. "Trust me, I'm careful."

"Good," Sloane says, raising her glass. "To staying on Jasmine's good side and rocking killer accessories!"

We clink glasses, and I try to push away the guilt gnawing at me. She's right. We shouldn't keep secrets from each other, and lately that's all I've been doing.

"So," I say, eager to change the subject, "tell me more about this family Christmas in Montauk. What exactly am I missing out on?"

Sloane's eyes light up. "Oh, where do I even start? There's Aunt Marge's infamous fruitcake—I swear it's more brandy than cake. And when there's enough snow, we have the snowman-building contest, which always ends in sabotage and tears . . ."

As Sloane regales me with tales of her family's holiday antics, I find myself laughing harder than I have in months. For a moment, I almost regret turning down her invitation. But then I remember the empty house waiting for me, filled with memories I need to face.

"It sounds amazing," I say when she finally pauses for breath. "Maybe next year?"

Sloane's expression softens. "Absolutely. And hey, if you change your mind at the last minute, there's always room for one more. Even if we have to stuff you in the chimney like Santa."

I smile, touched by her persistence. "I'll keep that in mind."

As we continue chatting and sipping our cocktails, my phone buzzes in my pocket. I pull it out, expecting another work email, but then I see the name on the screen.

Jack.

I smile as I read the words.

> JACK: Hey, Scrooge. Hope you're not drowning your sorrows in eggnog. Just want you to know I'm picking up a shift for a buddy, but when I'm off, we can make plans for our date and discuss our anti-Christmas agenda.

There's a flutter in my stomach as I read Jack's message. Part of me wants to respond immediately, but I hesitate, glancing at Sloane.

"Everything okay?" she asks, noticing my sudden distraction.

"Yeah, just . . . nothing," I lie, slipping my phone back into my pocket. I'll respond to Jack later, when I'm alone.

Sloane narrows her eyes and leans forward, her sweater jingling slightly. "Oh no, you don't get to 'just nothing' me. Spill it, Chloe. Who's got you smiling at your phone like that?"

CHAPTER FIFTEEN
CHLOE

Maybe it's the two peppermint martinis, or maybe it's Jack. But I feel my cheeks flush as the room increases in temperature and I have the sudden urge to remove the sweater I'm wearing. "It's nobody, really. Just . . . a friend."

"A friend, huh?" Sloane's grin widens. "A friend who makes you blush like that? Come on, give me something here. I'm seriously worried that you may die of boredom someday. Change my mind that you aren't actually living the most boring existence known to man."

I feign being offended, but she has no idea just how not boring I am. Living this double life as of late has been anything but dull.

I take a deep breath, weighing my options. On one hand, I don't want to lie to Sloane. On the other, I'm not sure I'm ready to share this . . . whatever it is with Jack.

"Okay, fine," I concede. "It's a guy I met recently. We're . . . getting to know each other."

Sloane squeals, earning us a few curious glances from nearby patrons. "I knew it! Tell me everything. Is he hot? Smart? Rich?"

"Safe," I say, shocking myself to hear that as the first word I use to describe Jack.

"Safe?" Sloane repeats, her brow furrowing. "That's not exactly a glowing endorsement. What do you mean by 'safe'?"

I take a sip of my drink, trying to find the right words. "I mean . . . he's a fireman."

Sloane's eyes widen, and she lets out a low whistle. "A fireman? Well, that certainly explains the 'safe' comment. But, girl, you're holding out on me! A fireman is definitely not boring."

I play-punch her arm. "I'm not boring, you know. I have some juicy secrets. You might just not know them all."

Oh yes. The martinis are most definitely taking hold.

Sloane inches closer, her eyes sparkling with intrigue. "Ooh, secrets? Now we're talking. Come on, spill! What juicy secrets are you hiding, Miss Boring?"

I bite my lip, realizing I've said too much. The alcohol is making me loose-lipped, and I need to be careful. "I . . . I meant that there's more to me than you might think."

"Clearly," Sloane says, eyeing me suspiciously. "First a hot fireman, now mysterious secrets. Who are you and what have you done with sweet Chloe?"

I laugh nervously, trying to deflect. "Maybe I'm just full of surprises."

"Well, don't stop now," Sloane urges. "Give me something. Anything. I'm dying here!"

I hesitate, weighing how much I can safely reveal. "Okay, fine. Let's say . . . I've been doing a side project. Not just for Hailey."

Sloane's eyebrows shoot up. "Cheating on me?"

"Not exactly," I hedge. "It's more . . . personal. Just exploring another side of me."

My friend's voice drops to a conspiratorial whisper. "Another side of you? What, like a secret identity? Are you moonlighting as a superhero or something?"

I laugh at the irony. If only she knew how close to the truth she was. "Not quite a superhero. But may involve . . . costumes." I take another sip. "And leather, whips, cuffs, and—" I shrug. "Maybe."

Sloane's eyes widen to the size of saucers, and she nearly spits out her drink. "Wait, what? Are you saying . . . are you doing some kind of . . . kinky stuff?"

My face burns, realizing I've gone too far. "I . . . it's not . . . I mean . . ."

"Oh my god," Sloane whispers, leaning in even closer. "You are! Little Miss Vanilla is secretly a dominatrix or something, aren't you?"

"Well, I'm far from vanilla. But I'm also not a dominatrix. But I do have an account on Dark Secrets. I have subscribers and I like to . . . perform. Do live videos and . . ."

Sloane's mouth drops open, her eyes widening in shock. "Dark Secrets? As in the adult content platform? Chloe, are you serious?"

I nod slowly, the full weight of my admission sinking in. There's no taking it back now.

"Holy shit," Sloane breathes. "I can't believe it. You're like . . . a camgirl?"

I wince at the term. "It's not exactly like that. It's more . . . artistic. Sensual. I don't do hardcore stuff, and I hide my face for the most part. I keep my identity private."

Sloane leans back, studying me with new eyes. "Wow. I never would have guessed. You always seemed so . . . reserved."

"That's kind of the point," I say, feeling strangely relieved to finally share this secret. "It's a way to explore a different side of myself. To be someone else for a little while."

Sloane nods thoughtfully. "Well, girl, I have to say—I'm impressed. And a little jealous. Here I thought you were spending your nights curled up with a book and a cup of tea."

I laugh, feeling lighter than I have in months. "Well, sometimes I do that too. A girl needs balance, you know?"

"And the fireman? Is that how you met him?"

I shake my head. "No. In fact, I think that's one of my hang-ups about the fireman. I've been with vanilla men all my life. I'm ready for a change."

Sloane leans back, a mischievous glint in her eye. "So, the fireman doesn't know about your . . . extracurricular activities?"

I shake my head, feeling a twinge of guilt. "No, he doesn't. And I'm not sure how to bring it up. Or if I even should."

"Oh, hon," Sloane says, patting my hand. "If you're serious about this guy, you'll have to tell him eventually. But maybe not on the first date."

I nod, grateful for her understanding. "It's just . . . complicated. I like Jack, I really do. But this other part of me . . . it's important too."

"Jack, huh?" Sloane grins. "So the fireman has a name. And a pretty hot one at that."

I roll my eyes but can't help smiling. "Yes, his name is Jack. And he's . . . he's different. Kind, funny, and yes, hot."

"But you want something less *safe*," she says.

I nod slowly, feeling conflicted. "Maybe. I don't know. And I'm probably overthinking this. Jack and I haven't even been on a real date yet."

Sloane takes a long sip of her drink, studying me thoughtfully.

"Maybe Jack has hidden depths too. Or maybe he'd be open to exploring new things with you. Plus, firefighters are used to handling heat, right?"

I groan at her terrible pun but a laugh still escapes. "That was awful."

"You love it." She grins. "But seriously, don't write him off just because he seems *safe*. Give him a chance. Maybe he'll surprise you. Also, don't hold back on this Dark Secrets thing either. Explore it. Live it. Fuck . . . maybe I need to as well."

I nearly choke on my drink. "You? On Dark Secrets?"

Sloane shrugs. "Why not? I could use some excitement in my life. Plus, it might be fun to explore my wild side a bit."

"Trust me, your wild side is plenty explored," I laugh, remembering some of Sloane's more outrageous escapades.

"Well, trust me on one thing," she says. "Now that I know this about you, we are going to have much more fun! No more cocktails at geriatric hour for us."

I giggle, feeling a mix of excitement and trepidation at Sloane's words. "Oh no, what have I unleashed?"

"Only the best kind of chaos," Sloane says with a wink. "Now, finish that drink and give me your username so I can look you up."

I nearly choke on my drink. "My username? Oh no, I don't think that's a good idea."

"Come on! I won't tell a soul," Sloane wheedles. "And I promise I won't judge. And who knows, maybe I'll even become a subscriber."

The thought of Sloane watching my videos makes me squirm. "That's . . . really not necessary. And obviously this stays between us."

Sloane pouts but nods. "Fine, keep your secrets. For now. But don't think this conversation is over."

I breathe a sigh of relief, grateful for the reprieve. "Thanks. And really, it's not that exciting. Mostly me in lingerie, maybe a little role-play . . ."

"Uh-huh," Sloane says, clearly unconvinced. "Well, whatever it is, I'm proud of you for exploring that side of yourself. But I also need to put on my corporate, responsible hat too. Be careful. Jasmine is conservative."

I nod. "I know about the morality clause in the contract. Trust me. It keeps me up at night."

Sloane's expression turns serious. "Good. Because as much as I love this wild side of you, I'd hate to see you lose your job over it. Jasmine can be unforgiving when it comes to the company's image."

I nod, feeling a knot form in my stomach. "I know. That's why I'm so careful about keeping my identity hidden. No face shots, nothing that could tie back to me or Moth to the Flame."

"Smart," Sloane says, finishing her drink. "But also . . . kind of sad, isn't it? That we have to hide parts of ourselves to keep our jobs?"

I sigh, tracing the rim of my glass. "Yeah, it is. Sometimes I wonder if it's worth it."

Sloane reaches out and squeezes my hand. "Hey, don't go there. You're talented, Chloe. Your work at Moth to the Flame is important. And if this . . . other thing . . . helps you express yourself, then more power to you. Just be careful, okay?"

I squeeze her hand back, thankful for her support. "I will."

As we sit in companionable silence, my phone buzzes again. I glance down to see another message from Jack.

> **JACK:** Hope I'm not interrupting anything. Just wanted to say good night and sweet dreams, Scrooge.

A smile tugs at my lips, warmth spreading through my chest that has nothing to do with the alcohol.

"Ooh, is that the firefighter again?" Sloane asks, noticing my expression.

I nod, feeling a mix of excitement and apprehension. "Yeah. He's . . . he's sweet."

Sloane grins. "Well, don't keep him waiting. Go on, text him back. I promise not to peek."

I laugh and pick up my phone, my fingers hovering over the keys. How do I balance these two sides of myself? The Chloe who's drawn to Jack's warmth and safety, and the one who craves the excitement and freedom of my alter ego?

Good night, Jack, I type. Sweet dreams to you too. And don't worry, no eggnog-drowning here. Just some holiday cheer with a friend. Looking forward to our date.

I hit Send and put my phone away, turning back to Sloane with a smile. "Now, where were we? I believe you were about to tell me about your family's infamous eggnog incident of 2018 again."

Sloane's eyes light up mischievously. "Oh, you're in for a treat. Picture this: my Uncle Fred, who fancies himself a mixologist, decided to 'improve' on Grandma's secret recipe . . ."

As Sloane launches into her tale, complete with dramatic reenactments and colorful impressions of her relatives, I find myself laughing harder than I have in months. The weight of my secrets, my conflicting feelings about Jack, and my worries about work all fade into the background, if only for a moment.

By the time we stumble out of the bar hours later, my sides ache from laughing and my head is pleasantly buzzing from the cocktails. The crisp night air hits us as we step onto the sidewalk, and I shiver, pulling my coat tighter around me.

"Well, that was fun," Sloane says, linking her arm through mine as we walk. "We should do this more often. But now I'm going to go home and find you on Dark Secrets."

I nearly trip over my own feet. "Oh Jesus."

"Night!" she shouts as she leaves before I can protest any further.

CHAPTER SIXTEEN
CHLOE

Okay, I'm buzzed. Maybe drunk. Peppermint martinis with Sloane was fun and surprisingly liberating. I can't believe I actually confessed my secret. I've never been so bold before, so open.

And now that I'm safe at home, sitting in front of my computer, I'm not ready for bed quite yet.

"Just going to read the comments," I whisper to myself, the peppermint still lingering on my breath.

I log in to my account, the Dark Secrets logo flashing across the screen. My heart races as I see the number of viewers already waiting. They don't know my real name, my day job, my fears. Here, I'm whoever I want to be.

I adjust my webcam, checking my reflection. My cheeks are flushed from the alcohol, my eyes glassy. I look like a hot mess and in no condition to go live, but that doesn't mean I can't—

And then I see the green light pop on next to my most recent commenter—WinterWatcher.

Maybe it's the alcohol clouding my judgment, or maybe it's the lingering high from my confession to Sloane, but I find myself reaching for the direct message button. I normally avoid DMs completely. I have never had a desire to look at strangers' dick pics or hairy anus shots (yes, that's a thing). But I want to see if the new message that popped up is him.

I hover over the message icon, my finger heavy as I click. The chat window opens, and there it is—a message from WinterWatcher.

Hey there. Couldn't sleep either?

No dick pics. No crude comments. Just . . . nice.

The words stare back at me from the screen, innocent enough but loaded with possibility. I bite my lip, debating whether to respond. This is new territory, dangerous even. But the peppermint martinis have lowered my inhibitions, and curiosity gets the better of me.

Not yet, I type back, my heart skipping.

No video tonight?

Not tonight. I was out and . . . not feeling it tonight.

The three dots appear, indicating he's typing a response. I hold my breath, unsure of what to expect.

That's okay. Sometimes it's nice to just chat. How was your night out?

I pause, surprised by the casual, friendly tone. This isn't the type of exchange I expected. I assumed I'd get the ick factor or feel too dirty. This almost feels . . . normal. Something about his easy manner makes me want to continue.

It was . . . enlightening, I reply, thinking back to my conversation with Sloane. Had drinks with a friend. Told her about . . . this. Dark Secrets.

Wow, that's brave. How'd she take it?

I smile, remembering Sloane's reaction. Better than expected. She called me a "camgirl" and wanted to know all about it.

Haha, sounds like a good friend. It must be nice to have someone to talk to about it.

His response makes me realize how lonely keeping this secret life has been. I've never had anyone to discuss it with, to share the excitement and fears.

Yeah, it is, I type, feeling a sudden warmth toward this stranger. What about you? Why are you up so late?

Insomnia, mostly. But talking to you is definitely making it worthwhile.

I feel a flutter in my stomach, a mix of alcohol and unexpected connection. This is treacherous territory, I remind myself. But I can't seem to stop.

So, WinterWatcher, what's the story behind your username? I ask, curiosity getting the better of me.

Ah, that's a tale for another time. But I will say it involves a snowstorm, standing outside a pretty girl's window, and well . . . watching.

There's something both intriguing and slightly unsettling about his response.

Sounds like there's quite a story there, I type, my fingers hesitating over the keys. Care to elaborate?

There's a long pause before another one of his responses comes through. Sorry, I didn't mean to freak you out. Nothing sinister, I promise.

It's okay, I type. We all have our stories, right? Our fantasies, our desires, and even our obsessions.

I stare at the screen, my heart racing. The alcohol in my system makes everything feel slightly surreal, like I'm watching this conversation unfold from outside my body.

You're right, WinterWatcher replies. We all have our stories. Our fantasies. Our obsessions. What's yours?

I hesitate, my fingers hovering over the keyboard. How much should I reveal? The anonymity of the platform emboldens me, but a small voice of caution still whispers in the back of my mind.

Mine? I type. Mine is . . . complicated, I type finally. It's about control, I guess. Being seen, but on my own terms.

Interesting, WinterWatcher responds quickly. Is that why you do this? The cam shows?

I consider his question, surprised by how perceptive it is. Partly, I admit. It's liberating in a way. To be desired, admired even, but still maintain distance.

I can understand that, he replies. The power of being watched, but still being untouchable.

What about you? I ask, deflecting. What's your fantasy?

There's a long pause before his response comes through. To be close to someone. To know them completely. Every detail, every secret. Not just know what she presents for the world to see, but really know her deepest and darkest desires.

How close is too close?

There's no such thing as too close, he replies almost instantly. Not when you truly want to know someone.

I swallow hard, my mouth suddenly dry. And how would you go about getting that close?

Carefully. Patiently. Building trust, piece by piece.
Learning every detail, every habit. Watching. Studying.
Becoming a part of their world, even if they don't realize
it at first.

I pause, unsure how to respond. The rational part of my brain tells me to end this conversation, to log off and forget about WinterWatcher. But something keeps me there, fingers poised over the keyboard.

And what if the person doesn't want to be understood that deeply? I ask.

Everyone wants to be understood, he replies. Even if they don't know it yet.

Yup, I have to be drunk for me to have the courage to type, Is that your fantasy? To watch?

Yes.

And what about me? I type, my heart racing. Am I part of that fantasy? Do you like watching me?

There's a pause that feels like an eternity before his response appears.

Yes.

I stare at the screen, my mouth dry. The single word *Yes* seems to pulse with an energy of its own. I'm not sure if it's the alcohol or the late hour, but I feel a strange mix of fear and excitement.

I studied you, he types. We like the same videos. We have favorited a lot of the same pics.

Is that so? I like knowing this. My kinks are eclectic. Give examples.

Well, WinterWatcher types, there's that video of the woman tied up in shibari rope, suspended from the ceiling. You favorited it and five others just like it.

My breath catches. He's right. I had been mesmerized by that video, the intricate knots, the vulnerability and strength of the model.

And then there's the album of vintage pinup photos, he continues. You've favorited almost every image.

Again, he's correct. I've always been drawn to the tease and glamour of those old photos.

And the spanking videos. You love those.

You've been doing your homework, I type.

I have, he responds quickly. I find you fascinating.

I pause, unsure how to proceed. Part of me wants to shut down the conversation, to log off and pretend this never happened. But another part, the part fueled by the battle I've had inside of me of danger vs. safe continues on.

Is that what you want to do? I type. Spank me?

Is that what you want? WinterWatcher replies. To be spanked?

I hesitate, my fingers hovering over the keys.

Maybe, I type finally.

I actually think you want more than that.

I stare at his words, my heart racing. He's right, of course. I do want more. But how could he know that?

What do you think I want? I type.

There's a pause before his response comes through. You want a man who doesn't ask. He just does. You want a man who takes control, who knows what you need before you even realize it yourself. I see a woman who craves intensity. Who wants to be pushed to her limits, to experience everything life has to offer. But I also see someone who's afraid. Afraid of losing control, of being truly vulnerable.

His words hit me like a physical blow. I feel naked, stripped bare by his perceptions.

I get up from my chair and pace my room, trying to sober up some. This is unlike me. I never peel back the curtain. And yet, here I am.

Something about WinterWatcher's words has me captivated.

I sit back down, my fingers hovering over the keyboard. Are you the kind of man who can make all those fantasies happen?

Yes, comes his swift reply.

How? I type, my fingers shaking. How would you do it?

There's a pause before his reply comes through. First, I'd make you wait. Build the anticipation. Make you think about all the possibilities until you're practically begging for it. I'd want your pussy wet without me even touching you.

Oh Jesus. Here we go . . . Is this officially sexting? I don't even know what to call this!

Then? I prompt, barely breathing.

Then, WinterWatcher types, I'd blindfold you. Take away your sight so every other sense is heightened. You'd feel the brush of my fingertips along your skin, never knowing where I'd touch next. The anticipation would drive you wild.

I swallow hard, my body responding to his words.

Go on, I type, my heart racing.

I'd tie your wrists, not too tight, but enough to make you feel restrained. Vulnerable. At my mercy. Then I'd explore every inch of your body with my hands, my mouth. Tasting you. Teasing you. Building you up slowly until you're quivering, desperate for release.

I squeeze my thighs together, feeling a familiar warmth building. And then? I prompt, switching to voice command for . . . ease.

Then, when you're on the edge, when you can't take it anymore, I'd spank you. Hard. Just once. The shock of it would ripple through your body, heightening every sensation.

I let out a shaky breath, realizing I've been holding it. Keep going, I dictate.

I'd alternate between gentle caresses and sharp slaps, never letting you know what's coming next. Then my fingers would lace around your throat. I'd tighten them enough to make you gasp, to feel that edge of danger. Your pulse would race under my fingertips as I whispered in your ear, telling you exactly what I was going to do to

you next. That I was going to fuck you so hard. Spread
your pussy with my cock until you screamed out my name.

I stare at the screen, my body flushed and clammy at the same
time. WinterWatcher's words have painted such a vivid picture, I
can almost feel his hands on my skin, his breath on my neck. I'm
breathing heavily, aroused beyond belief.

I let out a soft moan, my hand unconsciously moving to my
breast, pretending it's his touch.

Promises, promises, I somehow am able to say even though my
throat tightens.

Do something for me, he types.

I hesitate. What do you want me to do? I ask, my heart racing.

Take off your clothes, WinterWatcher replies. I want to imagine
you sitting there, naked, as we talk.

I'm surprised he's not asking me to turn on the camera.

No camera, he adds as if reading my mind. Just you and me . . .
and our fantasies.

I pause, considering his request. The alcohol in my system
makes me feel bold, reckless even. Without overthinking it, I stand
up and start to undress, my fingers fumbling slightly with the buttons of my jeans.

As I slip off my jeans and pull my top over my head, the cool
air of the room caresses my bare skin, making me shiver slightly. I
unhook my bra and let it fall to the floor, then slide off my panties.
I'm completely naked now, exposed and vulnerable in a way I've
never been before during my Dark Secrets sessions. Even though
the camera isn't on, I get this feeling as if he's somehow watching.
The fantasy of him doing exactly that—watching—heightens my
arousal to an even higher degree.

I sit back down in front of the computer, my heart feeling as if it's two sizes too big. Done, I say, my body feels . . . hot.

Good girl, WinterWatcher replies. Now spread your legs. Wide.

I slowly spread my legs, feeling alive and beyond turned on.

They're spread, I reply, licking my dry lips.

Perfect, he says. Now, I want you to touch yourself. Slowly.

CHAPTER SEVENTEEN
JACK

Yup, I'm going to hell on a sleigh ride. I'm double-fisting my ticket to hell.

I swore to myself over and over that I'd resist the urge to log on to the hidden nanny cam. I swore that even though I installed it, I wouldn't watch her.

And yet, here I am.

The soft glow of my laptop screen illuminates my guilty face as I stare at the live feed.

There she is, sitting in front of her computer, chatting with me but not knowing that I am WinterWatcher, and slowly moving her hand between her legs.

I stare at my phone where I've been chatting with her— username: BlackAsChlo.

I know it's her. She just doesn't know I know.

My finger hovers over the X to close the window, but I can't bring myself to do it. I'm transfixed, watching her every move like some digital voyeur.

The guilt gnaws at me, but the thrill of this forbidden knowledge is heady with lust. I watch as she leans back in her chair, her eyes closing briefly in pleasure.

Take off your clothes, I type. I want to imagine you sitting there, naked, as we talk. No camera. Just you and me . . . and our fantasies.

I don't want her to go live so everyone can see her. I want her all to myself. Alone with my secret camera stealing this scene before me.

My heart races as I watch her comply, slowly undressing even though no one is technically watching—that she is aware of. She thinks she's alone, and yet she still does what I ask.

She sits back down in front of the computer. Done, she types.

Good girl, I reply. Now spread your legs. Wide.

She slowly spreads her legs, performing like a true submissive would.

They're spread, she types, licking her lips.

Perfect. Now I want you to touch yourself. Slowly.

I watch, mesmerized, as her hand drifts lower. Her fingers trace delicate patterns across her skin, teasing herself. My breath catches in my throat.

I wish you could see me, she dictates into the computer. I'm doing as you ask.

I don't need to see you to know you are being the
perfect good girl you are. Move your fingers nice and
slow over your clit.

On the screen, I see her head tilt back, eyes fluttering closed as she follows my instructions. Her chest rises and falls with quickening breaths. I'm torn between watching her face and watching her hand as it moves in steady circles.

It feels so good, she says. I wish you could see how wet you make me.

My pulse races as I read her words. The camera's high-definition image leaves nothing to the imagination. I swallow hard, my mouth suddenly dry.

Tell me more, I type back. Describe how it feels. It's here when I decide to do the same thing she wisely did and turn my typing into voice control. I want my hands to be free.

As I wait for her response, I watch her hand trail up her body, cupping her breast. She pinches her nipple, and I see her bite her lower lip to stifle a moan.

It's like electricity, she replies. Every touch sends sparks through my body. I'm imagining it's your fingers instead of mine.

I'm directing this private show, orchestrating her pleasure from afar. Faster now, I instruct. Circle your clit faster. Use your other hand to slide two fingers inside.

I lean closer to the screen, captivated as she follows my commands. Her back arches slightly, her movements becoming more urgent. I can see the flush spreading across her chest, the rapid rise and fall of her breasts as her breathing quickens.

Oh god, she says, her fingers caressing her flesh. I'm so close.

My cock painfully presses against the fly of my pants. I free it from its confines and begin pumping the length of it, matching the rhythm and pace she's set. My own breaths become shallow and quick, trying to mimic hers.

She's beautiful, by far the sexiest woman I've ever seen—even more so in this vulnerable and erotic state. I can see the glisten of her arousal on her fingers as she continues to touch herself, her eyes closed tightly, lost in the throes of her own pleasure.

My own release builds, matching the pace of her fingers. My breath hitches as I watch her, my gaze locked on her hand guiding her closer and closer to the edge.

Don't come yet, I demand. Not until I tell you to. With one hand clutching my throbbing cock and my mind consumed by the sight of her pleasuring herself, I send a commanding message, Spread your pussy lips wide apart for me. I want to imagine how wet you are. How slick you'd be for my cock that is so fucking hard for you right now.

I watch as she follows my instructions, her fingers opening herself up for me, her lips parting and her juices coating her delicate flesh in the light of the screen. My heart pounds with excitement and anticipation. I'm one step away from finding release, and it's all thanks to this incredible performance she's putting on for me, unaware of how transfixed I am.

Now, touch yourself faster, I urge. Imagine my hands and fingers on you, guiding you toward the edge.

Her breathing is ragged, and her moans are growing louder with each passing second. I'm so close to climaxing myself, the grip on my cock tightening as I imagine feeling her flesh beneath my fingers, her wetness enveloping me, her body buzzing with pleasure.

I know we are both so close, but I need to do one more thing. I need to see how much dominance I have over her. Just how submissive is my Chloe?

I want you to lick your fingers and rub the wetness on your tight little asshole, I confess.

I can feel my heart rate increase, my breaths quickening as I watch her pause for a moment before following my command. Her hesitation only fuels my desire to see how far I can push her. She licks her fingers, her eyes fluttering open briefly to look at the computer screen, then she resumes her pleasure, sliding her fingers between her legs and gently probing the sensitive skin around her entrance. I feel like I'm in control, like I'm the one setting the pace of her desires.

Good girl, I praise. I know you like that, don't you.

Yes.

Put your finger inside your tight little ass. I want to
imagine how your body reacts.

She hesitates for a moment, but it's clear that she's trusting me
and this distance game we're playing. A moment later, I see her finger disappear into her tight opening, and I moan softly. Her fingers
splaying open, spreading herself for me, it's an intoxicating sight.

I wish you could see me, she leans forward, giving me a peek at a
different angle.

You like it when people watch you. Don't you?

I do.

Would you like us to fuck while people would watch? Is
that a fantasy of yours?

I'd love it.

Then we'll make that fantasy a reality someday, I promise. But not
yet. Tonight, you get to come because you are such a good girl. Pump
your fingers in and out, just like I'm fucking you. I issue another command. Imagine my cock sliding in and out of your tight hole, filling you
up, stretching you wide.

She obeys without hesitation. The sight before me is a potent
mix of vulnerability and strength. The surge of my own climax

builds within me, and I know it's only a matter of time before we both reach the pinnacle of pleasure together.

I watch as her breaths become shallow, her hips rising and falling in perfect harmony with the movements of her fingers. She's so close. I can see it in the way her chest rises and falls, the glistening sweat upon her skin. She's on the precipice of orgasm, just as I am.

Make yourself come, pretty girl. Come for me.

My words seem to ignite something within her, and her body responds with a wild intensity. Her hips buck wildly, her fingers moving faster. I can see her eyes are closed tightly, and her mouth is wide-open in a silent scream of pleasure.

I'm coming, I'm coming!

The moment of her release is matched perfectly by my own. I grip my throbbing cock tighter, my body shuddering with the force of my release. I can feel myself coming, my hot seed spilling onto my hand, my breath catching with the force of my climax.

Oh fuck, I groan, my voice hoarse from the intensity of the moment. My hand goes limp, and I look down at the mess of my release, feeling both satisfied and a bit dazed.

As the waves of pleasure subside, reality crashes back over me like a cold wave. What have I done? The guilt that had been simmering beneath the surface now boils over, churning my stomach. I quickly close the laptop, unable to look at the screen any longer.

My hands shake as I clean myself up, disgust and self-loathing coursing through me. I've crossed a line I swore I never would. I've violated her trust, her privacy, in the most intimate way possible.

The phone buzzes with a new message from her. **That was amazing,** it reads. **Thank you for making me feel so good.**

Each word is a dagger of shame. She has no idea of the depths of my betrayal. I can't bring myself to reply, to continue this charade. But if I don't, I could fuck with her head and give her self-doubt—the last thing I want to do to her.

I force myself to type a response, my fingers heavy with remorse. You're welcome. You were perfect. Such a good, good girl.

I've turned off the camera, and I can no longer see what she's doing. I desperately want to see her. I already miss watching her, even though I know it's wrong. My finger hovers over the laptop, tempted to turn it back on. Just one more look, I think. But I know if I do, I'll be right back where I started.

The room feels too small, suffocating. I need air. I stumble to the window and throw it open, gulping in the cool night breeze. But it does nothing to wash away the stain of what I've done.

My phone buzzes again. It's her. Are you still there?

I hesitate, unsure how to respond. Part of me wants to confess everything, to beg for forgiveness. But I know that would only hurt her more. So I type back, Yes, sorry. Just got distracted for a moment.

I was worried you'd left, she replies. I always feel a bit needy after . . . you know.

Her words twist the knife of guilt even deeper. She trusts me, feels safe with me, and I've violated that in the worst way possible. I want to comfort her, to reassure her, but every word feels like a lie.

I'm here, I type back. You're stuck with me.

There's a pause before her next message appears. I should get some sleep, she types. Work tomorrow. But this was . . . incredible. Can we do it again sometime?

My stomach churns. The thought of repeating this violation

makes me sick, but I can't let on that anything is wrong. Of course, I reply. I want to hear more about your fantasies.

I want to hear about yours as well.

I hesitate, my fingers hovering over the keys. How much further down this rabbit hole am I willing to go? But I can't stop now. I've already crossed so many lines.

Sweet dreams, I type back. We'll talk more soon.

CHAPTER EIGHTEEN
CHLOE

Confusion, slight guilt, and one hell of a doozy of a hangover has made this morning pretty brutal. I've never been more in need of my coffee and my favorite pastry from Pete's Café. As much as I wanted to stay in bed today, I forced myself out. I normally don't need to come into the office as often as I have been, but with the holiday season and my recent posts getting so much engagement, I'm starting to feel like a regular commuter.

The ferry ride, squinting against the harsh morning light only adds to my irritable mood. The sidewalk seems to sway beneath my feet as I make my way down the block. Thank god Pete's is only two streets over. The bell jingles as I push open the café door, the aroma of freshly ground beans hitting me like a much-needed slap to the face.

I don't know what the hell got into me last night. Oh I know . . . too many peppermint martinis. That's what. But regardless of the booze, I still can't believe I actually went online and sexted with a complete stranger. Not only sexted but masturbated. Part of me woke up this morning thinking it had to be a dream, right? Because no sane woman would do something like that.

I shuffle up to the counter, avoiding eye contact with the barista, mumbling my usual order as I fumble with my wallet. I wince at the sound of the espresso machine grinding, each whir feeling like a drill to my temples. As I wait for my order, I lean against the counter, my eyes closed, trying to will away the pounding in my head. The café chatter fades to a dull hum as my mind drifts back to last night's escapade. Flashes of explicit messages and blurry memories of sitting naked in front of my computer dance behind my eyelids, making my cheeks burn with embarrassment.

But embarrassment isn't nearly as bad as the guilt ripping me up. Why do I feel guilty? I've done nothing wrong. What I do in the privacy of my home and—I'm single. Sure, I've been talking to Jack, but it's not like anything has happened. We haven't even been on our first official date yet. It's not like we're exclusive. Hell, we haven't kissed yet, or even came close . . . much to my dismay.

I mean . . . is there even anything between Jack and me? Maybe we've stepped into friend zone.

"Order for Chloe!"

I jolt at the sound of my name, my eyes snapping open. The barista is holding out my coffee and pastry, a concerned look on her face. I must look as terrible as I feel.

"Thanks," I mutter, grabbing my order and shuffling to leave.

As I turn toward the door, I bump into a solid chest, spilling my precious coffee all over my white blouse. Strong hands steady me, and I look up, mortified, into the welcoming eyes of none other than Jack.

I stare at him, my mouth agape, unable to form words. Of all the people to run into, it had to be him. My face burns hotter, and I'm not sure if it's from embarrassment or the scalding coffee seeping through my shirt.

"Shit. Sorry," I stammer, finally finding my voice. "Just a little clumsy this morning."

Jack's eyes flick down to my stained blouse, then back up to my face. A small smile tugs at the corner of his mouth. "Rough night?"

If he only knew. I nod, trying to ignore the way my stomach flips at his proximity. "You could say that."

He reaches past me, grabbing a handful of napkins from the counter. "Here, let me help."

Before I can protest, he's dabbing at my blouse, his touch gentle but firm. I hold my breath, hyperaware of every point of contact between us. The guilt from earlier resurfaces, mixing with a confusing cocktail of attraction and shame.

"Ugh. Of course. I was headed into the office to pick up some new jewelry pieces. It'll be lovely to arrive like this."

Jack chuckles softly, his breath warm against my ear. "I think this shirt is a lost cause."

"Fuck my life."

Jack's eyes sparkle with amusement. "I have an idea," he says, stepping back slightly. "My apartment's around the corner. I've got a clean shirt you could borrow. It will be big but maybe you can tuck it in or knot it or something."

I hesitate, torn between the desire to escape this embarrassing situation and the unexpected thrill of being invited to Jack's apartment. My hangover-addled brain struggles to make a decision.

"I don't want to impose," I mumble, still acutely aware of his nearness.

Jack shakes his head, his smile widening. "It's no imposition at all. Besides, I'm partially to blame."

I bite my lip, weighing my options. On one hand, going to his apartment feels dangerously intimate, especially given my current state and the guilt still gnawing at me. On the other hand, I can't exactly show up to work looking like I've been in a coffee-based bar fight.

"Okay," I finally concede, my voice barely above a whisper. "Thank you."

Jack's smile widens, and he gently places his hand on the small of my back, guiding me out of the café. The warmth of his touch seeps through my damp shirt, and my mind becomes even foggier than it was when I started this day. I'm hyperaware of every step, every breath. The hangover, the guilt, and now this unexpected turn of events has my head spinning.

As we walk the short distance to Jack's apartment, I'm acutely aware of the silence between us. It's not uncomfortable, exactly, but it's charged with an energy I can't quite define. We reach an older, but clean and well-kept building, and Jack leads me inside, his hand still resting lightly on my back. The elevator ride is mercifully short, but it feels like an eternity as I stand there, coffee-stained and disheveled, next to Jack's put-together presence.

Jack's apartment is on the third floor, and as he unlocks the door, I find myself holding my breath. The space that greets me is surprisingly cozy—warm colors, well-worn leather furniture, and bookshelves lining one wall. It's lived-in but tidy. It also has a live Christmas tree in the far right corner that is full of ornaments and topped with an angel. Christmas lights line the windows, and tinsel covers the tops of his kitchen cabinets. I immediately feel both comforted and surprised that a single man would go all out in Christmas decor.

"Make yourself at home," Jack says, gesturing to the living room. "I'll grab you that shirt."

As he disappears down a hallway, I stand awkwardly in the

middle of the room, afraid to touch anything. My stare roams over the bookshelves, taking in titles ranging from classic literature to modern thrillers. A framed photo catches my attention—Jack, younger and sun-kissed, arm slung around an older woman who bears a striking resemblance to him. Mother and son, I assume.

"Here we go," Jack's voice startles me out of my observations. He's holding out a crisp white button-down. "It's the smallest I've got, but it should do the trick."

Our fingers brush as I take the shirt from him, looking around for what I had expected, to be greeted with sloppy kisses and large paws. "Where's your dog?"

He freezes with a look that almost appears to be confusion. "Dog?"

For a minute, I second-guess my memory. But I clearly remember him walking his dog when we first met. Hungover or not—but wait. I thought he lived in my neighborhood.

"Oh, right," Jack says, looking slightly flustered for the first time. "That wasn't my dog. I house- and dog-sit for a friend in the crew sometimes."

I nod slowly, trying to process this information through my hangover fog. Something about his explanation doesn't quite sit right, but I can't put my finger on why. Maybe it's the lingering confusion from last night clouding my judgment.

"Oh, I see. I just assumed," I mumble, clutching the shirt to my chest. "Um, where can I . . . ?"

Jack points down the hallway. "Bathroom's the second door on the left."

I shuffle toward the bathroom, my mind racing. As I close the door behind me, I catch a glimpse of myself in the mirror and wince. My makeup is smudged, my hair a tangled mess, and my blouse is a disaster. I look exactly how I feel—like I've been hit by a truck.

With shaky hands, I unbutton my ruined blouse and peel it off, tossing it into my purse. I splash some cold water on my face, trying to clear my head. I quickly put on Jack's shirt, rolling up the sleeves and tying it at the waist. It smells like him.

Taking a deep breath, I step out of the bathroom. Jack is in the kitchen, pouring two mugs of coffee. He looks up as I enter, his eyes widening slightly.

"Wow," he says, a smile playing on his lips. "You make that shirt look good." He extends a mug of coffee to me. "I can't make your latte, but this coffee does have creamer and sugar."

Man, this guy really is perfect.

I take the mug gratefully, wrapping my hands around its warmth. "Thanks," I say, taking a sip. The coffee is rich and smooth, infinitely better than what I usually make at home.

Jack leans against the counter, watching me over the rim of his own mug. There's something in his gaze that makes me feel both exposed and intrigued. The silence stretches between us, thick with unspoken words.

"You clearly like Christmas," I say, taking in more of his decorations. There is a Charles Dickens village set up on a side table, complete with tiny Victorian-era figurines and miniature snow-covered buildings.

"It was my mother's favorite holiday." Jack's eyes soften at the mention of his mother. "Yeah, she always went all out for Christmas. The little village was her favorite."

I nod, feeling a pang of sympathy. The photo I saw earlier flashes in my mind. "Is that her in the picture on your bookshelf?"

Jack's smile turns bittersweet. "Yeah, that's her. She passed away when I was fifteen."

"I'm so sorry," I say softly.

"The village was the one thing of hers that I managed to keep hold of after I went into the foster system. So, I guess you could say it's important to show it off and make the place festive."

"I'm sure she's happy you are."

He shrugs, takes in the decorations and says, "I hope so."

I instinctively reach out to touch his arm, moved by his moment of vulnerability. The moment my fingers make contact with his skin, I feel a jolt of electricity. Jack's eyes meet mine, and for a moment, the world seems to stand still.

I wait. And wait. And like the times before . . . nothing.

Yeah, I think it's fair to say that we crossed into friend zone. And maybe that isn't a bad thing. He's as vanilla as the flavor of creamer he put in my coffee, and after last night with WinterWatcher . . . I'm clearly as black as the coal that I deserve in my stocking.

"I, um, I should probably get going," I stammer, setting down the coffee mug. "I don't want to keep Sloane waiting for long. Thank you for the shirt and the coffee."

Jack nods, his expression unreadable. "Of course. Anytime."

I make my way to the door, feeling Jack's eyes on me as I go. Just as I reach for the handle, his voice stops me.

"Chloe, wait."

I turn, my heart suddenly racing. Jack takes a step toward me, his expression intense.

Come on, buddy. Throw me against the wall. Take me by the hair and plunge your tongue into my mouth. Do it! Do it!

Nothing.

"About that date of ours. True crime and Chinese food. I work for the next forty-eight hours, but maybe when I'm off shift?"

My heart sinks a little. Hearing him ask it like that is the same way Sloane would ask me to hang out.

Yup, friend zone.

"Oh," I say, trying to mask my disappointment. "Um, text me and we'll figure it out. But I really should be going."

Jack nods, his smile not quite reaching his eyes. "Sure, no problem. I'll text you."

I hurry out of his apartment, my mind a whirlwind of conflicting emotions. As I step into the elevator, I lean against the wall, closing my eyes and taking a deep breath. The scent of Jack's shirt lingers around me, a constant reminder of the confusing encounter I just had.

The elevator dings, and I step out onto the street, the chilly winter air shocking my system. I start walking briskly toward the office, trying to sort through my thoughts. On one hand, Jack was sweet and helpful, offering me his shirt and coffee when I was in a bind. But on the other hand, there was that moment—or rather, the lack of a moment—when we were so close, and nothing happened.

I can't shake the feeling that something's off. The dog explanation, the lack of chemistry . . . it all feels strange. I didn't even know he lived in Manhattan. He was only housesitting in my neighborhood?

As I round the corner toward Moth to the Flame, ready to get my jewelry, head home, and crawl in bed to erase this day completely, my phone buzzes in my pocket. It's a notification from Dark Secrets. I turned them on last night just in case. Just in case—

Last night was fun. Maybe we can do it again
sometime?—WinterWatcher.

CHAPTER NINETEEN
CHLOE

"How in the hell do you look so good, when I feel like death?" I ask as Sloane appears perfectly put together in her expensive designer suit, not a hair out of place. "We drank the same amount. It's not fair."

Sloane flashes me a brilliant smile, her teeth impossibly white. "Years of practice, my friend. And a little help from drug of choice." She gestures to the steaming travel mug in her hand.

I groan and rub my temples. "I think I've had enough coffee for one day." I look down at my borrowed shirt from Jack. "Coffee mishap this morning. Now I'm wearing Jack's shirt."

Sloane raises an eyebrow. "Jack's shirt, huh? Booty call last night?"

I shake my head. "I ran into him this morning. Literally."

Sloane chuckles, her perfectly manicured nails tapping against her coffee mug. "Sure . . ."

I roll my eyes, wincing as the movement sends a sharp pain through my skull. "Anyway," I continue. "Show me the new necklaces you told me about so I can get home and crawl back into bed. I'm questioning this trip to the office now."

Sloane's eyes light up, her hangover seemingly nonexistent as she practically bounces on her heels. "Oh, you're going to love them! Come on, they're in my office."

I follow her down the hallway, my feet dragging slightly. The fluorescent lights are doing nothing for my headache.

As we enter her office, Sloane heads straight for her desk, pulling out a small, velvet-covered box. She opens it with a flourish, revealing a stunning array of delicate gold necklaces, each adorned with a unique pendant.

"Voilà! What do you think?" she asks, her voice brimming with excitement.

I move closer, squinting slightly to focus on the intricate details. Despite my hangover, I take the time to admire the craftsmanship. "They're beautiful, Sloane. Really stunning work."

She beams at me, clearly proud of her latest creations. "I knew you'd love them. Tyler saw them yesterday and said they may be too basic, but he's a man, so what does he know."

Grrr, Tyler. I realize my groan was audible.

Sloane's eyes narrow, her smile fading slightly. "What's that about? You having issues with Tyler?"

I wave my hand dismissively, trying to backtrack. "No, no. It's just . . . my head. The hangover, you know."

Sloane doesn't look convinced. She sets down the jewelry box and crosses her arms, fixing me with a penetrating stare. "Come on, spill. I know he can be a pain in the ass sometimes. He follows every rule to a T, and can be super uptight. But he's harmless. You just have to know how to work with the man. Not against him. Is he riding your ass?"

I sigh, knowing I can't escape Sloane's interrogation. "It's nothing, really. He's just . . . Are you sure he's harmless? I get a weird feeling sometimes."

Sloane's perfectly arched eyebrow rises even higher. "Weird feeling? What do you mean?"

I hesitate, not sure how to put my vague suspicions into words. "I don't know exactly. It's just . . . sometimes I catch him watching me when he thinks I'm not looking. And he's shown up at my house twice now completely out of the blue."

Sloane's expression shifts from curiosity to concern. "At your house? That's . . . unusual."

I nod, relieved that Sloane seems to be taking me seriously. "Exactly."

"Has he done anything?"

I shake my head. "No. Not really. He's asked me on a date, I guess. But in a weird way. It's hard to explain. I'm trying to brush him off and not make it weird between us. But it's weird between us." I shrug. "I don't want to make anything of it because nothing really has happened. But—"

Just then, we hear footsteps approaching. Sloane quickly picks up the jewelry box again, resuming our facade of casual conversation. As the door opens, I turn to see who it is, my heart racing.

It's Tyler, his eyes immediately locking on to mine.

"Hey, ladies," Tyler says, his voice smooth as silk. "Hope I'm not interrupting anything important."

I force a smile, trying to keep my voice steady. "Not at all. Just girl talk."

Tyler's eyes linger on me for a moment too long before he turns to Sloane. "I need those quarterly expenses on my desk by five, Sloane. I know you've been busy with the latest designs, but Jasmine has asked me to hunt these down."

Sloane nods, her face a mask of professionalism. "Of course. I'll have them to you by four."

My stomach clenches. I glance at Sloane, who I can tell is studying every move Tyler makes. She's always been such a good judge of character. If Tyler is a creep, she'll pick up on it.

"I brought in some Christmas cookies," he adds. "They're in the break room if you guys want any."

A creep who bakes?

I force a smile. "Thanks, Tyler. That's . . . thoughtful of you."

Tyler's eyes flick back to me, a hint of something I can't quite place lurking behind them. "I made your favorite. Snickerdoodles."

How does he know my favorite cookie? I've never mentioned it at work. I try to recall if I've ever mentioned my favorite cookie to anyone aside from my deceased parents. Then I remember that I said it in passing on one of my lives as I was showing off a line of *Nightmare Before Christmas*–inspired pendants. It wasn't even one of my more popular posts.

But does Tyler really watch every single one of my videos? Does he take notes? How would he remember such a small detail?

"Oh," I manage, trying to keep my voice light. "That's . . . nice."

Sloane steps in smoothly, her tone cheerful but with an edge I recognize. "We'll definitely grab some later. Thanks, Tyler."

He lingers for a moment, his gaze uncomfortably intense. "Great. I hope you enjoy them." With a final nod, he turns and leaves, closing the door behind him.

As soon as his footsteps fade, Sloane whirls to face me. She leans in, her voice dropping to a whisper. "Your gut is telling you something's off."

I nod, grateful she understands. "I hope he catches on that I'm not interested, and this doesn't have to get awkward. I really don't want to make this into something bigger if I don't have to."

I really love my job and the last thing I want is to jeopardize it. I know that Tyler has Jasmine's ear, and while I hope I'd be taken seriously if I came forward, I'd rather not find out.

Sloane nods thoughtfully, her brow furrowed. "I get it. You don't want to rock the boat."

"I'm a contractor. Not an employee," I point out.

"I get it. But listen, if Tyler keeps this up, you need to say something formally. I can help you if you're not comfortable going to Jasmine yet."

"Deal."

"Okay, subject change," Sloane says, her tone lightening. "So last night got me thinking. Your bombshell of a secret really sunk in once I was sober."

My heart pounds at Sloane's words. The events of last night come flooding back, and I suddenly remember the drunken confession I'd made. "Oh god," I groan, covering my face with my hands. "I can't believe I told you about that."

Sloane's eyes sparkle with excitement. "Are you kidding? I'm glad you did! Which also means that we have plans Friday night. We're going to Naughty and Nice. No arguments."

"The nightclub? Isn't that like a sex club? I heard it was members only or something?"

Sloane waves her hand dismissively. "Oh please, I have connections. But Fridays are open to all anyway. They're having a holiday party and it's going to be packed. And it's not just a sex club—it's more of an upscale, exclusive venue for adults to explore their . . . interests. Perfect for people like us."

"Like us, huh?"

Sloane grins. "Exactly. People who are curious, open-minded, and ready to explore. Come on, it'll be fun. And who knows? Maybe you'll find someone who can help you *indulge*."

My thoughts instantly turn to WinterWatcher and how he and I indulged in our own way last night. A blush creeps up my neck, and I hope Sloane can't see. I'm not ready to tell her about him yet.

"It's just a party," Sloane insists. "You don't have to do anything you're not comfortable with. We'll go, have a few drinks, maybe dance a little. If you hate it, we'll leave. No pressure."

I bite my lip, considering Sloane's offer. Part of me is terrified at the thought of going to such a place, but another part—a part I've been trying to ignore for years—is thrillingly curious.

"I . . . I don't know, Sloane. It sounds intense."

"Come on, live a little! When was the last time you did something truly exciting?"

I think about my recent online encounters with WinterWatcher, but of course, I can't tell Sloane about that. "Fine," I sigh, unable to resist her enthusiasm. "But if I say I want to leave, we leave. No questions asked."

Sloane claps her hands together, beaming. "Deal!" Her eyes narrow, and I recognize the mischievous look immediately. "You know . . . you could always invite Fireman Jack to meet you. Maybe he can show you his naughty and his nice."

My cheeks flush at the mention of Jack. "Sloane! No way. I barely know him. Besides, I don't think he's the type for that kind of scene."

Sloane shrugs, a sly smile playing on her lips. "You never know. Sometimes the quiet ones are the wildest behind closed doors."

I roll my eyes, trying to ignore the guilt that runs through me at the thought of Jack just minutes after thinking of WinterWatcher. My thoughts have become a two-timing whore.

"Speaking of Jack," Sloane says, her eyes glinting with curiosity, "you never did tell me how exactly you ended up in his shirt this morning. Spill the details, honey."

I sigh, knowing my friend won't let this go. "It's really not that exciting. I was rushing to get coffee before work, not paying attention, and crashed right into him. Spilled my entire latte down my front."

I continue the story, glossing over the fact that my insides were torn to shreds because after my encounter with WinterWatcher, something was off between the two of us. I couldn't quite put my finger on it, but something was off. And it wasn't just the guilt I felt inside.

Sloane's lips curl into a knowing smirk. "You like him a lot, don't you? But you feel guilty because of your secret online profile."

She has no idea how right she is.

My face heats, caught off guard by Sloane's perceptiveness. "I . . . it's complicated," I stammer, not sure how to explain the tangled web of emotions I'm dealing with.

Sloane's expression softens. "Hey, I get it. You're exploring different sides of yourself. There's nothing wrong with that."

I nod, grateful for her understanding. "I don't want to hurt anyone, you know? Jack seems like a really good guy."

"And you're a really good girl. You deserve to find happiness after everything you've been through," Sloane prompts with a tone that reminds me of my mother's. Comforting. Warm. Like a loving hug.

I smile weakly at Sloane's words, touched by her support but still feeling conflicted. "Thanks, Sloane. I just . . . I don't know what I want right now." I rub my temples. "And this hangover isn't exactly helping. I need to get home and lick my wounds."

"All right, all right," she says, her tone softening. "Go home and rest. But don't think you're getting out of Friday night. I'll text you the details later."

I nod, grateful for the reprieve. "Thanks. I'll see you then."

As I make my way out of the office, my phone buzzes in my pocket. My heart skips a beat when I see it's a notification. A message from WinterWatcher.

Hey there. Can't stop thinking about last night. I keep
logging on in hopes to find another one of your videos.
I'm craving . . . to watch.

CHAPTER TWENTY

JACK

I shouldn't be doing this while I'm at the station. I know this. It's not breaking rules or anything or grounds for termination. What firefighters do in the privacy of their bedrooms at the station once they go to bed is on them. As long as we are prepared to spring into action the minute the alarm goes off. But tonight has been extremely quiet, and I'm hoping that I can log on to my laptop undisturbed.

My fingers hover over the keyboard as I glance toward the door, half expecting the chief to burst in, somehow knowing I'm going to log in to the nanny cam and spy on the girl I've been stalking for years. But the hallway remains silent, save for the distant snores of my fellow firefighters.

With a deep breath, I type in the password and wait for the feed to load. The familiar layout of her bedroom appears on the screen, dimly lit by the glow of a computer left on. My heart races as I scan the room, searching for any sign of movement.

There she is. Curled up on the bed, fast asleep. Her long dark hair cascades over a pillow, and I can barely make out the rise and fall of her chest as she breathes. I put my face closer to the screen, drinking in every detail.

I know I shouldn't be doing this. I'm not completely delusional. But I can't help myself. I've been watching her for so long, learning her routines, her habits. In a way, I feel like I know her better than anyone else in her life.

A creak in the hallway makes me jump. I quickly minimize the window, my pulse ringing in my ears. But it's just the old building settling. I let out a shaky breath and return to the feed.

A voice in my head screams that this is wrong, that I'm crossing a line I can never come back from. But another part of me, a darker part, whispers that this is the closest I'll ever get to her.

That I need this.

Chloe stirs in her sleep, and for a moment I'm afraid she'll wake up. But she just rolls over, pulling a blanket tighter around herself. I wonder what she's dreaming about. Does she ever dream about me? The nice firefighter who bought her hot cocoa. Or does she dream of WinterWatcher, not knowing that we are the same person but offering her something completely different.

I know it. I see it.

Jack offers her light. WinterWatcher offers her dark. The question is, who is the real me?

I shake my head, trying to clear these thoughts. This has to stop. I need to close the laptop, delete the app, and forget about her. But as I try to bring myself to do the right thing, she mumbles something, rolls over, and reaches for her phone. I freeze, captivated once again by this woman.

My hand hovers over the laptop, ready to close the window at a moment's notice. But Chloe doesn't wake fully. She fumbles for her phone, squinting at the bright screen before dropping it back onto the nightstand. I release a breath I didn't realize I was holding.

The soft glow of her phone illuminates her face for a brief moment, and I'm struck again by her beauty. The curve of her cheek, the slight pout of her lips as she drifts back to sleep. I've memorized every detail but seeing her like this never fails to take my breath away.

I glance at the clock. It's well past midnight now. I should try to get some sleep in case we get a call. But I can't tear myself away from the screen. Just a few more minutes, I tell myself. Just a little longer.

Suddenly, Chloe sits up in bed, fully awake now. My heart races as I watch her get out of bed and head over to her computer.

Is she going to log on? To chat with WinterWatcher? The thought both delights and terrifies me.

I'm not prepared for this. I haven't planned what to say, how to act. But as her fingers move across the keyboard, I find myself reaching for my own. Ready to become the persona she knows online, to step into that dark world we've created together.

My phone buzzes with a notification. I glance down at my phone, my body tensing. It's a message from Chloe to WinterWatcher.

Are you there? she types. I can't sleep and was hoping you'd be awake. Actually, I have no idea where you even live. It could be midday where you are.

I type back, I live in New York. Maybe it's dangerous sharing that fact about me, but the words come out before I can truly process the ramifications.

Really? Me too.

Part of me wants to backpedal, to lie and say I'm actually in California or Europe. But another part, the part that's been yearning for a real connection, pushes me forward.

What a coincidence, I type back. Small world, huh?

I watch her smile on the screen, her face illuminated by the soft glow of her computer. She tucks a strand of hair behind her ear, a gesture I've seen her do countless times before.

Very small, she replies. What part of New York?

Manhattan, I type. It's vague enough, I reason. More than a million people live in Manhattan.

I work there. Her excitement is obvious, even through the screen. We could have passed each other on the street and never known it.

If only she knew how many times that has actually happened.

I've been thinking of you, I type.

I watch as Chloe's eyes widen at my words. She bites her lip, hesitating before she responds.

I've been thinking of you too, she types back. More than I probably should.

My heart races. This is dangerous territory we're entering, but I can't stop myself.

What have you been thinking about? I ask.

There's a long pause. On the screen, I see Chloe take a deep breath, steeling herself. When her response comes through, it's more forward than I expected.

About my fantasies. Fantasies that include you.

I swallow hard, my tongue sticking to the roof of my mouth. This is escalating quickly, and a part of me knows I should put a stop to it. But the darker part, the part that's been watching her all this time, urges me on.

Tell me about these fantasies, I type, ignoring the hardening of my cock.

On the screen, I see Chloe blush. She takes another deep breath before responding.

I imagine meeting you in person, she types. I picture you in a mask. A mask that is almost pagan in style. It will have horns or something demonic in nature. I imagine it covering most of your face. But not your lips.

Go on, I type, my fingers feeling heavy.

I watch as Chloe shifts in her chair, clearly affected by the fantasy she's sharing. She bites her lip again, a gesture that never fails to drive me wild.

In my fantasy, you approach me slowly, she continues. I can't see your eyes clearly, but I can feel the intensity of your gaze. You don't say a word, but your presence is overwhelming. When you're close enough, you reach out and touch my face. Your fingers are cool against my skin, and I shiver.

My breath catches in my throat. I can almost feel her skin beneath my fingertips, can almost smell her perfume. The line between fantasy and reality is blurring dangerously.

What happens next? I ask, both dreading and craving her answer.

There's a pause as Chloe considers her words. I watch her chest rise and fall with quickened breaths.

You lean in, she types slowly, and kiss me. It's gentle at first, but then it deepens. Your hands tangle in my hair, pulling me closer. I reach up to touch your mask, but you catch my wrists, pinning them above my head.

I groan softly, thankful that the walls of the station are thick. The image she's painting is vivid, and I find myself lost in it. For a moment, I forget about the camera, about the distance between us. In this moment, we're together, sharing this fantasy.

Do you want me to stop? Chloe asks after a moment of silence.

No, I type back quickly. Don't stop.

On the screen, I see her smile, a mix of shyness and desire. She takes a deep breath before continuing.

You press me against the wall, she types. Your body is hard against mine. I can feel every inch of you. Your lips move to my neck, and I gasp. Your teeth graze my skin, and I beg you to fuck me. I plead for your cock.

I exhale sharply.

And do I give you what you want?

On the screen, Chloe squirms in her chair, her cheeks flushed. She hesitates before responding.

Not right away. You tease me first. Your hands roam my body, touching me everywhere except where I need it most. I'm whimpering, begging you to take me.

My cock strains against my uniform pants. I shift uncomfortably, trying to focus on the screen and not my own burning desire.

Tell me how you beg, I type, my breath ragged.

Please, she types. Please fuck me. I need you inside me. I need to feel your cock stretching me open. Please, I'm yours. Take me. She continues to type. But you won't. Not yet. You're waiting for . . . them. They haven't arrived yet.

Who are they? I prompt.

The others, she finally types. The ones who watch.

You want to be watched as I fuck you.

Yes. More than anything.

How many others? I type.

A roomful, she responds quickly. I want everyone to see my pussy as you spread me.

And what do I do next?

You slide your hand between my legs, feeling how wet I am. You tell the others how ready I am, how desperate. Then you push two fingers inside me, making me cry out.

I stifle a groan, my arousal almost painful now. On the screen, I can see Chloe's breathing has quickened, her chest rising and falling rapidly.

You fuck me with your fingers, slowly at first, then faster, she continues.

I'm lost in the fantasy now, picturing every detail. The heat of her skin, the sound of her moans, the feeling of her tight around my fingers.

And then? I ask, desperate to know more.

Then you pull your fingers out, she types. You bring them to my lips, making me taste myself. And finally, finally, you unzip your pants and pull out your cock.

I watch as Chloe's fingers hover over the keyboard, her chest heaving. She's clearly as aroused as I am.

You tease me with the tip of your cock, she types. Rubbing it against my clit, making me whimper. The crowd watches, their eyes hungry. You ask me if I'm ready, if I'm sure I want this.

The need to be inside her is unbearable.

I beg you, she replies. I tell you I've never been more ready for anything in my life. I wrap my legs around your waist, trying to pull you closer.

I need to fuck her. I need to fuck her now.

You thrust into me in one smooth motion. I cry out, overwhelmed by the feeling of fullness. You start to move, slowly at first, then faster. The room is filled with the sound of skin on skin, of my moans and your grunts. You're fucking me hard now, she continues. Your hands are gripping my hips so tightly I know there will be bruises tomorrow. I love it. I want everyone to see the marks you've left on me.

I'm so hard it hurts.

I'm moaning your name, begging for more. I—

Suddenly, the fire alarm blares through the station. I jump, slamming the laptop shut instinctively. My heart pounds as I hear my fellow firefighters stirring, boots hitting the floor as everyone rushes to respond.

I can't simply leave Chloe wondering where I had to run off to, so I open my laptop and quickly type, I have to go, pretty girl. Someone is at my door. I'm sorry. But know that I'll be jacking off to this later.

I scramble to my feet, adjusting myself and trying to compose my thoughts as I rush to join my team. This girl is going to be the death of me, or at the very least, the giver of some gnarly blue balls.

CHAPTER TWENTY-ONE
CHLOE

I somehow get the courage to type, I'm going to Naughty and Nice in the city tonight. Maybe you're free to meet me there? I'll be wearing a red ribbon around my neck tied in a bow. I'll also be in a green, silky dress. Come and unwrap me.

My fingers hover over the send button for what feels like an eternity. Have I lost my mind? Yes, I think that is fair to say. I never thought I would be going to a sex club party with Sloane. And as much as I'd like to say it's due to my best friend's urging and that this was all her idea, I actually am excited. She didn't really have to force this on me.

I press Send. It's done. No turning back now. I stare at my message to WinterWatcher, now a part of reality forever.

I pace around the room, my palms sweating, my mind a whirlwind of vivid expectations and terrible anxieties.

Was that too bold? Yes, it was. I don't even know this person.

I don't even know this person! Now I just told him where I'd be tonight.

I'm not a naive girl. I've lived in New York all my life. I know better than this and yet . . .

I look at the clock and know I no longer have time to overthink if he'll come or not, and if he does, whether he's a serial killer or a Boy

Scout. I need to go if I'm going to catch the ferry in time to meet Sloane. I glance again at my phone. No response yet. Should I feel relieved? Disappointed? It's hard to decide. As I gather my purse and keys, one last look at that agonizingly silent device makes me wince.

I tug my emerald dress into place and check the red ribbon around my neck one last time in the mirror before stepping outside. And freezing my ass off. I quickly decide to travel to the club by vehicle instead of boat.

By the time I reach Naughty and Nice, I've managed to calm my nerves, taking slow, deep breaths as I step out of the cab and join Sloane, who's waiting for me out front. Classic Sloane style, she's decked out in fishnet stockings and a red leather corset, her fiery red hair cascading down her back.

"Holy shit, Chloe! Look at you!" She looks me up and down. "Damn, girl."

I blush under her compliment and stand straighter with more confidence, revealing the emerald dress that clings to my figure. For the first time ever, I don't feel as if Sloane has outdressed me. I don't feel like the mousy hermit lurking in her shadow.

The pulsating beat of the music from inside the club seeps out onto the street, mingling with the lively chatter and laughter of the partygoers milling about. Sloane loops her arm through mine, her eyes sparkling with excitement. "Are you ready for this?" she asks, her voice barely audible over the noise. "Let's go inside and see what kind of trouble we can get into."

I nod, my heart pounding in my chest. I am ready; or at least, I want to be. I want to let go of all my fears and doubts, to embrace this wild, uninhibited side of myself that has been hiding for so long. I can't hide behind a phone forever.

As we make our way through the crowded club, Sloane confidently leads me to the bar, where she orders us each a drink. The air is thick with the scent of sweat, alcohol, and something else: desire. The room is dimly lit, with flashes of neon light illuminating the faces of everyone. At least the faces I can see. Many people are wearing masks, some holiday in theme, others made of leather or lace. Simply being around so many masks unlocks a deep-rooted fantasy inside of me. I love the fact that the room is a blend of secrets and open passion.

As I take a sip of my drink, the music and energy of the club sizzle into my core. Why have I hidden from this for so long? Inside of me there's a sense of freedom that I've never experienced before. My dress hugs every curve to my body, making me feel sexy and powerful. I sway to the beat of the music, losing myself in the moment. This feels right. So right.

Sloane grins at me, her eyes filled with mischief. "Let's go dance," she shouts over the music, grabbing my hand and pulling me onto the dance floor.

We dance as the rhythm and the bass vibrate through my body, and I can't resist scanning the crowd for my mystery man. Not that I know what he looks like. But maybe he's watching me. Maybe he's one of the masked men in this room. Maybe he's spotting my red ribbon right now and getting ready to approach.

Just as I let myself indulge in the tantalizing fantasy, a strong hand grips my waist from behind. I gasp, spinning around to find myself face-to-face with a man wearing a black velvet mask adorned with silver filigree. His dark eyes pierce through the slits of the mask, sending a thrill down my spine. The mask only covers the top of his face, leaving his lips revealed. He's also wearing a black hood, long black sleeves, and he seems to vanish behind the mask so I can't make out any of his features.

"Dance with me," he commands, his voice deep and husky. With the music as loud as it is, I can barely make out his voice.

I nod, unable to find my words as he pulls me close, our bodies moving in sync with the pulsating beat. His touch is electric, igniting a fire within me that I can't quench.

Is it him? Or is this just another clubgoer?

As we dance, his hand traces the line of my rib cage, brushing against the red ribbon around my neck. My breath hitches as he tugs gently, pulling me even closer. The scent of sandalwood and musk intoxicates me, and there is something familiar about the smell. Something so strong it makes me want more.

My heart races as I look into his eyes, trying to discern who he is beneath the mask.

Do I really want to know?

No. Yes. Maybe. Although the idea of being with a complete stranger sends jolts of electricity straight between my legs.

He whispers something in my ear, but the words are lost in the thundering beat. All I can focus on is the heat of his breath against my skin and the way his hands never stop moving.

His lips trace a path down my neck, leaving a trail of shivers. I gasp as his teeth graze my collarbone, the hint of pain only heightening my arousal. I arch my back, silently begging for more.

Who could this man be? Is he the guy on my phone? Maybe he's just a banker, a doctor, a police officer, a firefighter . . . Jack. A fireman like Jack.

The mystery man spins me around, pressing my back against his chest. His strong arms encircle me, holding me tight as we continue to move to the beat. The tempo of the music speeds up, mirroring the racing of my heart. I lean my head back against his shoulder, closing my eyes and giving in to the sensations that flood through me. His lips find the sensitive spot below my ear, and I let out a soft moan. The thought of Jack fades away, replaced by the overwhelming desire for this stranger.

He reaches up, gently tracing the edge of my jaw with his thumb. "Is it time for me to unwrap you?" His voice is extremely deep . . . too deep, as if he's doing it to disguise his voice. But I don't care.

He came! It's him!

The realization hits me like a tidal wave, and I smile as I turn around to face him. "You came," I breathe, my voice barely audible over the music. "I wondered if you would."

His fingers deftly untie the red ribbon, letting it fall to the floor as his eyes never leave mine.

I see Sloane in the distance dancing with a man of her own, and our eyes lock in silent communication. This is where our night together ends and where we part to explore the next stage of the night. She gives me a wicked smile, and I know exactly what's she's telling me to do.

Should she be concerned I'm dancing with a masked man? Should I be?

He takes my hand and leads me through the writhing mass of dancers, guiding me toward a secluded corner of the club. The shadows envelop us as he pushes me gently against the wall, his body pressing into mine. His lips find mine in a passionate kiss, and I surrender to the intensity of the moment.

Our tongues dance together in perfect harmony, just as our bodies had on the dance floor. His hands explore my body, leaving a trail of fire in their wake. I moan into his mouth as his fingers trace the edge of my dress, teasing the sensitive skin beneath.

Maybe I should ask for him to remove the mask, but I don't want to. I like the feel of the velvet against my face as we kiss.

My fingers tangle in the fabric of his cloak as I pull him closer, desperate for more. The taste of him, the feel of him, it's all-consuming.

His hands slide up my thighs, lifting my dress just enough to give him access to the bare skin beneath. I gasp as his fingers brush against the lace of my panties, and he growls low in his throat.

In response to my gasp, he deepens our kiss, leaving me breathless and wanting. The teasing touch of his fingers sends waves of pleasure through me, and I rock my hips against his hand, silently begging for more.

He obliges, slipping his fingers beneath the lace and finding my wetness. I moan into his mouth as he begins to stroke me, his expert touch sending pure eroticism crashing over me. I cling to him, my nails digging into his shoulders as I look around at the hundreds of clubgoers who don't seem to notice. It's not like we are the only ones in sexual acts in the room, but I've never been so exposed before. I've never done anything in the open. But just like the fantasy I described to him in our chat . . . I craved this.

The world around us fades away, and all that exists is the booming music and the feel of his body pressed against mine.

Breaking the kiss, he mouths, *Come.*

He takes my hand and leads me through the writhing mass of dancers, toward a door at the back of the club. My heart pounds, and my breath seems trapped in my chest as we make our way up a narrow staircase and into a dimly lit hallway. He stops in front of a door, his hand reaching for the knob.

I consider running before he pushes the door open, revealing a dimly lit room with plush red curtains draped over the walls. The scent of incense fills the air, and the distant and muffled sound of music from the club below filters in through the walls.

He guides me inside, closing the door behind us, and locks it. Even though we are alone in the room, we aren't really alone. There are two huge floor-to-ceiling windows revealing people in a room on the other side. The viewers watch with rapt attention, their faces illuminated by the soft glow of the room. They are close enough to see us, but far enough away that their features are indistinct.

A rush of heat forms between my legs as I return my attention to my masked man, uncertain if I can actually go through with this.

He steps closer, his fingers brushing a stray hair from my face. "You said this was your fantasy." His voice is low and husky, and I now know he's trying to conceal its natural sound, which only adds to the sexy mystery of this entire experience.

I hesitate for a moment, my eyes darting toward the windows and the shadowy figures beyond.

"I did," I say. "But I never thought it would actually happen."

He takes my hand and leads me toward the center of the room, stopping in front of a large, ornate bed. The red velvet curtains surrounding the bed create a sense of intimacy, despite the voyeurs beyond the windows.

People are watching. Oh god, people are watching!

He softly runs his fingers along my jawline, tilting my face up toward his so our eyes connect. I swallow hard, my body wanting to collapse to a pile of goo on the floor.

I nod, giving him my silent consent.

With a wicked smile, he slowly undresses me, his touch leaving a trail of goose bumps on my exposed skin. The cool air of the room contrasts with the heat of our breaths.

He whispers in my ear as my dress pools at my feet, "Remember, they're watching." His words only serve to heighten my arousal.

I try not to look at the windows in fear that I'll chicken out and run out of the room with a failed fantasy to haunt me forever. Instead, I stand before him, clad only in my lace panties and heels.

He takes a step back to admire me. A low growl escapes his lips as he takes in my nearly naked form. The hunger in his eyes, and the knowledge that strangers are also watching my every move, sets my body ablaze.

His fingers hook into the lace of my panties, slowly pulling them down my legs. I step out of them, feeling extremely exposed in the best possible way. His lips find mine again, his kiss dominating and possessive.

For the first time since entering the room, I steal a peek at the windows. Several pairs of eyes are fixed on us, observing our every move with unabashed curiosity. The heat between my legs intensifies as I realize how many people are truly watching, and I press myself closer to him, eager to put on a show.

I reach up and unfasten his shirt, revealing the muscular chest beneath. And tattoos . . . holy shit . . . so many tattoos. My fantasy truly coming to life.

He groans as my fingers trace the intricate patterns inked onto his skin. I try to push his shirt off his shoulders, but he stops me and shakes his head. He wants to keep the cloak on, the mystery, and I'm fine with that. More than fine.

With a smirk, I undo his belt buckle and slide the leather through the loops. His pants have to go, however.

I glance back at the window and give a smirk to the viewers. Yeah, that's right. He's mine for the night.

CHAPTER TWENTY-TWO
JACK

Fucking Chloe in this room with everyone watching on the other side of the thin glass is most definitely a fantasy of mine, and I know it's one of hers as well. Me wearing a mask, though not my first choice, makes this night possible without me being detected. A convenience that Chloe gushed about how erotic she thought a masked man would be.

She's tracing her fingertips on my tattoos which makes me nervous. Flames and axes, and other classic firefighter tats mark up a majority of my chest and arms, and I'm hoping they won't give my identity away. Luckily for me, Chloe doesn't seem to be examining them too closely, and even if she does discover it's me beneath the mask, is that really that bad?

My lips brush against her ear. "Can you feel their eyes on us?" I whisper, my voice low and husky and as disguised as I can possibly make it. It borders on sounding ridiculous.

Chloe gasps, her breath hitching in her throat. "Yes," she whispers back, her voice barely audible. "It turns me on."

"They can see your bare pussy," I growl. "And now they're going to see me lick every inch of it."

Chloe whimpers as I slide my hand up her thigh, my fingers

inching closer to her wetness. I can see the hungry gazes of the onlookers beyond the glass. It's a thrill like no other, knowing that we're the center of their attention, and I'm about to give them so much more. It's my mission to not disappoint.

I pull her to the edge of the bed and spread her legs wide, exposing her fully to our audience. Chloe bites her lip, her cheeks flushing with desire as I lower myself to my knees. The scent of her arousal fills the air, casting an animalistic spell over me. I waste no time in devouring her, my tongue teasing her clit as I slide two fingers inside her.

Chloe cries out, her body vibrating with pleasure. She grabs onto my cloak, pulling me closer as I continue my relentless assault on her senses.

Jesus, she tastes good. Really good.

"Oh god," Chloe moans, her voice breathy and desperate. "Don't stop."

I have no intention of stopping. I'm too far gone, lost in the taste and feel of her. I curl my fingers inside her, hitting that sweet spot that makes her cry out even louder. I suck her clit into my mouth, flicking my tongue over it relentlessly.

Chloe's back arches off the bed as she cries out, "Jack!" even though she doesn't realize it's me.

Wait . . . did she just call out my name? I freeze, and she sits up, eyes wide.

Her gaze darts to the window, back to me, and she clears her throat. "Make them *jack off* to what you're doing to me," she clarifies.

She appears nervous, or maybe I'm the one nervous. There's no way she could know that this is me. She'd say something surely.

Not wanting to kill the moment, I give her a smirk, nod, and lick my lips, ready to return to my task with renewed vigor.

I glance up at the glass, meeting the gaze of some of the onlookers. Some of them are touching themselves. It's a heady feeling, knowing that Chloe and I are responsible for their pleasure.

I turn my attention back to Chloe, who's breathing heavily, her chest rising and falling with each ragged breath. Her eyes are closed, her head thrown back in ecstasy. I slide my fingers out of her and replace them with my tongue, lapping up her wetness as I insert three fingers inside her, spreading her wide.

Chloe's hips buck against my face, her thighs shaking as she nears her peak. I curl my fingers inside her, searching for that spot that I know will send her over the edge. Her hands tangle in the fabric around me, pulling me closer, urging me on.

"Oh god, yes," she moans, her voice hoarse with desire. "Right there, don't stop!"

I increase the pressure of my tongue, flicking it rapidly over her sensitive bud as I pump my fingers in and out. The wet sounds of her pussy fill the air, mingling with Chloe's cries of pleasure and the muffled groans from our audience.

God, I want to fuck her. But not here. Not now. So instead, I focus all my energy on bringing her to climax. I want to hear her scream, to feel her body convulse around my fingers. I want to taste her release on my tongue.

Jesus Christ, her taste . . . It's like honey, sweet and intoxicating. I can't get enough. I lap at her greedily, my tongue delving deeper, exploring every fold and crevice. Her thighs clamp around my head, holding me in place as her hips grind against my masked face. I can feel her getting close, her inner walls starting to flutter around my fingers.

"Oh god, oh god, oh god," she chants, her hips bucking wildly against my face.

I redouble my efforts, sucking her clit into my mouth.

She gasps, her body quivering as she climbs higher and higher toward her climax. I can feel her walls tightening around my fingers, and I know she's close. I suck on her clit harder, flicking my tongue over it rapidly as she cries out, her body convulsing with pleasure.

I don't stop until she's fully ridden out her orgasm, her body limp and spent. I pull back, licking my lips as I savor the taste of her. She opens her eyes, looking up at me with a satisfied smile on her face.

"That was amazing," she says, her voice husky and full of desire. "But it's your turn now."

I stand up, and she gets on her knees in front of me as I lower my briefs, my erection springing free.

I step closer, pressing myself against her as I whisper in her ear.

"I'm going to make you swallow every last inch of me," I say, my voice low and full of promise. "And they're all going to watch you do it like the good girl you are."

Chloe nods, her eyes hungry, as I wrap my hand around the back of her head, guiding her toward my cock. She licks her lips, her gaze locked on to mine as she takes me in inch by inch. I groan as she circles the tip before taking me deeper into her mouth.

The onlookers beyond the glass seem entranced, their eyes following every movement as Chloe works her magic. I can see some of them stroking themselves in time with her rhythm, their pleasure building alongside mine.

I grip the back of Chloe's head, guiding her movements as she takes me deeper still. She moans around my length, the vibrations sending waves of pleasure coursing through my body. I can feel myself getting closer, my muscles tensing as I approach the edge.

Just as I'm about to release, I pull back, teasing Chloe with shallow thrusts. She whimpers, her eyes pleading with me to let her finish me off. But I'm not ready yet, not when others are depending on this entertainment to get off themselves.

Patience, as hard as it is.

"Put your ass in the air," I command. "So everyone can see how perfect it is as you suck on me."

Chloe complies eagerly, getting onto her hands and knees and arching her back so her ass is prominently displayed.

I step closer to her, running my hands over her curves before slapping her ass sharply. She gasps, her body jolting forward at the sudden impact.

"You like that, don't you?" I say, giving her ass another slap. "You like being on display, knowing that everyone out there is watching you."

She nods, her breath coming in short pants. I can see the desire in her movements, the way she's pushing back against me, silently begging for more.

I slide my hand between her legs, feeling her wetness as I tease her clit. She moans, her hips bucking as I push two fingers inside her.

"That's it," I say, my voice low and husky. "Show them how much you love it. Show them how much you want it."

Chloe whimpers, her body jerking as I continue to finger her. I can feel her walls tightening around me, her orgasm building again. I can see the pleasure etched on her face, the way her eyes roll back as she moans loudly. I reach around and grab her breasts, squeezing them roughly as I continue to thrust my fingers in and out. She cries out again, her body shaking as she comes for a second time.

Now I can have my turn.

I circle around, place my cock back at her lips and slide into her mouth, my movements slow and deliberate. I can feel the hunger in her as she takes me in, her tongue swirling around my length. The onlookers are getting louder now, their moans and gasps filling the room. I thrust deeper into Chloe's mouth, my grip on her hair tightening as I find my rhythm.

Her mouth works in tandem with my movements as my climax builds, my muscles tensing as I get closer and closer. With a final push, I release into her mouth, my body shuddering as I fill her with my seed. Chloe swallows it all, her eyes locked on to mine as she milks every last drop from me.

We take a moment to glance at the onlookers, noticing the crowd grew in number. Chloe and I share a satisfied smile.

As we catch our breath, I lean down to whisper in Chloe's ear, "Did that live up to your fantasy?"

She nods, still trying to catch her breath. "More than I could've ever imagined."

I help her up and pull her close, kissing her deeply. She tastes like me and something uniquely her own, and I can't get enough of it. But I need to break away. I got too comfortable, and I spoke way more than planned. I don't want to get sloppy.

"Thank you for the invite," I say, willing myself to leave her even though it's the last thing I want to do.

"Wait. You're leaving?"

I give her one last kiss, savoring the taste of her before dressing, gathering my belongings, and turning to leave. "Until our next fantasy."

CHAPTER TWENTY-THREE
JACK

I had to leave her. I couldn't fuck her there. I wanted to. God, I wanted to. But I didn't want our first time to be at a sex club, with me wearing a mask, and her having no idea who I even am.

I'm fucked up.

But not that fucked up.

I stumble out of the club, the throbbing bass still pulsing through my veins. The cool night air hits my face as I rip off the mask, gulping in deep breaths. My head spins, a cocktail of satisfaction and self-loathing.

I lean against the grimy brick wall, trying to get my bearings. What the hell am I doing here? This isn't me. Or is it? The line between who I thought I was and who I'm becoming is blurring more each day.

Chloe's face flashes in my mind—flushed with arousal, eyes hungry, lips parted. She had been so willing, so eager. And I walked away.

I push off the wall, my legs unsteady as I start the walk home.

Wait. I need to make sure she makes it home safely. I pace outside, torn between leaving and staying. I can't let her see me—

Jack—without the mask. But I can't exactly walk the streets of New York in my demon mask either.

I settle for a compromise, ducking into a nearby alley and peering around the corner. I'll wait until I see her leave, then follow at a distance to ensure she gets home okay. It's the least I can do after abandoning her in there.

Minutes crawl by like hours. The thundering music from the club seems to mock me, reminding me of what I left behind. What kind of man walks away from a willing woman? The kind who's too afraid to face his own desires, apparently. But this same question could be asked—and I have asked time and time again—why would I stalk her? Why would I stand outside her window night after night freezing off my balls? It absolutely doesn't make any sense, and at the same time . . . it somehow does. At least to me.

Finally, the club door swings open. My breath catches as I spot her stepping out—alone. Where is her friend? Why would she leave and head home alone? Does she not know what the buddy system is?!

I shadow her as she starts walking, keeping to the darker edges of the street. She's heading in the general direction of the subway but taking a route I know is less safe. She should be waiting for a cab. It's late! Too late! My protective instincts kick into overdrive.

A group of rowdy guys rounds the corner ahead, laughing and shoving each other. I tense, ready to intervene if needed. Chloe hugs the building wall as she passes them, head down. One of them wolf-whistles, but they keep moving. Thank god she seems to have some street smarts.

I trail her for several more blocks, my heart racing every time she gets too close to someone or passes a shadowy alleyway. Why isn't she more careful? Doesn't she know the dangers lurking in this city at night?

Suddenly, Chloe stops and fumbles in her purse. She pulls out her phone, the screen illuminating her face in the darkness. Is she calling for a ride? Texting a friend? I strain to hear, but I'm too far away.

She starts walking again, this time with more purpose. Her pace quickens, and I have to jog to keep up. I've been so focused on her, that I haven't been paying attention to exactly where we are going. It's not the subway station it's—

As we turn onto my street, I hang back, not wanting to risk her seeing me. She reaches my building and pauses at the entrance, looking up toward my floor as if I'm up there and by chance looking down.

Why am I not up there looking down? Crap! She's here to see me, and I'm not here.

I freeze, my mind racing. What do I do? I can't simply waltz up to my own apartment building while she's standing there. What would be my excuse for being out so late? And I'm still wearing this damn cloak.

Chloe pulls out her phone again, probably to text me. My pocket vibrates—thank god I had the presence of mind to silence it earlier. I watch as disappointment flashes across her face.

She lingers for a few more minutes, shifting from foot to foot, occasionally glancing up at my dark windows. I'm torn between wanting to comfort her and knowing I can't reveal myself. Finally, she sighs and turns away, shoulders slumped.

As she walks back the way we came, I trail her again, making sure she gets to the subway safely this time. Only when I see her disappear down the steps do I finally head back to my own apartment.

I take the stairs two at a time, bursting through my door and immediately pulling out my phone to text her when I notice a missed call and voicemail. Who leaves voicemails anymore?

My thumb hovers over the play button, both dreading and longing to hear her voice.

"Hi, Jack. It's Chloe. I know it's late, and you may even be at work, but I was in the neighborhood and thought . . . Well, never mind. I'll catch up with you later."

Jesus, she was just with another man. Wait . . . no. She was with me. But she didn't know it was me. And then she leaves one man to come to me. This twisted mess is getting more tangled by the second. I collapse onto my couch, head in my hands. What am I doing? What is she doing? This double life, this obsession—it's consuming me.

Am I jealous? Jealous of *myself*?

I replay the events of the night in my mind. The way Chloe looked at me in the club, not knowing it was me behind the mask. The heat of her body as we nearly fucked. The disappointment in her voice just now, thinking I wasn't home.

I can't keep doing this. I can't keep living two separate lives, torn between the man she thinks I am and the man I become in the shadows. But I'm in too deep now. How can I possibly explain any of this to her?

Oh hey, Chloe. Guess what? I've been stalking you for years. Yeah, no big deal. I'm not a psychopath. Promise. But anyway, wanna date now?

The thought sends a bitter laugh through me. There's no way out of this mess that doesn't end with Chloe hating me or thinking I'm completely insane. Or both.

I drag myself to the window, peering down at the empty street where she stood minutes ago. The city never sleeps, they say, but right now it feels like the quietest place on Earth. The silence is deafening, filled only with the echo of my racing thoughts.

I'm wired, my nerves frayed and crackling with nervous energy. I need to see her, to talk to her, to explain . . . what? That I'm not who she thinks I am? That I'm both more and less than the man she knows?

I need to at least go make sure she got home okay. I'll just stand outside her window—again—and check. Real quick.

Yeah . . . this line of thinking is what got me into this mess in the first place. But I can't help myself. I'm already grabbing my jacket, heading for the door.

When I arrive at Chloe's, I see a faint light glowing from her window. She's home. She's safe. I should leave.

But I can't. I'm rooted to the spot.

This is how it started. There was something about her after the accident that made me want to check up on her. To make sure she was okay after her parents' death. Could I have knocked on her door, introduced myself as the fireman who worked the scene, and then told her that I was only making sure she was okay?

Yes. I could have.

But at the time, it seemed intrusive. It seemed inappropriate. It seemed wrong.

So what did I do?

I became a goddamn stalker instead. Because that's not intrusive, inappropriate, or wrong at all, right?

I take my usual position by her window. There's no recent snow, so no footprints for me to worry about.

My mind drifts back to the club, to the heat of her body pressed against mine. The way her fingers trailed down my chest, how her breath hitched when I pulled her close. God, I wanted her. I still want her.

But not like this. Not with lies and masks between us.

After crawling into bed, she turns toward the window and stares out, and for a moment I think she's looking right at me. But then she turns away, and the light to her room clicks off.

This has to stop. I can't keep living this double life, can't keep lying to her—and to myself.

Tomorrow. Tomorrow, I'll tell her everything. I'll lay it all out—the stalking, the club, my feelings for her. She'll probably run screaming, but at least it'll be over. At least I'll have been honest.

CHAPTER TWENTY-FOUR
CHLOE

A kink love triangle for the holidays? Yes, that's what I've found myself in. My own fault, of course.

This isn't me. This is not who I am. I'm a one-man-at-a-time kind of gal. And yet, here I am.

I should be working but instead I keep looking at my notifications on Dark Secrets to see if WinterWatcher has messaged me—he hasn't. I keep looking at my texts to see if Jack has texted me back—he hasn't.

Maybe I'm delusional in thinking either are interested in me. Am I reading too much into things?

I sigh and put my phone down, trying to focus on the jewelry displayed in front of me. I need to come up with some catchy content. The perfect song or maybe lip-syncing? But my thoughts blur together, my mind wandering back to memories of last night. On how WinterWatcher made me come in front of all those people.

But then there's Jack. Sweet, funny Jack who I still thought of as WinterWatcher had his fingers buried inside of me. I don't want to admit that fact, but it's true. Jack remained.

And when I found myself standing at Jack's apartment building last night, had he been home . . . I would have fucked him. I needed to fuck him.

But was I imagining the spark between us? He's barely made a move on me. Not really anything. Not a kiss. Just . . . some flirting and a sweet connection.

"Focus," I mutter to myself, picking up a delicate silver necklace. I hold it up to the light, trying to think of a clever caption. But all I can picture is WinterWatcher fastening it around my neck to the point where I can barely breathe.

Yes . . . choke me with it.

I shake my head, trying to clear the erotic thoughts. This is getting out of hand. I need to work, for god's sake. I need to be professional.

But as I set the necklace down, my phone buzzes. My heart leaps into my throat. Is it him? Which him?

I grab my phone, fumbling in my haste. It's Sloane, no doubt checking on me from last night. I went looking for her after my experience with WinterWatcher, she was nowhere to be found. I know Sloane is a big girl and could take care of herself, but it's still good to see her finally call me back.

"You alive?" I say the minute I answer. "I've been texting you."

"Yeah, I'm alive," Sloane's voice comes through, sounding a bit groggy. "Sorry, I crashed hard last night. Didn't even hear my phone."

"Hot night?"

"Jesus no," she groans. "When you went off with Sexy Masked Man, I was left with this guy who kept trying to impress me with his crypto portfolio. I swear, if I hear the word 'blockchain' one more time, I'm going to scream."

I laugh, picturing Sloane's exasperated face. "Oh no, that sounds awful."

"It was. I ended up faking a phone call and bolting. How about you? Did Mr. Mysterious live up to expectations?"

My cheeks flush hot as the memories flood back. "He, um . . . he certainly did."

"Ooh, spill the tea, girl! I want all the juicy details."

"Let's just say it was intense. Very intense. And very public."

Sloane gasps. "You didn't! You fucked right there at the club?"

"Not quite, but . . . close enough. God, Sloane, I don't know what came over me. I've never done anything like that before."

"Hey, no judgment here."

"I know, I just . . . I feel so conflicted. It was amazing in the moment, but now I'm questioning everything."

"That's totally normal," Sloane reassures me. "First time experiences like that can be overwhelming. But hey, you're a consenting adult. As long as you felt safe and respected, there's nothing wrong with exploring your desires."

"I guess," I say, still uncertain. "It's just . . . there's more to it."

"More? What do you mean?"

"The fireman," I remind. "I actually called out Jack's name as I was getting ready to come."

She gasps. "You. Did. Not."

"I covered fast. Or at least I think I did, but yeah. The first name that came to mind was Jack's. And then afterward, when the night was over, I went to Jack's apartment."

"You fucked the fireman!"

"No. But I wanted to. He wasn't home."

I can hear Sloane's sharp intake of breath through the phone. "Oh, honey, you've got it bad."

"I know," I groan, rubbing my forehead. "I don't know what to do. It's like I'm losing my mind."

"Okay, let's break this down," Sloane says, her voice taking on that no-nonsense tone she uses when she's about to dispense advice. "You've got the mysterious, kinky guy who clearly knows how to push all your buttons. And then you've got the sweet, funny fireman who you can't stop thinking about. Am I getting this right?"

"Pretty much," I admit.

"And playing with both is out of the equation?"

"I can't do that. I'm a one-man kind of girl. Look how torn I am now, and I'm not even officially dating either of them. Jack and I haven't even had a kiss or a real first date yet. And I don't even know Mystery Man's real name."

"All right, all right," Sloane says, her voice softening. "I get it. You're not built for the poly life. So let's think about this logically. What does each guy bring to the table?"

I pause, considering. "WinterWatcher . . . he's exciting. Dangerous, almost. He makes me feel things I've never felt before. But Jack . . . he makes me laugh. He makes me feel safe and protected."

"Hmm," Sloane hums thoughtfully. "Sounds like you've got quite the dilemma on your hands. But let me ask you this—which one do you see a future with?"

I pause, caught off guard by her question. It's not something I've allowed myself to consider yet. "I . . . I don't know. I mean, I barely know WinterWatcher. He could be anyone behind that mask. And Jack . . . well, we're just getting to know each other too."

"True but humor me. Close your eyes and picture yourself a year from now. Who do you see by your side?"

I do as she says, letting my eyes drift shut. In my mind's eye,

I see a cozy living room, a Christmas tree sparkling in the corner. And there, on the couch . . .

"Jack," I whisper, opening my eyes. "I see Jack."

"Well, there you have it," Sloane says, a smile in her voice. "Sounds like your heart knows what it wants, even if your libido is a bit conflicted."

"But what about the excitement? The passion?" I ask, thinking of WinterWatcher's skilled touch.

"I think having a fireman's hose inside you is exciting enough," Sloane says with a loud laugh.

"Sloane! You aren't helping."

"Well, here you are telling me that a fireman isn't exciting. I'm calling you out on your bullshit. Find me a fireman. I want to be a badge bunny or a hose hoe. Sign me up!"

"Hose hoe? Are you kidding me? There are names?" I'm laughing even though I shouldn't be.

"Oh yeah. Fireflies, bunker bunny. They all want to join the circle jerk. I can't say I blame them. So see? Keeping Jack is a good thing."

"But I want . . . I have fantasies. Dark Secrets has opened something up deep inside of me."

"Honey, passion can be cultivated. If Jack's the one you want a future with, then you two can explore and grow together. Who knows? Maybe he's got a kinky side waiting to be unleashed."

There's no way I can't laugh at that. "Maybe you're right."

"Of course I'm right. I'm always right," Sloane says smugly.

But then I think of ending it with WinterWatcher and my gut twists. I don't want that. Waiting for his message is like waiting for Christmas morning as a kid. Yes, I know nothing about this man other than what gets him hard. But . . . I don't want to let him go either.

"I've been the good girl my entire life. The people pleaser. The one that settles. Accepts. Being on Dark Secrets . . . it lets me unleash another side of myself." I pause, surprised by what I'm realizing. "I really, really like that side. And this WinterWatcher guy, he gets that. I think Jack may represent the side of me that's safe and familiar. The side everyone expects me to be."

Sloane is quiet for a moment, considering my words. "I get that. But who says you can't be both? You don't have to choose between being 'good' and being 'dirty.' The right person will accept all sides of you."

I sigh, fiddling with the necklace again, remembering how WinterWatcher had untied the ribbon around my neck. Jesus, the man was hot. So fucking hot.

"I suppose you're right. It's just . . . I'm not sure Jack is that person."

"Well, then, maybe you need to end it with Jack," Sloane suggests, and I hate those words just as much as ending it with WinterWatcher.

I groan, feeling more confused than ever. "I don't know if I can end it with either of them."

"Then maybe you need more time," Sloane says gently. "You don't have to make a decision right this second. Why not spend more time with both of them and see how things develop?"

"But isn't that leading them on?" I ask, guilt gnawing at me.

"Not if you're honest about where you're at," Sloane points out. "You can tell them both that you're exploring your options and not ready for anything exclusive yet. That way, everyone's on the same page."

I consider this, turning the idea over in my mind. It feels a bit uncomfortable, but also . . . freeing. "I guess that could work. But what if they're not okay with it?"

"Then that's valuable information too," Sloane says. "If either of them can't handle you taking the time you need to figure things out, then maybe they're not the right fit for you anyway."

She has a point. I take a deep breath, feeling some of the tension leave my body. "Okay. Yeah. I think I can do that. I may feel guilty though."

"Screw guilt. You aren't doing anything wrong. It's not like you are declaring your love, nor are they. Yet."

I take a deep breath.

"And you shouldn't spend the holidays alone anyway. This is good for you. You deserve this after all the pain you've been through. It's about time you had a holly jolly holiday."

"You're right. I am tired of moping around and feeling sorry for myself."

"That's my girl," Sloane says warmly. "Just remember, you're allowed to take your time. You're allowed to explore. And most importantly, you're allowed to put yourself first. It's time to do you. Chloe era."

As I'm about to respond, my phone buzzes with a new notification. My heart leaps as I see it's a message from WinterWatcher on Dark Secrets.

"Oh god," I whisper.

"What? What is it?" Sloane asks, concern in her voice.

"It's him. WinterWatcher. He just messaged me."

"Well, don't leave me hanging! What does it say?"

I swallow hard, my finger hovering over the notification. "I . . . I haven't opened it yet."

"Girl, if you don't open that message right now, I swear I'll reach through this phone and do it myself!"

Laughing nervously, I tap the notification. The app opens, revealing his message:

Last night was unforgettable. I can't stop thinking about you. When can I see you again?

My breath catches in my throat. "Oh wow."

"What? What did he say?" Sloane demands.

I read her the message, my voice shaky.

"Damn," Sloane whistles. "Sounds like Mr. Mysterious is just as smitten as you are."

"Yeah," I say, staring at the screen. "What do I do now?"

"Well, if you're going with the explore-your-options plan, I'd say you message him back. Set up another meeting. But be clear about where you stand."

I nod, even though she can't see me. "Right. Okay. I can do that."

CHAPTER TWENTY-FIVE
JACK

I know I promised myself that I'd confess my stalking ways to Chloe today, but when morning comes . . . I can't. I'm not ready to let her go. Not just yet.

Does that make me a monster? Maybe.

Does it make me the villain in the story? I hope not.

But when I woke up today, I had two choices. Go to her house and confess, or log on to the secret camera and watch her work from home.

Since I'm staring at my computer right now, mesmerized by Chloe's every move, it's obvious what choice won.

As Chloe stretches in her chair, I lean closer to the screen. She's wearing the black sweater I love, the one that brings out her eyes. I imagine I can smell her fruity shampoo through the pixels, that I can feel the warmth of her body as it innocently brushes up against me.

On-screen, Chloe stands and walks out of frame. I hold my breath until she returns, coffee mug in hand.

This has to stop. I know it does. I've always known it. But not today. Today, I'll watch a little longer. Tomorrow, I'll be brave. Tomorrow, I'll face the consequences.

She's done with her live, and I'm hoping she's in the mood to log in to Dark Secrets. Today, I want her to make the first move.

As if on cue, a notification pops up on my screen. Chloe is on Dark Secrets. My heart races as I switch tabs, eager to see what she'll say. Will she confide in me today? Share another intimate detail of her life? Confess some deep and erotic fantasies that I can only hope to give?

I wait, fingers hovering over the keyboard, ready to respond. But minutes tick by, and she remains silent. I switch back to looking at the nanny cam footage to see if she's changed her mind, perhaps wrestling with her own demons.

I catch her as she's removing her pants, her black sweater I love so much, and reveals a lacy black bra and matching underwear. She looks stunning, and a familiar ache settles in my chest.

Jealousy nearly knocks the air out of me. No. She's getting ready to go live for all her subscribers. All of them. Not just me. I type out a message to tell her to stop, delete it, type again. No, I can't. I can't play the possessive boyfriend when I am anything but.

But I don't want to share. Or do I?

I watch, transfixed, as Chloe settles in front of her camera. She's adjusting the lighting, primping her hair. My fingers itch to reach through the screen and touch those silky strands. I've imagined running my hands through her hair countless times, but this . . . this is different. This is real, raw, unfiltered Chloe.

The chat on her live stream explodes with comments. I can't bear to look at them, can't stand to see other men lusting after her. But I force myself to watch, to be a silent guardian in the shadows of her digital world.

"I know it's been a couple of days," she begins. I can't see her face as she's been careful to angle the camera where it's shadowed, but now that I know BlackAsChlo is Chloe, it's so obvious. "Before we continue," she says, her voice soft but clear, "I want to share something with you all. I've been talking to someone . . . someone special."

She leans forward to read all the comments. Comments that are saying "No!" "Choose me!"

"Don't be jealous, everyone. He likes to share. We already did a little show for all to see. He's a mystery right now," Chloe continues, her voice a sultry purr. "But I think I might be able to convince him to join me on camera soon. Would you all like that?"

The chat explodes again, a cacophony of enthusiasm and jealousy. I can barely breathe. My mind races, trying to piece together what's happening. A flashback of our night at Naughty and Nice crashes into my mind like a tidal wave. Clearly it made as much of an impression on Chloe as it did on me.

Chloe giggles, the sound both innocent and knowing. "Oh, you naughty people. Always so eager. But patience is a virtue, you know."

She leans back, giving her audience a tantalizing view. She runs a finger from her breast, down her stomach, down to the waistband of her panties. I can't tear my eyes away, even as a part of me screams that this is wrong, that I should stop watching.

"Maybe I'll give you a little preview," Chloe says, her voice husky. "Just a taste of what's to come."

She hooks her thumb under the lace of her underwear, slowly pulling it down. I'm frozen, caught between desire and rage, unable to look away but hating the idea of anyone else watching.

Possessive. That's how I'm feeling.

If I was being honest with myself, it's been there all along, but now that I've had a taste . . . it's suffocating.

I think you've given them enough, pretty girl, I find myself typing. I don't want to share. Call me an asshole, but I don't want anyone seeing her pussy but me. Or at least without me being there making it obvious to all who are watching that though we may be showing her pussy . . . it's still mine.

Possessive jerk? I guess so.

Should I have resisted? Doesn't matter. It's too late now. The message is out there, floating in the digital ether, making its way to Chloe's screen.

I watch as Chloe pauses. Her hand stills on her underwear, and I can almost see the wheels turning in her head. She leans forward, presumably reading my message, and for a moment, I'm terrified she'll get angry and everything will come crashing down.

But then she laughs, a sound that I will never tire of hearing. "Well, well," she purrs, addressing her audience. "Looks like my mystery man has decided to join us after all. And he's feeling a bit . . . possessive."

The chat explodes again, a mix of disappointment and taunts. I can barely focus on the words scrolling by; all I can see is Chloe, all I can hear is the blood rushing in my ears.

"What do you think, everyone?" Chloe asks, her voice teasing. "Should I listen to him? Or should I give you the show you've been waiting for?"

I hold my breath, watching as she reads the responses. My fingers hover over the keyboard, itching to type something else, to beg her to stop, to claim her as mine. But I resist.

No. Fuck that shit. I quickly type a warning on the public feed for all to see, BlackAsChlo . . . naughty girls get punished.

"Hmm," Chloe muses, tracing lazy circles on her thigh. "It seems we have a bit of a split decision. I might like what my Winter-

Watcher has in mind for my punishment. I've never claimed to be a good girl."

The temptation to spank her ass has never been so strong. Hearing her plead for mercy as she promises to be the good girl I know she can be. Then she falls to her knees, wraps her lips around my cock and—

"But you know what? I think I'm going to listen to my mystery man tonight."

Relief washes over me, quickly followed by a surge of domineering pride. She chose me. She listened to me.

"Don't worry though," Chloe continues, her voice a seductive whisper. "I promise we'll make it up to you next time. Maybe with a special guest appearance?"

The minute she logs off, I instantly get a private message. A punishment, huh?

Yes, I quickly type back. Clearly you deserve one.

Don't like sharing?

I'm treading dangerous waters now, but I can't stop myself.

No, I don't like sharing, I type back. Not unless I'm there to make it clear who you belong to.

There's a pause, and I wonder if I've gone too far. Then her reply pops up. Mmm, jealous possessive. I like it. So tell me, WinterWatcher, how would you claim me?

My fingers fly across the keyboard, unleashing all the pent-up fantasies I've harbored for months.

I'd start by wrapping my hand in your hair, pulling your head back to expose your throat. I'd mark you there, where everyone can see. I'd punish you in front of everyone so all your subscribers can see what happens when you're a bad girl and perform for them without me. I pause and add, You deserve discipline for what you did.

Oh really? And what do you have in mind, WinterWatcher?

I'm going to spank that ass of yours until it's bright red, until your pussy is dripping, and until you are moaning my name.

I stare at the screen, my dick hardening to uncomfortable levels as I wait for Chloe's response. The seconds stretch into an eternity.

Finally, her reply appears. Mmm, promises, promises. But can you deliver?

Oh, if only she knew. I've imagined this scenario a thousand times, planned it out in exquisite detail.

I don't make promises I can't keep, I type back. The question is, can you handle it?

I watch the nanny cam footage as Chloe reads my message. I can almost see the wheels turning in her head, weighing the risks and rewards.

Is that your fantasy? she replies.

Pretty girl, I have so many. That's just one of hundreds when it comes to you.

Tell me another, she says. The biggest one of all.

I pause, considering if I should reveal my truest fantasy of all. The one thing I've wanted since I first stood outside her window.

My biggest fantasy, I type slowly, is to not have to spend Christmas alone.

I hold my breath, watching the screen intently. Have I said too much? Have I gone from sexy dom to pathetic cinnamon roll?

Seconds tick by with no response. On the nanny cam, I see Chloe staring at her screen, her expression unreadable.

Finally, a message appears. That's a fantasy of mine as well. I didn't realize it until now.

A pretty girl like you shouldn't be alone for Christmas.

You aren't the first to tell me that.

For a moment, I forget about the cameras, the stalking, the lies. All I can think about is the possibility of spending Christmas with her, of waking up next to her on a cold winter morning, of sharing hot cocoa and stolen kisses by a fireplace.

Two people alone for Christmas, huh? I reply, feeling as if I'm walking on eggshells. I don't want to be too forward too fast.

I want to invite myself over. I want to suggest we spend Christmas together. But I can't. Not yet. It's too soon, too risky. I have to play this carefully.

But I wasn't lying when I told her that my biggest fantasy is not having to spend Christmas alone. Ever since my mother died . . . I can't bring myself to finish that thought. The pain of losing her is still too raw, even after all these years. Instead, I focus on Chloe, on the possibility of a future where I'm not alone.

Maybe we don't have to be alone, Chloe types back. What if . . . what if we spent it together? You gave me one of my fantasies at Naughty and Nice. It seems only fair that I give you one of yours.

How can I pull this off? How can I spend Christmas with Chloe and her not discover who I am? It's one thing wearing a mask and a cloak in a dark club. I could speak in a low tone, covered by the sound of loud club music. It's another spending intimate time together in the hushed comfort of her house. I can't exactly wear a mask on Christmas Eve and practically growl out commands, now can I? How far can the masked caveman act go?

Giving me one of my fantasies? I begin typing, thinking of every possibility to keep my charade alive. Whatever I want for Christmas?

I see her smile as she answers, Yes. My Christmas gift to you. That's if you've been a good boy and you're on Santa's nice list.

Oh, I've been good. Very, very good.

I'm sure you have, Chloe replies. I can almost hear the teasing lilt to her words. So yes, you get your Christmas present however you want it. Just tell me.

I want my present wrapped in a bow on Christmas Eve, I type.

A bow?

Yes. I want you blindfolded when I arrive at your house.
A red ribbon tied tightly around your perfect face. I want
you completely naked, legs spread wide-open, lying on
your bed waiting for me.

I can do that—

I'm going to arrive at ten p.m. on Christmas Eve. I'm
going to knock on your door and give you two minutes
to get ready. When I enter, I want to see you exactly as
I described. Do you understand?

Yes, I understand, Chloe replies. Ten p.m. on Christmas Eve. Blind-folded, naked, with a red ribbon. I'll be waiting.

I stare at her words, a mix of disbelief and primal need coursing through me. This is really happening.

Good girl, I type back. And remember, no peeking. The blindfold stays on the entire time.

On the nanny cam, I see Chloe squirm in her chair, clearly aroused by the idea. Okay, she types. I trust you.

Those three words hit me like a punch to the gut. She trusts me. If only she knew the truth.

But I push the guilt aside. This is what I've wanted for so long. I'm not going to let anything ruin it now.

You won't regret it, I type back. I promise to make it a Christmas Eve you'll never forget.

I watch as Chloe reads my message, her lips curving into a smile. She types back, I haven't done Christmas in a really long time.

Same.

My house isn't decorated.

You in a red bow is the only decoration I need.

I've never done anything like this, she continues to confess.

Inviting a masked man you nearly fucked at a club to your house is not your norm, you say? I type, smirking as I do.

I see and hear her laugh. I smile, watching her through the camera.

My fingers hover over the keyboard. I want to reassure her, to tell her she has nothing to fear from me. But how can I do that without revealing too much?

I would never hurt you, I type finally. You can trust me.

She's quiet for a long moment, and I watch her face on the camera, trying to decipher her thoughts. Finally, she responds.

I know. I don't know why, but I do trust you. This is wild.
Borderline insane. If anyone in my life knew I was doing
this . . .

I'm worried that she may start to talk herself out of this, so I type, Until Christmas Eve, I want you to think about what might happen. I want you to imagine my hands on your body, my lips on your skin. But you're not allowed to touch yourself. Not until Christmas Eve.

I see her squirm in her chair again, clearly affected by my words. Can she last two days without touching herself?

That's cruel, she types back, but I can almost hear the playful tone in her voice.

Consider it part of your punishment for earlier, I reply. And motivation for good behavior.

And if I'm not good? she asks.

Then maybe Santa will have to leave coal in your stocking
instead of me in your bed.

She laughs out loud at that, the sound carrying through my speakers. It's a magical sound, one that makes my heart soar.

I'll be good, she promises. The best you've ever had.

If only she knew how good she already is, how perfect she is in my eyes. But I can't tell her that. Not yet.

We'll see, I type instead. Now, it's getting late. You should get some sleep.

You're right, she agrees. *Good night, WinterWatcher. Sweet dreams.*

Good night, BlackAsChlo, I reply. *Give me your address, and I'll see you soon.*

I watch as she shuts down her computer and gets ready for bed. As she slips under the covers, I lean back in my chair, my mind racing with possibilities.

Christmas Eve can't come soon enough.

CHAPTER TWENTY-SIX
JACK

I've looked at the text exchange far too many times. I'm trying to not overanalyze or read into it too much, but it's hard to resist.

> **ME:** Chinese food and movie tonight? Your place or mine?

> **CHLOE:** Uh . . . tonight? sure. My place works.

What does the . . . mean? Why didn't she capitalize the *s* in *sure*? Maybe she's just busy and distracted. Or maybe she's not really excited about our plans. The "Uh" feels hesitant, like she's trying to come up with an excuse. Now I've worked myself into a frenzy over two tiny punctuation marks. Or the lack thereof.

My thumb hovers over the call button. I could just ask her directly if everything's okay. But what if I'm being paranoid? I don't want to come across as needy or insecure. Or maybe the real issue is that I know I need to come clean and tell her who I am. Tell her what I've been up to the past two years.

I lock my phone screen and toss it onto the couch, trying to push the nagging thoughts from my mind. But they creep back in, persistent as ever. The truth is, I'm terrified of how Chloe will react when she learns about what I've done. Will she understand why I had to watch over her—from afar? Or will she feel betrayed, scared, creeped out and call the police to report me as the stalker that I am?

I pace around my apartment, my mind racing. The walls feel like they're closing in, reminding me of all the secrets I'm keeping. It's still too early to head over to Chloe's for our date, but I can't wait around any longer. I'll make a stop at the florist before I pick up the Chinese food and get her something. Something that might soften the blow of my confession.

I grab my keys and head out, my stomach churning with anxiety. The late afternoon sun setting feels too bright, too exposed. I squint as I make my way to my truck, constantly glancing over my shoulder out of habit. It will be dark soon. But not dark enough for me to hide in the shadows like I'm used to.

The florist's shop is a riot of colors and scents. I wander the aisles, touching petals absently as I try to decide. Roses feel too cliché, too romantic for what I'm about to do. Lilies are too funereal. My eyes land on a poinsettia. On theme for the night, friendly, unassuming. Perfect.

Back in the truck, I place the plant carefully on the passenger seat. The Chinese restaurant is busy, filled with the sounds of sizzling woks and rapid-fire Mandarin. I give my name for the pickup order, then wait, shifting from foot to foot.

My phone buzzes. It's Chloe. Don't forget the hot mustard. Nothing screams getting in the holiday spirit like cleaned-out sinuses.

I text back, Will do. See you soon. I add a smiley face emoji, trying to keep things light.

The woman behind the counter calls my name, handing over

two large paper bags. The smell of garlic and ginger wafts up, making my mouth water despite my nerves. I ask for extra packets of hot mustard, remembering Chloe's text.

As I drive to her house, my mind races through different scenarios. Should I tell her everything right away? Or ease into it over dinner? Maybe I should wait until after the movie. But no, that feels dishonest somehow, like I'm trying to manipulate her emotions.

I pull up to Chloe's house, my hands shaking slightly as I gather the food and flowers. The porch light is on, casting a warm glow over the front steps. I take a deep breath, trying to steady myself, before ringing the doorbell.

Chloe opens the door, her smile bright and welcoming. "Hey, you're early! Come on in." She's wearing a soft-looking sweater and leggings, her hair pulled back in a messy bun. She looks beautiful, and my heart aches with the weight of my secrets.

"I, uh, brought you this," I say, thrusting the poinsettia toward her awkwardly.

Her eyes light up. "Oh, how festive! Thanks, that's so sweet." She takes the poinsettia, her fingers brushing mine for a moment. "Let me put this down and we can dig into that food. I'm starving!"

I follow her into the kitchen, setting the bags on the counter.

"Nice place," I say. That's what someone who's never been in the house would say, right? I'm trying to play it cool, and to be *normal*, but I feel anything but.

"Thanks. It was my parents' and then it became . . . thanks."

As she fusses with the poinsettia, I start unpacking the containers of food. The familiar routine feels surreal, knowing what I'm about to do.

"So, what movie did you want to watch?" Chloe asks, her back to me as she finds a spot for the plant.

Okay, I'll tell her after dinner and the movie. No sense in ruining the entire night.

I hesitate, my hands pausing over the containers of fried rice and kung pao chicken. "I didn't actually pick one out yet. I thought maybe we could choose together? Only rule is it has to be Christmas. No Scrooge allowed, remember." I give her a smile and it feels good to release some of my built-up tension.

Chloe turns around, a playful smirk on her face. "No Scrooge, huh? Well, that rules out *Die Hard*, then."

I chuckle, grateful for the moment of lightness. "Come on, that's totally a Christmas movie!"

"Agree to disagree," she says, reaching for the plates in the cupboard. "How about *It's a Wonderful Life*? Classic, heartwarming, and definitely Christmassy."

"Sounds perfect," I reply, my voice a little too enthusiastic. I'm trying so hard to act normal, to push down the anxiety bubbling in my chest.

We settle on the couch with our plates piled high with food. Chloe starts the movie, and for a while, I lose myself in the familiar story. Jimmy Stewart's earnest face fills the screen, his character's struggles echoing my own inner turmoil.

As George Bailey contemplates ending his life, I feel a lump form in my throat. How many times have I stood on the edge, metaphorically speaking, wondering if my actions were justified? If the path I've chosen was the right one?

Chloe must sense my discomfort, because she reaches over and squeezes my hand. "You okay? You seem a little . . . off tonight."

I swallow hard, knowing this is my chance. The moment I've been dreading and anticipating in equal measure. "I'm fine. Just . . . missing my mom, I guess."

Fucking coward. Tell her!

"I know. I miss my parents too." She mutes the TV, turning to face me fully. "What are you doing for Christmas?"

"Working," I half lie, half tell the truth. I am working Christmas Day and night, so that's not completely a lie. "I try to work one of the firefighters' shift who has kids so they can be home for at least some of the holiday. Even though I'm technically off as Christmas doesn't fall on my shift, I feel it's only right."

Chloe's eyes soften with sympathy. "That's really sweet of you."

I shrug. "I hope to be paid back someday when I have my own young kids."

We turn our attention back to the movie, but I can barely focus on the screen.

"This is nice," she says. "I can't believe the Scrooge in me is admitting this fact. But I'm actually enjoying this."

I nod, trying to smile, but my chest feels tight. The weight of my secrets is crushing me, making it hard to breathe. I can't keep this up any longer. I have to tell her.

"Thank you," she adds. "My holidays have been pretty shitty for a while, and well . . . this year feels different. I'm determined to not have another bad one. So thanks for helping me with that."

Guilt floods in. She has no idea how much I've been involved in her life, how I've watched over her through those "shitty" holidays. I take a deep breath, steeling myself for what I'm about to say.

But she just got done telling me she wants a good holiday and is on the path of having one. I don't want to be the cause of fucking that up for her. Not when she actually is smiling and seeming genuinely happy for once. I decide to hold off on my confession, at least for tonight. Maybe it will be my New Year's resolution to tell her.

Plus, I don't want to ruin tomorrow night. Our Christmas Eve.

Or is that my dick speaking, and he's much louder than my mind?

"I'm glad I could help," I say, forcing a smile. "Everyone deserves a good holiday."

We finish the movie in comfortable silence, but my mind is still racing. As the credits roll, Chloe stretches and yawns.

"That was nice," she says, smiling at me. "Thanks for suggesting this."

"You're welcome," I reply, my voice sounding strained even to my own ears. "I'm glad you enjoyed it."

Chloe tilts her head, studying me. "Are you sure you're okay? You seem distracted."

I force a laugh, but it comes out hollow. "Just tired, I guess. Long shift yesterday."

She nods, but I can see the concern in her eyes. "Well, don't let me keep you if you need to get some rest. I appreciate you coming over, even if you're exhausted."

Her kindness only makes me feel worse. I stand up abruptly, nearly knocking over my empty plate. "I should probably head out. Early shift tomorrow."

Chloe looks surprised by my sudden departure but doesn't argue. She walks me to the door, and I can feel her eyes on me as I fumble with my jacket.

"Thanks again for tonight," she says softly. "It really meant a lot to me."

I turn to face her, my hand on the doorknob. Her eyes are warm, trusting. I open my mouth, ready to spill everything, but the words catch in my throat.

"Anytime," I manage to say. "Good night, Chloe."

I step out into the chilly night air, my breath visible in small puffs. As I walk to my truck, I hear the soft click of Chloe's door closing behind me. The sound feels final, like a missed opportunity.

The drive home is a blur. My mind keeps replaying the evening, analyzing every moment, every word left unsaid. I grip the steering wheel tightly, my knuckles turning white.

At least I get to see her tomorrow night.

CHAPTER TWENTY-SEVEN
CHLOE

I hate Christmas.

Those are the words I'd easily say when this holiday season started. In fact, I could easily say those words ever since the car accident that took my parents. But not right now. Right now, I'm rushing around my house, trying to do last-minute decorating in preparation for my blind date with a stranger. An *almost* stranger.

I watched a Christmas movie! That has to be saying something.

With tinsel in hand, I frantically drape it over the mantel, cursing under my breath as I snag my sweater on an errant hook. The clock on the wall ticks mercilessly, each second bringing me closer to the moment he'll arrive.

Ten o'clock, he said. Be blindfolded, naked, legs spread, and waiting for him.

My heart races as I glance at the clock again. Nine thirty. I've wasted too much time on these pointless decorations. What was I thinking? This isn't about Christmas cheer. It's about following his instructions to the letter.

I hurry to my bedroom, shedding clothes as I go. The sweater falls to the floor, followed by my jeans and undergarments. Goose bumps cover my legs and arms from anticipation and nerves.

The blindfold sits on my nightstand, a strip of red silk that will soon plunge me into darkness.

I glance at the time again: 9:36.

Is time even moving? I can't exactly stand here naked and wait for twenty-four minutes.

Impatience grips me, and I start to pace. What if he's early? What if he's late?

I force myself to take a deep breath. I need to calm down. This is what I wanted, isn't it? To feel something other than the emptiness that's consumed me since the accident. To push my boundaries, to lose control.

Sitting on the edge of the bed, fingers tracing the silk blindfold, I try to soothe the manic raging within. The material of the red silk is cool against my skin, a stark contrast to the heat building within me.

It's 9:38. Yeah . . . time is nearly frozen. It has to be.

I get up to check the front door to make sure it's unlocked. It's only the seventh time I've done this, but why not be sure?

As I reach for the doorknob, a rational thought occurs to me. What if someone else walks in? What if it's not him? What if he arrives with a gang and— I shake off the paranoid thoughts and confirm the door is indeed unlocked. Returning to my bedroom, I catch a glimpse of myself in the full-length mirror.

I'm naked. I hardly recognize the woman staring back at me— eyes wide with a mix of fear and fire, cheeks flushed, hair slightly disheveled from my frantic decorating. Is this really me? Am I really going through with this?

What would Jack say if he saw me like—

What. The. Fuck.

Why is Jack entering my thoughts? I haven't even heard from

him since our Chinese food and movie date last night. Our date was so sweet, so much fun and so . . . vanilla. The man didn't even kiss me. When was that going to happen? Was it even going to happen at all?

I shake my head, trying to banish thoughts of Jack from my mind. This isn't about him. This is about me, about exploring a vital part of myself that I've kept locked away for far too long. I take a deep breath, steeling my nerves.

Nine forty-five. Fifteen minutes to go.

I can't wait any longer. With trembling hands, I sit on the edge of the bed, pick up the blindfold and secure it around my eyes. The world goes dark, and my other senses immediately heighten. The chill of the air against my skin feels more pronounced, the sound of my own breathing louder.

I position myself on the bed as instructed—legs spread, ready, waiting. The silk sheets beneath me feel cool and smooth, a stark contrast to the heat coming from my body. I try to steady my breathing, but it's impossible. My heart is racing, my mind a whirlwind of anticipation and fear. Every sound makes me jump. Is that him at the door? No, just the house settling. A car passing outside. The neighbor's dog barking.

Time loses all meaning in the darkness. Has it been minutes? Hours? I resist the urge to remove the blindfold and check the clock. Following his instructions is crucial. It's all part of the game, the surrender of control.

It's just me and my thoughts right now. Did I shave my legs well enough? I rub my heel on my shin to test the smoothness. Yes, I did. But what about—

The sound of knocks on the door, just as he said he would, jolts me from my thoughts. I tense. Three knocks. Slow, deliberate.

I know I have to wait two minutes now. That was his dictate. His rules.

Two minutes. It feels like an eternity. My body shakes, every nerve ending alive with anticipation. I count the seconds in my head, trying to keep my breathing steady. One hundred and twenty seconds. That's all.

All this counting, all these numbers.

I hear the door open, then close. Footsteps, slow and measured, make their way through my house. My heart pounds so loudly I'm sure he can hear it. The footsteps pause, then continue, growing closer. He's in the bedroom now. I can sense his presence, feel his eyes on me.

"Good girl," he says, his voice low and husky. It almost sounds as if he needs to clear his throat or cough. It's not natural. His voice is familiar, but different than when I heard it at the club. I can't quite put my finger on—

The bed dips as he sits beside me, his warmth radiating against my skin.

I spread my legs even wider, showing off how much of a good girl I am.

His hand touches my cheek, fingers trailing down my neck, across my collarbone. I gasp at the contact, my body arching involuntarily toward him. His hand moves lower, tracing the curve of my breast. I bite my lip, stifling a moan. Every nerve ending in my body feels like it's on fire, hyperaware of his touch, his presence.

He isn't speaking. I wish he was. Maybe I should speak. What will I say?

My breath hitches as his hand splays across my stomach, the heat of his palm searing my skin.

He shifts on the bed, and suddenly I feel his breath on my inner thigh. I tense, anticipation coiling tightly in my core. His lips brush against my skin, soft at first, then more insistent. He kisses a path up my thigh, maddeningly slowly, each touch sending sparks through my body.

He spreads my thighs apart even wider. His hands grip my thighs firmly as he settles between them. I can feel his hot breath against my most sensitive area, making me squirm with need. But he doesn't touch me there, not yet. Instead, he places light, teasing kisses along my inner thighs, occasionally nipping at the tender skin.

I whimper, frustrated by his teasing. "Please," I whisper, my voice breathy and desperate.

His tongue finally makes contact, a long, slow lick that has me gasping and arching off the bed. He takes his time, exploring every fold and crevice with meticulous attention. It's maddening and exquisite all at once.

As he works me with his mouth, one of his hands slides up my body to cup my breast. His thumb brushes over my nipple, causing it to harden into a tight peak. He pinches it lightly, the slight pain mixing with the pleasure building between my legs.

I'm lost in a haze of sensation, my hips moving of their own accord as I chase my release. Just as I'm about to tumble over the edge, he pulls away. I cry out in frustration, my body nearly vibrating with need.

I hear the rustle of fabric, the clink of a belt buckle. He's undressing. Oh god, if only I could see. The wait is almost unbearable as I lie there, listening to the soft sounds of clothing hitting the floor.

The bed dips again as he positions himself over me. I feel the heat of his body, so close but not quite touching. His breath fans across my face, mingling with mine. The scent of him fills my nostrils—a mixture of cologne and something uniquely male that makes my head spin.

His hand cups my cheek, thumb tracing my lower lip. Without thinking, I part my lips, my tongue darting out to taste his skin. He groans softly, the sound sending a pulse of pleasure straight to my exposed, and very wet, pussy.

His lips crash onto mine, hot and demanding. The kiss is intense, passionate, stealing my breath away. His tongue invades my mouth, exploring, tasting, claiming. I respond hungrily, my hands reaching up to tangle in his hair, pulling him closer.

This kiss will be my undoing. His lips move against mine with a familiarity that catches me off guard. There's a tenderness beneath the passion that I wasn't expecting. My mind races, trying to make sense of the conflicting signals.

His hand slides down my body, fingers trailing fire across my skin. He positions himself between my thighs, the hard length of him pressing against my entrance. I arch up, silently begging him to take me.

"Not yet," he whispers against my lips. I can barely hear him as he issues his command.

CHAPTER TWENTY-EIGHT
JACK

I want to speak freely so badly. I want to praise her every move. Compliment her perfect, naked body displayed for me like the best Christmas gift a man could ask for. But if I do, she'll recognize my voice. She'll know it's me, and that red blindfold won't be enough to keep me concealed.

My cock is so close to her pussy, and as much as I want to thrust it inside of her, I hold back, savoring the wait. Her body quivers with each shallow breath, goose bumps rising on her flushed skin. I trace a finger lightly along her inner thigh, feeling her shudder at my touch. She moans softly, arching her back, silently begging for more.

I lean in close, breathing in her intoxicating scent. My lips brush against her neck and I plant feather-light kisses along her collarbone. She gasps and I have to bite my tongue to keep from whispering her name.

Every fiber of my being aches to fully possess her, to claim her as mine. But I force myself to go slowly, to draw out this exquisite torture for us both. My hands roam her body, caressing and teasing. I cup her breasts, feeling their perfect weight, circling her hardened nipples with my thumbs. She whimpers and arches into my touch.

I trail kisses down her stomach, reveling in the taste of her skin. Her hips buck as I near her center. I pause, my hot breath ghosting over her most sensitive areas. She's trembling now, her chest heaving. I can see how wet she is, glistening and ready.

Unable to resist any longer, I run my tongue along her slit. She cries out, a sound of pure ecstasy. I lap at her greedily, savoring her sweetness. Her hands fist in the sheets as I focus my attention on her clit, circling it with my tongue before taking it between my lips.

Her thighs clamp around my head as I suck gently, feeling her body tense. I slide two fingers inside her, curling them to stroke her most sensitive spot. She's close now, her breathing ragged and interspersed with breathy moans. I increase the pressure and speed of my tongue, matching the rhythm of my pumping fingers.

Just as she's about to tumble over the edge, I pull back. She whines in frustration, her hips lifting off the bed, seeking more friction. I kiss my way back up her body, kissing her lips so she has no choice but to smell and taste her own arousal.

She surprises me by deepening the kiss, her tongue seeking mine hungrily. Her hands find my shoulders, nails digging in as she pulls me closer. I groan into her mouth, my resolve crumbling.

Slowly, torturously, I position myself at her entrance. She's so wet, so ready. I ease in just the tip, relishing her warmth. Her hips buck, trying to take me deeper, but I pull back teasingly. I want to draw this out, to make her squirm and beg. To drive her wild without saying a word. I also need to slide on a condom before I do anything stupid.

I reach for one of the foil packets I placed on the nightstand when I first entered, carefully tearing it open. The crinkle of the wrapper seems deafening in the silence of the room. Her head turns slightly at the sound, a small smile playing on her lips. She knows what's coming.

In one swift motion, I thrust inside her. We both cry out at the sensation. She's so tight, so wet, enveloping me in liquid heat. I have to pause, overwhelmed by the feeling of finally being joined with her.

She wraps her legs around my waist, urging me deeper. I begin to move, setting a slow, deep rhythm. Each thrust sends sparks of pleasure through my body. I watch her face, captivated by the way her lips part in silent gasps.

"Oh yes, more," she begs, arching her back to meet each thrust. Her nails dig into my shoulders, marking me as hers.

Her breaths become ragged, her moans louder, fueling my desire to give her everything she craves.

The bed creaks under our weight, the only sound aside from our panting and the slapping of skin.

I increase my pace, driven by her passionate cries. My hips snap against hers, driving deeper with each thrust. She's so close, I can feel it in the way her walls clench around me, in the tensing of her thighs.

I slip a hand between us, finding her swollen clit. I circle it with my thumb, applying just the right pressure. Her back arches off the bed, a keening wail escaping her lips.

I grind against her, hitting that perfect spot inside while my fingers work her clit. She's writhing beneath me now, her body coiled tight like a spring about to snap.

And then something wild and insane comes into me. It's time. It's time to reveal who I truly am. Before I lose my courage, I reach for her blindfold.

Time seems to slow as I gently pull it away, revealing her eyes. They're squeezed shut at first, overwhelmed by sensation. Then slowly, they flutter open, adjusting to the dim light of the room.

Our gazes lock. For a breathless moment, neither of us moves. I see the shock register on her face, followed quickly by confusion, then understanding. Her lips part, forming a silent "oh" of recognition.

I hold my breath, waiting for her reaction. Will she push me away in disgust? Scream? Call me a pervert and storm out?

But then, something unexpected happens. A slow smile spreads across her face, her eyes lighting up with a mixture of surprise and . . . is that delight?

"It's you," she whispers, her voice filled with wonder. "I should have known."

Relief floods through me, quickly followed by a surge of renewed passion. I capture her lips in a searing kiss, pouring all my pent-up emotions into it. She responds with equal fervor, her fingers tangling in my hair, pulling me closer.

With a final, deep thrust, she shatters. Her body convulses, inner muscles clamping down on me as waves of pleasure crash over her. I hold still, letting her ride out her orgasm, drinking in the sight of her coming hard on my cock.

As her tremors subside, I start to move again, chasing my own release. She moans softly, oversensitive but still eager. Her hands roam my back, nails raking my skin.

I'm close now, heat building at the base of my spine. My thrusts become erratic, harder and faster. She meets me thrust for thrust, urging me on.

"Come for me," she whispers, and it's my undoing.

With a guttural groan, I bury myself deep inside her as my orgasm hits. Pleasure courses through me in pulsing waves as I empty myself into the condom.

We stay like that for a long moment, both panting and processing.

As our breathing slowly returns to normal, I gently withdraw from her and dispose of the condom. She watches me with hooded eyes, a satisfied smile playing on her lips. I settle back onto the bed beside her, unsure what to say now that the moment of revelation has passed.

I break the silence first. Seems only fair considering the bomb I just dropped. "Are you mad?"

She reaches out, tracing my jawline with her fingertips. "Mad? No, not at all," she says softly. "Surprised, yes. Extremely confused. But . . . pleased."

"Pleased?" I echo, hardly daring to believe it.

She nods, her fingers still caressing my face. "I've wanted this," she confesses. "I wasn't sure you felt the same way."

I pull her closer, loving the feeling of her naked body against mine. "I've wanted this. Longer than you know," I murmur against her hair. "To finally be able to touch you, to show you how I feel."

She tilts her head up, capturing my lips in a tender kiss. When we part, her eyes are narrowed. "So you've been WinterWatcher all along, huh? The masked man."

"Guilty as charged," I admit, searching her face for any sign of anger or disgust. But I see only curiosity and a hint of amusement in her eyes.

She props herself up on one elbow, regarding me with a raised eyebrow. "So all those chats, those steamy messages . . . that was you the whole time?"

I nod, feeling a mix of relief and nervousness.

She considers this for a moment, then smirks. "Well, I have to admit, you had me fooled. But now that I know . . ." She trails off, her hand sliding down my chest. "I think we have a lot of lost time to make up for."

My breath catches as her fingers dance lower. "You mean you want to . . . ?"

"Oh yes," she purrs, pushing me onto my back and straddling my hips. "I want to explore every inch of you, now that I can put a face to all those delicious messages."

I groan as she grinds against me, already feeling myself hardening again. "God, you're incredible," I breathe, running my hands up her thighs.

She leans down, her lips brushing my ear, and then freezes. Pulling back, she says, "Wait. How? How did you know BlackAsChlo was me? Or that I was her?"

Shit. Shit!

CHAPTER TWENTY-NINE
CHLOE

What the hell is going on right now? I just had the best sex of my life, blindfolded, only to discover that the mystery man is actually Jack! Jack rocked my world in ways I didn't think were possible, and as I try to process what just happened, I also feel sick.

How did he know that I was BlackAsChlo? Did he know all along? Was this some crazy coincidence? Or . . .

"Did you see my face when I was filming? I know I got careless one night and—" I look up into his eyes. "Did you realize it was me then?"

Jack's eyes widen. He runs a hand through his tousled hair, taking a deep breath before answering. "I . . . I did see your face that night," he admits, his voice low and husky. "But I wasn't sure at first. I thought maybe my mind was playing tricks on me."

"And that's when you became a subscriber. To see for yourself?"

Jack nods slowly, guilt flashing across his face. "I couldn't believe it might actually be you. I had to know for sure."

My stomach churns. "So you've known this whole time? Every conversation we've had since then, every time we hung out . . . you knew?"

He reaches for my hand, but I pull away. "I'm sorry, I should have said something sooner. You have every right to be mad."

I should be. I should be furious, right? But why am I not?

I close my eyes, trying to sort through the tangle of emotions swirling inside me. Anger, betrayal, confusion . . . but also a strange sense of relief. And underneath it all, a lingering spark of desire that I can't quite extinguish.

"I don't know how to feel," I admit, my voice barely above a whisper. "Part of me wants to scream at you, but another part . . ."

Jack moves closer, his presence both comforting and unsettling. "Another part what?" he prompts.

I look up at him, really seeing him for the first time. Not just sweet Jack. But sexy as hell, dominant Jack. The man who just gave me earth-shattering pleasure. The person who's known my deepest secret for weeks.

"Another part of me is glad it's you," I confess, the words tumbling out before I can stop them. "I was torn between you—Jack, and WinterWatcher."

"Torn how?"

"Between good and bad," I admit. I take a deep breath, trying to gather my thoughts. "You were the safe choice, the sweet guy that rescues kittens from trees and shovels my neighbor's walkway. But WinterWatcher . . . he represented everything exciting and forbidden. I never thought they could be the same person."

He smiles softly, a hint of that dominant energy flickering in his eyes. "And now that you know they are?"

"I don't know," I whisper, my heart racing. "It's like two worlds colliding. I'm scared, excited, confused . . . everything at once."

Jack reaches out, his fingers gently brushing my cheek.

I lean into his touch, despite my better judgment. "But why didn't you tell me sooner? Why go through with this?" I gesture vaguely at the rumpled sheets, the lingering scent of our passion still heavy in the air.

"Being a masked man was a fantasy of yours," he reminds me. "My goal—" he lifts the red blindfold and dangles it in front of me "—is to grant you every single fantasy you have."

His words hang in the air between us, heavy with implication. I search his face, looking for any sign of deception, but all I see is sincerity and desire. My breath catches in my throat as I realize the full weight of what he's offering.

"Every fantasy?" I whisper, my voice cracking slightly. His proximity is addictive, and I find myself leaning toward him almost unconsciously, never wanting this to end.

Jack nods, his eyes never leaving mine. "Every single one," he confirms, his voice low and husky. "I've seen your videos, Chloe. I know what you like, what you crave. And I want to give it all to you."

My heart races as I process his words. The rational part of my brain screams that I should be angry, that I should feel violated. But the part of me that craves excitement, that yearns for the forbidden, is thrumming with hunger.

He turns his head toward my computer. "If I remember correctly, you promised your subscribers a viewing with a guest."

I gasp, my eyes widening as I follow Jack's gaze to my computer. The realization hits me like a tidal wave. I had indeed promised my subscribers a special show with a mystery guest. But I wasn't being serious. Or was I?

"Oh my god," I breathe.

Jack's lips curve into a knowing smirk. "Well, we wouldn't want to disappoint your loyal fans, would we?"

I swallow hard, my mind racing. This is crazy, right? Completely insane. And yet, the thought of performing with Jack, of sharing our passion with my eager audience, makes it impossible to resist this offer.

"I . . . I don't know," I stammer, even as heat pools low in my belly. "We can't show our faces."

Jack moves closer, his hand cupping my face gently. "We don't have to. I think you and I can figure out the lighting, the angle, and the shadows perfectly."

I take a deep breath, weighing my options. The responsible part of me says this is a bad idea, that I should take some time to process everything that's happened. But the part of me that craves excitement, that yearns for new experiences, is screaming to take the leap.

"Okay," I whisper, my voice barely audible. "Let's do it."

"That's my good girl."

Jesus, the man knows how to make me melt.

We spend the next few minutes setting up the camera, adjusting the lighting, and making sure our faces will remain hidden. We also make sure the laptop is in a place we can see the comments. As we work, I can feel the need building, a delicious tension crackling between us.

Finally, everything is ready. Jack stands behind me, his strong arms wrapped around my waist, as I reach for the button that will start the live stream.

"Ready?" he whispers in my ear.

I nod, taking a deep breath. "Ready."

As I click the button, I feel a rush of adrenaline. The familiar green light blinks on, signaling that we're live. I can already see the viewer count climbing rapidly.

"Hello, everyone," I purr, slipping into my BlackAsChlo persona. "I hope you're ready for a very special show tonight."

Jack's hands slide down my sides, his touch igniting sparks across my skin. I lean back against him, feeling his solid chest pressed against me.

"As promised, I have a special guest with me tonight," I continue, my voice husky with desire. "Say hello, mystery man."

"Hello, everyone," Jack's deep voice rumbles.

"Tell us something about yourself," I say with a gasp as his hand caresses my belly.

"I like to watch," is all he says.

The chat explodes with excited messages, our viewers clearly thrilled by this unexpected development. I scan the comments, grinning at their enthusiasm.

"Oh, they're definitely ready," I moan, turning my head to look at Jack. "The question is, are you? Time to be watched rather than watch."

In response, Jack's hand slides up to cup my breast, his thumb brushing over my nipple. I gasp, arching into his touch.

"I think that answers your question," he murmurs, his lips brushing my ear.

We begin our dance, a sensual choreography of touches, kisses, and caresses. Jack's hands explore my body with a familiarity that still thrills me, knowing now that it's him—sweet, kind Jack—unleashing this passion.

As we move together, I'm acutely aware of the camera, of the hundreds of eyes watching us. But instead of making me nervous, it only heightens my arousal. I feel powerful, desirable, completely in my element.

"BlackAsChlo has been very, very naughty," Jack says to the viewers. "I've promised this naughty girl a punishment, and I'm a man of my word."

My breath catches in my throat at Jack's words. The dominant energy I've only experienced through a screen is now radiating from him in person, and I want more.

"That's right," I purr to the camera, playing my part. "I've been such a bad girl. Whatever shall you do with me? Do I get coal in my stocking?"

Jack's hand tangles in my hair, gently but firmly tilting my head back. "I think you know exactly what's coming," he growls in my ear, loud enough for the mic to pick up.

The chat is exploding with messages, but I barely register them. All my focus is on Jack—his touch, his voice, the heat of his body against mine. We are both completely naked, in front of hundreds, live on Dark Secrets playing out something I only dreamt of.

Jack's hand slides down my back, his touch both gentle and commanding as he moves to the side. "Bend over," he orders, his voice low and authoritative.

I comply, positioning myself over the edge of the bed, my back arched and my ass exposed to both Jack and the camera.

"Count them out," he instructs, and I nod, bracing myself.

The first smack lands, a sharp sting that quickly blooms into warmth. "One," I gasp, my voice breathy.

Jack alternates between cheeks, each spank carefully measured. The pain mingles with pleasure, sending me from bliss to erotic agony all at once. By the time I count "Ten," my skin is tingling and I'm panting and writhing in need.

"Good girl," Jack says, his hand now gently caressing my heated flesh. "You took your punishment so well."

I whimper at his praise, pressing back against his touch. "Please," I beg, not caring how desperate I sound.

"Please what?" Jack teases, his fingers dancing along my inner thigh.

"Please fuck me," I moan, loud enough for the microphone to pick up. The chat goes wild, but I barely notice.

Jack spins me around to face him, his eyes dark with desire. "Ready to give them a real show?" he asks, his voice dominant, and yet it soothes me.

I nod, breathless with anticipation. "Yes, please."

He lifts me effortlessly, and I wrap my legs around his waist as he carries me to the head of the bed. We fall onto the mattress together, a tangle of limbs and heated kisses.

As Jack's lips trail down my neck, I catch sight of the chat out of the corner of my eye. It's moving so fast I can barely read the messages, but I catch glimpses of sexual commands they want us to do, declarations of awe and more than a few of envy.

I smile to myself, closing my eyes and surrendering to the sensations. Let them watch. Let them see how good it can be when fantasy becomes reality.

I know how the camera is positioned, and I want the viewers to get a good view of my grip on Jack's cock. I reach down between us, my fingers wrapping around Jack's hard length. I angle my body slightly, making sure the camera captures the moment as I stroke his massive size.

I guide Jack's impressive length toward my entrance, teasing myself with the tip. The viewers can see everything—my glistening folds, Jack's thick shaft, the way my body trembles with need.

"Please," I whimper, loud enough for the mic to pick up. "I need you inside me."

Jack's eyes lock with mine, a silent question. I nod, giving him permission to take control.

"Safety first, ladies and gentlemen," he says as he reaches for a condom that rests on a stack on the nightstand. Then in one smooth motion, he thrusts forward, burying himself to the hilt. I cry out in pleasure, my back arching off the bed.

"Oh god, yes!" I moan, my fingers digging into his shoulders.

Jack sets a relentless pace, each powerful thrust sending waves of ecstasy through my body. I'm dimly aware of the chat exploding with activity, but all I can focus on is the incredible sensations Jack is creating within me.

"You feel so good," Jack growls. "So tight, so wet for me."

I wrap my legs tighter around his waist, urging him deeper.

"Harder," I plead. "Please, I need more."

Jack obliges, his hips snapping forward with increased intensity. The sound of skin slapping against skin fills the room, punctuated by our moans and gasps of pleasure.

I can feel my climax building, a familiar tension coiling low in my belly. Jack must sense it too, because he shifts his angle slightly, hitting that perfect spot inside me with each thrust.

"Are you going to come for me?" he asks, his voice low and commanding. "Are you going to come for all your viewers?"

The reminder of our audience sends a fresh wave of arousal through me. I nod frantically, words failing me as the pleasure builds to an almost unbearable level.

"Then do it," Jack orders. "Come for me. Now."

His command, coupled with a particularly deep thrust, sends me over the edge. I cry out, my body convulsing with waves of intense pleasure. Jack doesn't let up, prolonging my orgasm as he chases his own release.

With a guttural groan, Jack buries himself deep inside me one last time. I can feel him pulsing, filling me with his warmth. We stay locked together for a long moment, both of us panting and trembling in the aftermath of our shared climax.

Finally, Jack pulls out slowly, careful to keep our faces hidden from the camera. I turn my head toward the computer, seeing the chat absolutely exploding with excited messages and generous tips.

"I hope you all enjoyed the show," I say, my voice still breathless. "Until next time . . ."

I get out of bed and reach over and end the live stream, the room suddenly quiet without the constant ping of incoming messages. Jack pulls me into his arms, pressing a tender kiss to my forehead.

"That was . . ." I trail off, unable to find the right words.

"Incredible," Jack finishes for me, his voice soft and filled with awe. "You're incredible."

I look up at him, searching his face. The dominant energy from moments ago has faded, replaced by the gentle warmth I've always associated with Jack. It's a stark reminder of the duality I'm still trying to reconcile.

"What happens now?" I ask, my voice barely audible.

Jack's arms tighten around me. "That's up to you," he says. "We can take things slow, figure this out together. Or—"

"Or?" I cut in, my heart racing.

A hint of that dominant energy flashes in his eyes. "Or we can dive in headfirst. Explore every fantasy, every unexplored passion. No holds barred."

"I vote for package number two," I say, my voice stronger than

I expected. "I want to explore everything with you, Jack. No holds barred."

A slow, wicked grin spreads across his face. "That's what I was hoping to hear from my good girl."

"I like being your good girl," I moan, running my hands down his chest. "But I also like being very bad too."

CHAPTER THIRTY
JACK

Best Christmas Eve ever. My mind is at ease, my body is humming in sexual bliss, my cock still tingling from the intense orgasm I just had. I've lost count of how many I've had now.

Chloe lies next to me, her chest rising and falling as she catches her breath. The twinkling lights outside her window cast a warm glow across her naked body. I always wondered what the lights I hung looked like from her point of view, and now I know. And seeing what they do to her perfect body . . . worth the effort.

I trace lazy circles on her skin, savoring the afterglow and the intimacy of the moment.

"Mmm," Chloe purrs, snuggling closer. "I think you broke me."

I kiss her forehead. "Rest up," I murmur. "I'm not done yet."

"Mercy!"

"Never."

Chloe giggles and playfully swats at my chest. "You're insatiable."

"Only for you," I reply, capturing her hand and bringing it to my lips.

We lie in comfortable silence for a while, listening to the soft carols playing from her Bluetooth speaker. The scent of cinnamon and pine mingles with the musky aroma of our lovemaking. Outside, a light snow is falling, blanketing the world in peaceful white.

Chloe props herself up on one elbow, her tousled hair falling around her face. In the soft glow of the Christmas lights, she looks absolutely radiant.

"You know," she says, a mischievous glint in her eyes, "I have a present for you."

"Oh?" I raise an eyebrow, intrigued. "And here I thought you were my present."

She laughs, a melodious sound that makes my heart skip. "Well, consider this an . . . added bonus."

Chloe slides out of bed, the sheets falling away to reveal her curves. I watch appreciatively as she pads across the room to her closet. She rummages around for a moment before pulling out a small, wrapped package.

"Is the present for Jack or WinterWatcher?" I call to her, chuckling as I do.

She looks over her shoulder and playfully glares. "Jack. I was hoping I'd see you even though we didn't make plans to."

I smile warmly at her words, feeling a surge of affection. "I couldn't stay away," I admit softly.

Chloe returns to the bed, present in hand. She settles beside me, cross-legged, not bothering to cover herself. The Christmas lights dance across her skin, highlighting the curves I've spent the night exploring.

"Well, I'm glad you came," she says, her voice low and sultry. She holds out the gift. "Merry Christmas, Jack."

I sit up, taking the small package. It's beautifully wrapped in silver paper with a red bow.

"Since I haven't bought a present for anyone in years, this is a pretty big step. Being a Scrooge and all," she says. "But when I saw this in an antique shop, I knew I had to get it for you."

I carefully unwrap the gift. Chloe watches me intently, biting her lower lip—the cutest quirk of hers when she's nervous or thinking hard. As I remove the last of the paper, I reveal a small velvet box.

Inside is a beautiful silver pocket watch. The cover is intricately engraved with snowflakes and pine trees—a perfect winter scene. I gently lift it out, admiring the craftsmanship.

"Open it," Chloe urges softly.

I press the latch, and the cover springs open. Inside, along with the watch face, is an inscription:

TO JACK. THANK YOU FOR WATCHING OVER ME THIS CHRISTMAS.
LOVE, SCROOGE.

She smiles. "What's ironic is I bought this before I knew you were WinterWatcher, and I used the word *watching*. Funny, right?"

I'm momentarily speechless. I should completely confess how on the nose her engraving is, but I can't. Not tonight. Not Christmas Eve when it is literally the most perfect night of my life. Instead I get up and head to the other room where I placed her Christmas present in hopes I'd find the right time to give it to her.

"Do you like it?"

"More than you know."

"Good. I know pocket watches can be old-school. But something about you screams old-fashioned in some ways."

"Hold on," I say. "Let me get yours."

I return to the bedroom, a small, elegantly wrapped box in my hands. Chloe's eyes widen with surprise and delight.

"You got me something too?" she asks, her voice soft with wonder.

I nod, settling back onto the bed beside her. "Of course. I couldn't let Christmas pass without giving the Scrooge something so her heart can grow."

I hand her the box, watching as she carefully unwraps it, her fingers tracing the golden ribbon before gently pulling it loose. She lifts the lid, and I hear her sharp intake of breath.

Inside lies a delicate silver necklace, a small snowflake pendant hanging from the chain. Tiny blue stones are set into each point of the snowflake, catching the light and sparkling brilliantly.

"Jack, it's beautiful," Chloe whispers, lifting the necklace from its velvet cushion. "It's too much."

I shake my head, gently taking the necklace from her hands. "It's not too much. It's perfect for you."

I move behind her, brushing her hair to the side. As I fasten the clasp around her neck, I place a soft kiss on her shoulder. The snowflake pendant settles right above her breasts, glittering in the Christmas lights.

"There," I murmur, my breath warm against her skin. "Beautiful."

Chloe turns to face me, her eyes shining with emotion. She touches the pendant gently, then looks up at me. "Thank you, Jack. I love it." Her eyes meet mine, shimmering with unshed tears. "Thank you for making this year . . . not so hard."

I cup her face in my hands, thumbs brushing away the tears that have started to fall.

She leans in, pressing her lips to mine in a kiss that's both tender and passionate. When we part, she rests her forehead against mine, her fingers toying with the snowflake pendant.

"What a crazy night," she says.

I smile at her words. "Crazy good, I hope?"

"The best," she affirms, her eyes sparkling. "I never thought I'd enjoy Christmas Eve again, but here we are."

I pull her closer, wrapping my arms around her waist. "Here we are. And I wouldn't want to be anywhere else."

Chloe snuggles into my embrace, her head resting on my chest. I can feel her heartbeat, steady and strong, against my skin.

"But," I add with a sigh, "I do have to be at the station at seven a.m."

Chloe pulls back slightly, looking up at me with a mix of admiration and disappointment. "You're working on Christmas Day? For one of the firefighters? I remember you saying that."

I can see the conflict in her eyes. She doesn't want me to leave, but she also appreciates the gesture. I stroke her cheek gently.

"I know, I'm sorry. I made the promise before . . . well, before tonight happened," I explain softly. "I don't have any kids or family, so—"

"I think it's sweet," she interrupts.

"But the other guys and I are cooking Christmas dinner at the station. We're allowed to invite family and guests to come join us, and I'd love to have you come if you don't have any other plans tonight."

Chloe's eyes light up at my invitation, but I can see a flare of hesitation cross her face. "Really? You want me to come to the fire station for Christmas dinner?"

I nod, running my fingers through her hair. "Absolutely. I know it's not a traditional Christmas dinner, but—"

"No, it sounds perfect," she says, her smile growing. "I'd love to come. I just . . . I'm not family. Are you sure it'll be okay?"

"Of course it's okay. The guys will be thrilled to have another guest. We always cook way too much food anyway. But fair warning . . . we are still on shift. So if there's a call, we may have to get up in the middle of dinner and bolt. So as long as you're flexible and know you might be left with the other fire wives or girlfriends."

Chloe's face lights up. "That sounds amazing, actually. I've never experienced anything like that before." She pauses, a thoughtful look crossing her face. "Will I need to bring anything?"

I shake my head, pulling her close again. "Just yourself. And maybe a big appetite."

She laughs softly, her breath warm against my chest. "I think I can manage that. Especially after tonight's . . . activities."

I chuckle, running my hand down her back. "Speaking of which, we should probably get some sleep if we want to be functional tomorrow."

Chloe sighs contentedly, snuggling closer. "You're right. But I don't want this night to end."

"*We* don't have to end," I murmur, kissing the top of her head. "This is just the beginning."

We settle into bed, Chloe's back pressed against my chest, my arm draped over her waist. The Christmas lights continue to twinkle softly, casting a warm glow over the room. Outside, the snow falls silently, blanketing the world in white.

Just before sleep claims me, I hear Chloe whisper, "Merry Christmas, Jack."

"Merry Christmas, Chloe," I reply back, my heart full.

As consciousness fades, my last thought is of tomorrow. Of Chloe at the firehouse, sharing a meal with my colleagues, becoming a part of my world. It's a future I never dared to imagine, but now I can't imagine a life without her.

I stare at the window, knowing it wasn't that long ago that I stood on the other side. Watching. Picturing what it would be like to hold her. To be with her. And now here I am, her warm body pressed against mine, her soft breathing soothing the raging guilt I still battle. The guilt of my past actions—the watching, the secrecy—tugs at the edges of my consciousness. I know I'll have to come clean eventually. But for now, I push those thoughts aside, focusing instead on the feel of Chloe in my arms, the scent of her hair, the rhythm of her breathing.

As I drift off to sleep, my mind wanders to the future. I imagine more nights like this, more Christmases spent with Chloe. I want this—want her—more than I've ever wanted anything. But the weight of my secret hangs heavy.

Morning comes too soon. The alarm on my phone chimes softly, and I carefully extricate myself from Chloe's embrace. She stirs, mumbling sleepily.

"Shh," I whisper, kissing her forehead. "Go back to sleep. I'll see you later at the station and will text you the address."

She nods, already drifting off again. I dress quietly, pausing at the door to look back at her. The morning light filters through the window, casting a soft glow on her sleeping form. My heart swells with emotion.

I don't want to fuck this up.

Please don't let me fuck this up.

CHAPTER THIRTY-ONE
CHLOE

I've never walked into a fire station before. Walked past, driven by, but never really paid attention to the exterior and how it differs from other buildings. The large red bay doors dominate the facade, each wide enough to accommodate a massive fire engine. Above them, a row of windows reveals glimpses of the second floor, where I imagine firefighters spend their downtime between calls.

It's Christmas, and I'm here for dinner with the crew and their families, but I'm uncertain if I overdressed or underdressed. I didn't ask Jack what the dress attire was and felt silly sending a text after he left this morning to ask.

I take a deep breath and push open the side door, the one meant for people rather than trucks. The warmth hits me first, along with the mingled scents of food and . . . man. Voices and laughter spill out from further inside, and I follow the sounds down a short hallway.

The community room is decked out in full holiday splendor. A massive Christmas tree dominates one corner, its lights twinkling merrily. Garlands drape across the ceiling, and a long table groans under the weight of potluck dishes. I spot Jack across the room, chatting with a couple of his colleagues. He's wearing navy pants, and his navy fire T-shirt is stretched across his broad shoulders. A wave of relief washes over me; my outfit of a simple red sweater and black slacks seems to fit right in with the casual yet festive atmosphere.

Jack catches my eye and his face lights up with a smile. He excuses himself from his conversation and makes his way over to me, weaving through the small clusters of people scattered around the room.

"You made it," he says warmly, pulling me into a quick hug. The familiar scent of his cologne mixed with a hint of smoke envelops me. "I was starting to worry you might have gotten lost."

"Sorry I'm a little late," I reply, feeling a blush creep up my cheeks. "I, uh, spent more time than I'd like to admit second-guessing my outfit choice."

Jack chuckles, his eyes crinkling at the corners. "Well, you look perfect. Come on, let me introduce you to everyone."

As we move through the room, I'm struck by the sense of camaraderie that permeates the air. These people aren't just coworkers; they're a family. Children dart between the adults' legs, their laughter punctuating the steady hum of conversation. The firemen are in the large industrial-style kitchen cooking while the fire wives and girlfriends stand nearby chatting casually. Jack introduces me to so many people that the names start to blur together, but everyone is warm and welcoming. I find myself relaxing, drawn into conversations about holiday traditions and funny stories from the firehouse.

It's quite the scene watching four firemen in their casual uniforms moving about the kitchen with grace. The food smells amazing and I can't help but be impressed by their culinary skills. Jack notices my gaze and leans in close, his breath warm against my ear.

"Firefighters make the best cooks," he whispers with a wink. "We've got plenty of practice feeding hungry crews after long shifts. It's a requirement of the job."

"To cook?"

He nods. "We all take turns cooking dinner, so yeah, we learn really quick how to cook. Tonight we all pitch in for you guys—our guests."

"Can I help in any way?"

"No. You just get yourself a drink over there," he says, pointing to a table with sodas and tea, "and I'll go check on the pumpkin pies I made."

I nod and make my way to the drink table, selecting a cup of spiced apple cider. The warmth of the mug seeps into my hands as I take a sip, the sweet and spicy flavors dancing on my tongue. I turn back to observe the room, feeling more at ease now that I've settled in.

A young woman approaches me, her curly hair bouncing as she walks. She's wearing a festive green sweater with tiny reindeer prancing across it. "Hi there! I'm Melissa, Tom's wife. You must be Jack's new girlfriend?"

Girlfriend? Um . . . how do I answer that? I don't even know what we are.

"I'm Chloe," I answer, hoping that's enough.

Melissa shakes my hand enthusiastically. "Oh, we've all been dying to meet you! Jack's been so secretive, but we could tell something was different. He's been smiling a lot more lately."

Butterflies flutter in my chest at her words. "Really? That's . . . that's good to hear."

I catch a glimpse of Jack in the kitchen. He's laughing with his colleagues, a dish towel slung over his shoulder as he pulls a golden-brown pie from the oven. The sight of him so at ease, so in his element, makes my heart swell.

Melissa follows my gaze and smiles knowingly. "They're quite a sight, aren't they? All that masculinity crammed into a kitchen." She laughs softly. "But don't let the tough guy act fool you. These men are some of the most caring, compassionate people you'll ever meet."

I nod, still watching Jack as he carefully places the pie on a cooling rack. "I'm starting to see that," I say.

Melissa and I continue chatting, and I instantly warm to her bubbly personality. She introduces me to a few other wives and girlfriends, and soon we're all swapping stories and laughing together. It feels good to be included, to be part of this tight-knit community, even if I'm not quite sure where I fit in yet.

As the evening progresses, the aroma of roasted turkey and savory sides fills the air. Jack calls everyone to gather around the long tables that have been set up in the center of the room. I find myself seated between Jack and Melissa, with children excitedly squirming in their seats across from us.

Captain Rodriguez stands at the head of the table, his salt-and-pepper hair neatly combed and his kind eyes sweeping over the gathered group. He clears his throat, and a hush falls over the room.

"Before we dig into this wonderful meal," he begins, his voice warm and rich, "I'd like to say a few words. First, to our newest guests." He nods in my direction and a couple of others. "Welcome to our fire station family. We're glad you could join us tonight."

Jack's hand squeezes my knee under the table, and I can't hide my smile.

The captain continues, "As we celebrate this holiday season, I'm reminded of how fortunate we are. Not just for the food on our table or the roof over our heads, but for the bonds we share. This job isn't easy. We see things that most people never have to face. But we face them together, and that makes all the difference."

There's a murmur of agreement around the table. I glance at Jack, seeing a mix of pride and solemnity in his eyes.

"So tonight," the captain says, raising his glass, "I'd like to propose a toast. To family—both the ones we're born with and the ones we choose. To the loved ones who support us, worry about us, and welcome us home after every shift. And to those who couldn't be with us tonight, whether they're working or watching over us from above. Cheers!"

"Cheers!" The room echoes with the sound of clinking glasses and heartfelt responses.

As we begin to eat, the conversation flows easily. I listen to stories of daring rescues and comical mishaps, of sleepless nights at the station and unexpected acts of kindness from the community. With each tale, I gain a deeper understanding of the world Jack inhabits.

Halfway through the meal, the station's alarm suddenly blares to life. The firefighters, including Jack, immediately push back from the table, their expressions shifting from relaxed to focused in an instant.

"Sorry, duty calls," Jack says, leaning in to place a quick kiss on my cheek. "Save me some pie?"

Before I can respond, he and the others are rushing toward the bay. The remaining guests watch in respectful silence as the engines roar to life and pull out of the station, sirens wailing into the night.

I turn to Melissa. "So what do we do now?"

She shrugs. "You can wait here and see how long it takes for them to come back. Some will leave knowing it's a crapshoot. It's up to you."

"How long do these calls take?"

"Could be half an hour, or it could be hours." She glances at their half-eaten plates. "At least they got some food in them this year. Thanksgiving they all had to rush out the door right as the turkey was being carved."

"I think I'll stay, if that's okay. I'd like to see how this all works."

Melissa smiles warmly. "Of course it's okay. Welcome to the life of a firefighter's . . . friend." She winks at me, and I feel my cheeks heat again.

The remaining guests continue eating, but some get up and start gathering their things. Especially the ones with younger children. I don't have anywhere else better to be, so I figure I might as well wait for Jack. I just hope it doesn't take all night.

I join a group clearing the table and packing up leftovers. As we work, I listen to them swap stories about past Christmases interrupted by calls, emergencies narrowly averted, and the unique challenges of loving someone in such a demanding profession.

As we finish cleaning up, I find myself gravitating toward the large windows at the front of the station. The night is clear and cold, stars twinkling in the inky sky. I wonder where Jack is right now, what kind of emergency he's facing.

My heart leaps as I spot the red truck approaching after an hour or so. The engines pull into the bay, and a few moments later, Jack and the others file back into the community room. They look tired but satisfied, a thin layer of soot dusting their clothes and faces and the smell of grease announcing their presence.

Jack's eyes find mine immediately, and he makes his way over. "Sorry about that," he says, running a hand through his tousled hair. "Just a small kitchen fire. Turkey fryer incident. We have at least one a holiday."

I reach up to wipe a smudge of soot from his cheek. "I'm just glad you're back safe. And look—" I gesture to the table where I've set aside a plate "—I saved you some pie."

His face breaks into a grin. "You're the best, you know that?" He pulls me into a hug, not caring about the stink of grease fire transferring to my clothes.

As we rejoin the group, I notice the easy camaraderie between the firefighters and their families. They slip seamlessly back into the celebration, as if nothing had happened. And I realize that this is their normal—this constant readiness, this ability to switch gears at a moment's notice.

"Hey," Jack says, leaning in to me. "Want me to show you around? Show you the bay?"

"I'd love that," I reply, eager to see more of Jack's world.

He takes my hand and leads me toward the large bay doors. As we step into the cavernous space, the smell of diesel and rubber intensifies. The massive fire engines gleam under the bright overhead lights, their red paint still wet from the recent call.

"This is Engine Five," Jack says, patting the side of the nearest truck affectionately. "She's my baby."

I run my hand along the cool metal, marveling at the size and complexity of the vehicle. "It's incredible," I say. "I had no idea they were so . . . big."

Jack chuckles. "Yeah, they're pretty impressive. Want to see inside?"

Before I can answer, he's already opening the door and offering me a hand up. I climb into the cab, settling into the passenger seat as Jack slides in behind the wheel.

"This is where the magic happens," he says, his eyes shining with pride. He begins pointing out various gauges, switches, and communication devices, explaining their functions. I try to follow along, but I'm more captivated by the passion in his voice than the technical details.

As Jack explains the intricacies of the fire engine, I find myself imagining him in action—racing through the streets, sirens blaring, ready to face whatever danger awaits. It's a stark contrast to the man sitting beside me now, his face animated as he describes the truck's water pumping capacity.

"And this," he says, reaching across me to point at a small button near the dashboard, "is the air horn. Want to try it?"

I hesitate. "Won't it be too loud?"

Jack grins mischievously. "Nah, it's fine. Go ahead, give it a press."

Tentatively, I reach out and push the button. The resulting blast is deafening, echoing through the bay and making me jump in my seat. Jack bursts out laughing at my startled expression.

"Sorry," he chuckles, not looking sorry at all. "I couldn't resist."

I playfully swat his arm, trying to look stern but failing to hide my own smile. "You're terrible."

"Yeah, but you like me anyway," he says, his eyes bright.

Our gazes lock, and for a moment, the air between us feels charged with possibility. I'm acutely aware of how close we are in the confines of the cab, the warmth of his body next to mine.

"You know," I begin. "I thought we were crossing into friend zone. Before you became WinterWatcher, that is."

Jack reaches out, gently tucking a strand of hair behind my ear. "I most definitely don't only want you as a friend."

I subtly move toward his touch, feeling brave. "I'm glad to hear it."

Jack's hand lingers on my cheek, his thumb gently stroking my skin. The intensity in his eyes makes my heart race. Slowly, he leans in, giving me plenty of time to pull away if I want to. But I don't want to. I close the distance between us, our lips meeting in a soft, tender kiss.

His lips are warm and slightly chapped, tasting faintly of smoke and pumpkin pie. The kiss deepens, and I feel myself melting into him, my hands finding their way to his chest.

A sudden knock on the truck's window startles us apart. Melissa and her husband, Tom, are standing there, an amused expression on their faces. "Sorry to interrupt the lovebirds, but I'm getting ready to leave and wanted to say goodbye," she says.

Jack and I quickly scramble out of the fire engine. No doubt I'm blushing furiously. I smooth down my hair, acutely aware of how disheveled I must look. This man has the ability to knock the wind out of me with a simple kiss.

"Sorry about that," Jack says, rubbing my lower back in comfort. "We were just, uh . . ."

"Inspecting the equipment?" Tom supplies with a smirk.

Melissa elbows her husband playfully. "Oh, leave them alone. It's about time Jack found someone special." She turns to me with a warm smile. "It was wonderful meeting you, Chloe. I hope we'll be seeing more of you around here."

"I'm just glad the man finally made a move," Tom says with a laugh.

Jack tenses beside me, and though I didn't catch the look Jack must have given Tom, I do see Tom's face fall as he realizes his mistake. Melissa quickly intervenes, giving Tom a pointed look.

"Well, I should get going. The babysitter's waiting," she says, tugging on Tom's arm. "Walk me to my car, babe." She smiles again at me. "Merry Christmas, you two!"

As they walk away, I turn to Jack, raising an eyebrow. "Finally making a move?"

"Um . . ." He runs his hand through his hair. "I might have mentioned to the guys how we've met several times at the coffee-house."

I can't hold back the laugh at Jack's discomfort. "So you've been talking about me to the guys, huh?"

Jack's cheeks flush slightly. "Maybe a little. They've been giving me a hard time about being single for so long. When I mentioned meeting you at the coffee shop, they wouldn't let it go."

"And the WinterWatcher thing?" I prod gently.

"I've kept that to myself."

"Oh." I give a wicked grin. "Don't want to share our kinky side with all the boys?"

Jack's eyes widen slightly at my bold comment, but then a slow smile spreads across his face. He leans in close, his breath warm against my ear as he whispers, "Those are just for us."

He clears his throat and takes a small step back, though his hand remains on my lower back. "We should probably head back to the party," he says, his voice a little rough. "Before someone else comes looking for us."

I nod, trying to calm my racing heart. As we walk back toward the community room, Jack's hand slides from my back to intertwine with mine. It's a simple gesture, but it feels significant somehow.

The party is winding down when we return. A few families are gathering their things, children yawning and rubbing their eyes. Captain Rodriguez catches my eye and gives me a warm smile and a nod.

"So," Jack says, turning to face me. "What do you think of your first fire station Christmas?"

I look around the room, taking in the lights, the lingering scent of good food, and the easy chitchat of the people around us. "It's been wonderful," I say honestly. "Thank you for inviting me."

"I'm glad you came," Jack replies, squeezing my hand. "And I'm sorry about having to run out like that. It's part of the job, but—"

I cut him off with a quick kiss. "I understand. It's who you are, Jack. I wouldn't want you any other way. It's nice getting to know you better. You aren't such a mystery now."

"Merry Christmas, Chloe," he says, pressing a kiss to my temple.

"Merry Christmas, Jack," I murmur, snuggling closer to him.

CHAPTER THIRTY-TWO
JACK

The fire crew for the next shift are arriving, and I'm gathering my things to head home. Well . . . to head to the café to meet Chloe. It hasn't even been twenty-four hours since I've last seen her but I already miss her smile, the way her eyes light up when she talks to me, and her awkward little movements when she's nervous around me.

As I stuff my gear into my locker, Tom approaches. "Hey man, I never got a chance last night to apologize. I didn't mean to over-share like I did."

"Remind me not to tell you shit," I say, although my tone isn't aggressive or even mean. Frankly, I'm not holding a grudge. I know it was a slip on his end and I can't hold the fact that I am a fucking stalker and Chloe has no idea against him. "She doesn't know I've been keeping an eye on her since the accident."

Tom's eyes widen slightly, and he lowers his voice. "Right, right. I get it. Sorry again, man. I wasn't thinking."

I nod, accepting his apology. "It's fine."

He claps me on the shoulder. "I'm happy you finally made the move though. It's long overdue. She seems to make you really fuck-ing happy."

A smile tugs at my lips as I think about Chloe. "Yeah, she does. Meeting her for coffee in a bit, actually."

"Nice." Tom grins. "You two make a cute couple."

I finish packing up my gear and close my locker. "Thanks, man. I appreciate it."

The walk to the café feels both too long and too short. I keep replaying our interactions, overthinking if I was too soft, or too hard. I love the fact that Chloe is truly a sexual vixen, but I also know my tastes can scare—and have scared—others away. I don't want to push too fast or come off as too strong.

Years of fantasy and I've imagined these scenarios countless times, but the reality is so much more intense.

When I reach Pete's, I spot Chloe through the window. She's already here, sitting at a small table near the back, her hands wrapped around a steaming mug. My heart rate picks up as I watch her for a moment. She hasn't noticed me yet, and I drink in the sight of her—the way she tucks a strand of hair behind her ear, how she bites her lower lip as she checks her phone.

Taking a deep breath, I head inside. Chloe looks up as the bell above the door chimes, and her face breaks into a radiant smile when she sees me. God, I love that smile. I've seen it so many times from afar, but having it directed at me is surreal.

"Hey," I say as I approach her table. "Sorry if I kept you waiting."

"Not at all," she replies, gesturing for me to sit. "I got here a few minutes ago myself."

I slide into the seat across from her, my eyes never leaving hers. "You look beautiful," I say, unable to stop myself. She's wearing a simple gray sweater, her hair loose around her shoulders, and she's the most gorgeous thing I've ever seen.

Chloe blushes, her cheeks turning a delightful shade of pink.

"Thank you," she says, looking down at her coffee. "You look good too. How was your shift?"

"Long," I admit. "But worth it to be here with you now."

Her eyes flick back up to mine, a mixture of shyness and desire in their depths. "I'm glad you made it. I . . . I couldn't stop thinking about everything that has happened the last couple of days. It's a whirlwind of . . . I don't know."

"Neither can I," I confess, reaching across the table to take her hand. Her skin is soft and warm against mine. "You're all I can think about."

She intertwines her fingers with mine. "I know we just met, and our story isn't exactly normal, but . . . this feels different. Special."

It's true, even if she doesn't know the full extent of it. I've watched her for so long, dreamed of this moment, but the reality is so much better than anything I could have imagined.

Chloe's eyes sparkle as she looks at me. "I was worried I might be imagining things or moving too fast."

"No, you're not imagining it," I assure her. "And as for moving too fast . . . well, I think we can set our own pace. There's no rule book for this."

"Maybe I like breaking rules," she says beneath hooded eyes.

I inch nearer, lowering my voice. "I think we might have that in common."

Chloe's lips curve into a mischievous smile. "I feel like you and I both are Jekyll and Hyde. We have the good side—the firefighter and jewelry influencer—and then we have the very bad side—WinterWatcher and BlackAsChlo."

"I like it when you're a good girl," I say. "But I also like it when you are a very bad, bad girl."

Chloe's eyes darken, and she licks her lips unconsciously. "I think you just want to spank me again."

"Guilty."

Chloe's breath catches, and I can see the desire flaring in her eyes. She glances around the café quickly before meeting my gaze again. "I think we should go to your place."

I stand up, offering her my hand. "Let's go."

Chloe's hand is warm in mine, and I can feel her pulse racing. We walk quickly, barely speaking, the tension building with each step.

When we reach my apartment, I fumble with the keys, distracted by Chloe's closeness. As soon as we're inside, I push her against the closed door, my body pressing into hers.

"Do you want it hard or soft?" I ask, my lips brushing her ear.

"Hard," she breathes. "So fucking hard."

I trail kisses down her neck, reveling in the soft sounds she makes. My hands slide under her sweater, caressing the smooth skin of her waist.

"Tell me what you want," I say, my voice low and commanding.

Chloe's eyes meet mine, dark with desire. "I want you to make me your bad girl."

"Strip," I order.

Chloe's eyes widen slightly at my commanding tone, but a smirk plays on her lips as she slowly begins to remove her clothes. She maintains eye contact as she pulls her sweater over her head, revealing a lacy black bra underneath. Her fingers trail down to the waistband of her jeans, unbuttoning them teasingly slowly.

I watch her intently, drinking in every inch of exposed skin. My hands itch to touch her, but I force myself to stay still, savoring the show she's putting on for me.

As she shimmies out of her jeans, I notice she's wearing matching black lace panties. The sight of her standing there in only her lingerie makes my breath catch.

"Good girl," I praise, stepping closer to her. "Now turn around and put your hands on the door."

Chloe complies, her breathing quickening as she faces the door. I run my hands down her sides, feeling her shiver under my touch.

I run my hands over the curves of her ass. "Now, I think you've been very naughty, teasing me in the café. What do naughty girls get?"

"Spanked," Chloe whispers, arching her back slightly.

"That's right," I say, bringing my hand down firmly on her right cheek. Chloe gasps, her body jerking slightly at the impact. I alternate between her cheeks, each slap growing progressively harder. The pale skin of her ass turns a delicious shade of pink.

Chloe moans, a mix of pain and pleasure. "More," she begs.

I oblige, continuing my assault on her ass. The sound of skin on skin echoes through the room, punctuated by Chloe's gasps and whimpers. I can see the wetness gathering between her thighs, her arousal evident.

After a particularly hard slap, I pause, running my hand soothingly over her heated skin. "What if I tell you I want this ass of yours? Has anyone ever taken you here before?" I run my fingertip down the seam of her ass.

Chloe's breath catches at my words. She turns her head slightly, looking back at me with a mixture of nervousness and excitement. "No," she admits softly. "I've never . . . but I want to. With you."

A primal surge of possessiveness rushes through me at her words. I'll be her first, claiming a part of her no one else has touched.

"Are you sure?" I ask, my voice low and husky. "Once we start, I don't know if I'll be able to stop."

Chloe nods, her eyes dark with desire. "I won't ask you to stop. I want this. I want you." She wiggles her ass invitingly, and I have to take a deep breath to maintain control.

A growl escapes me as I turn her around and capture her lips in a fierce kiss. She responds eagerly, her fingers tangling in my hair. I lift her, and she wraps her legs around my waist as I carry her to the bedroom.

I lay her on the bed, drinking in the sight of her. Her hair is tousled, her lips swollen from our kisses. She looks up at me with a mixture of trust and hunger that makes my heart race.

I reach for the drawer where I keep my lube and condoms, never taking my eyes off Chloe's beautiful form. Her skin is flushed, her breathing rapid with want.

"Bend over the bed," I instruct her, and she complies eagerly, presenting herself to me. The sight of her like this, so willing and trusting, nearly undoes me.

I take my time preparing her, using plenty of lube and starting with one finger. Chloe gasps at the initial intrusion, her body tensing slightly.

"Relax," I say, rubbing soothing circles on her lower back with my free hand. "That's it, baby. Just breathe."

Gradually, I work up to two fingers, then three, stretching her carefully. Chloe's gasps of discomfort turn to moans of pleasure as she adjusts to the new sensations.

"Please," she whimpers. "I need you inside me."

I position myself behind her, the head of my cock pressing against her entrance. "Are you sure?" I ask one last time.

"Yes," Chloe breathes. "Please, fuck me."

Slowly, carefully, I push inside her. The tight heat envelops me, and I have to grit my teeth to keep from losing control. Chloe lets out a long, low moan as I fill her completely.

"Oh god," she gasps. "It's so much . . . so full . . ."

I hold still, giving her time to adjust. "You're doing so well, baby," I praise her. "You feel amazing."

When she relaxes around me, I start to move, setting a slow, steady rhythm. Chloe's moans grow louder with each thrust, her hands fisting in the sheets.

"Harder," she demands. "Please, I can take it."

I increase my pace, my hands gripping her hips tightly. The room fills with the sound of skin slapping against skin and our mingled moans of pleasure.

"You're mine," I growl, lost in the sensation of claiming her. "All mine."

"Yes," Chloe cries out. "Yours, only yours."

My orgasm builds, a tightening in my lower abdomen. I reach around to rub Chloe's clit, determined to make her come first.

Chloe's body shudders under my touch, her moans growing more frantic. I can feel her tightening around me as she nears her peak.

"That's it, baby," I encourage her, my fingers working her clit in tight circles. "Come for me. Let me feel you."

With a cry that's almost a scream, Chloe comes undone. Her body convulses, clenching around me so tightly it nearly pushes me over the edge. I slow my thrusts, letting her ride out her orgasm.

As her tremors subside, I resume my pace. The sight of Chloe, flushed and satiated beneath me, is the most powerful control a woman could hold over me.

"Where do you want me to come?" I ask, my voice strained with the effort of holding back.

"In my ass," Chloe gasps. "I want to feel you. I want you to claim what's yours and will only be yours."

Her words are my undoing. With a few more powerful thrusts, I bury myself deep inside her and let go, my orgasm washing over me in intense waves. Chloe moans softly as she feels me pulsing inside her.

For a moment, we stay connected, both of us catching our breath. Then, carefully, I withdraw and collapse onto the bed beside her. Chloe turns to face me, her eyes bright and a satisfied smile on her lips.

"That was . . ." She trails off, seemingly at a loss for words.

"Yeah," I agree, pulling her close. "It was."

We lie there in comfortable silence, our bodies intertwined. I run my fingers through Chloe's hair, marveling at how perfectly she fits against me.

"I think I'm falling for you," Chloe whispers suddenly, her voice barely audible.

My heart swells at her words. I've waited so long to hear them, dreamed of this moment countless times. But the reality is so much sweeter than any fantasy.

"I've already fallen," I admit, tightening my arms around her.

CHAPTER THIRTY-THREE
CHLOE

> **SLOANE:** We need to meet.

> **ME:** Oh my god we do! I have so much to tell you. Are you back from your trip yet?

> **SLOANE:** Yes. Tonic in an hour? Can you meet me there?

Drinks sound perfect. I can't wait to tell Sloane about my Christmas Eve and Christmas with Jack.

> **ME:** See you soon.

I arrive at Tonic a few minutes early, eager to see Sloane and share my news. The bar is quiet for a weeknight, with a few patrons scattered at tables. I find Sloane in our usual spot at the bar, her copper hair gleaming under the dim lights. As I approach, I notice her brow is furrowed, and she's fidgeting with her phone.

"Hey, you!" I slide onto the stool next to her. "How was the trip?"

Sloane looks up, her green eyes clouded with worry. "It was . . . fine. Listen, I need to tell you something important."

My excitement deflates a bit. "Is everything okay?"

She takes a deep breath. "I just got back from the office."

My heart skips a beat. This can't be good. Oh god, is she about to tell me my contract isn't going to get renewed at the beginning of the year? I need this job. I really, really need this job. There is no way I can afford to keep my parents' home and pay my bills for even a month without it. I try to keep my voice steady as I ask, "What's going on at work?"

Sloane leans in closer, lowering her voice. "I fucked up. I fucked up bad."

My stomach drops.

"Before I left for my trip, I logged on to Dark Secrets from work. I wasn't thinking about the ramifications of using a company computer and—" She runs her fingers through her hair. "You told me you had a secret identity on there, and I was curious. I wanted to find you."

The blood must have drained from my face. My heart races as I process Sloane's words.

"And," I ask, my voice raising an octave. "Did you find me?"

She looks away, unable to meet my eyes. "I did. And frankly, you were beautiful and sexy and I didn't think much of it. But," she says, taking a deep breath, "Tyler came into my office today. He was checking in after the holiday and . . ."

I'm going to be sick. My hands start to shake, and I grip the edge of the bar to steady myself. "And what, Sloane?" I manage to choke out.

"He told me that during the holiday time off, our tech department were running an audit or doing some regular maintenance on our computers. Basically, my search history came into question. And well, Tyler was coming in to tell me that he covered for me. That he has friends with HR and he's tight with Jasmine so even if she gets wind of it, he can soothe the waters. But . . ."

"But what?" I whisper, my heart hammering so hard I can barely hear my own voice.

Sloane takes a shaky breath. "But he saw your profile too. And he recognized a piece of Moth to the Flame jewelry—a necklace you were wearing. And he started to put it together and now suspects it's you in those videos and pics."

The room starts to spin. I grip the bar even tighter, my knuckles turning white. "Oh god," I breathe. "Oh god, no."

Sloane reaches out to touch my arm, but I flinch away. "I'm so sorry," she says, her voice cracking. "I never meant for this to happen. I was curious, and I didn't think—"

"You didn't think?" I repeat, my voice hollow. "You didn't think about the consequences? About my privacy? About my job? I signed a contract with a morality clause, Sloane! There's no way I can walk away from this with my job still intact. Dark Secrets is a kinky sex site! I'm fucked!"

Tears well up in Sloane's eyes. "I know. I know, and I'm so, so sorry. I told Tyler it wasn't you. I said it was someone else I knew and well . . . we'll deny, deny, but—"

"But what?" I snap, suddenly angry. "This is Tyler we're talking about, and there's no way he's stupid enough to fall for that. He'll use this as leverage over me."

"He doesn't know. He might suspect—"

"Do you really believe that?"

Sloane looks away, unable to meet my gaze. "I don't know if he believed me. He didn't seem convinced, but he has no proof it's you."

I close my eyes, trying to steady my breathing. My mind races through all the possible outcomes, each one worse than the last. My career, my reputation, everything I've worked for—it could all come crashing down because of one stupid mistake.

I take a deep, shaky breath, trying to calm the panic rising in my chest. "Okay," I say, more to myself than to Sloane. "Okay. We need to think this through. What exactly did Tyler say?"

Sloane fidgets with her glass, her voice low. "He said he was surprised to see your profile. He made some comments about . . . about your photos. And he said he never would have guessed you were into that kind of thing."

My cheeks burn with humiliation. The idea of Tyler—awkward, leering Tyler—looking at my private photos and videos makes me want to crawl out of my skin.

Ugh, is he a subscriber of mine now? The idea makes me want to puke.

"I told him I gave the necklace to another friend of mine, the person whose profile it was. I tried. I swear. I never admitted it was you."

I sigh. "But he knows." I sigh again to try to steady my breathing. "Did he say anything about telling anyone else?" I ask, dreading the answer.

Sloane shakes her head. "He never made a threat, but . . . you know Tyler. You're right in your thinking. He likes to have leverage over people."

I nod, my mind racing. "We need to get ahead of this. Maybe . . . maybe I should talk to HR first? Come clean before Tyler has a chance to spread rumors?"

"I don't know," Sloane says, biting her lip. "That could backfire. What if they decide to fire you on the spot?"

I run my hands through my hair, feeling trapped. "You're right. God, this is such a mess. I can't believe this is happening."

Sloane reaches out and squeezes my hand. "I'm so sorry. This is all my fault."

I want to be angry with her, but I can see the genuine remorse in her eyes. Besides, I need an ally right now. "We'll figure this out," I say, trying to sound more confident than I feel.

Sloane nods slowly. "He seemed . . . almost gleeful when he told me. Like he enjoyed having this secret. We need to convince him that it's not worth the risk of raising it to Jasmine."

"And if he threatens me?" I ask, voicing the fear that's been gnawing at me.

Sloane's expression hardens. "We'll stick to the story that it's someone else. Other than the necklace you were wearing, he can't prove anything."

I nod, trying to quell the nausea in my stomach.

"I'm sorry," she repeats. "I got sloppy and didn't think."

I take a deep breath, steeling myself. "It's not all your fault. I got sloppy too. I can't believe I kept on jewelry that didn't belong to me and . . . what was I thinking? That's not how Moth to the Flame wants me to influence people to buy their jewelry. It's my fault that you and Tyler were even able to make the connection between my profiles."

Sloane nods, her eyes still filled with guilt. "Maybe, but I'm the one who accessed the site from work. I should have known better. I'm so fucking sorry."

We sit in silence for a moment, both lost in our own thoughts. The weight of the situation hangs heavy between us.

"He may drop it," she says as she takes a sip of her drink. "Trust what I said."

"Maybe." But I don't believe it. Something tells me that Tyler knows the gold mine he's sitting on and is going to use this information to his gain. "Let's think this through. What's the worst-case scenario?"

Sloane grimaces. "Tyler tells HR, and we both lose our jobs. The news spreads through the office grapevine, and suddenly everyone knows about your . . . extracurricular activities."

I wince at the thought. "And the best-case scenario?"

"Tyler does nothing, and this all blows over," Sloane says, but her tone suggests she doesn't believe it either. "At least Tyler didn't get to see you having sex or anything. It was just a little showing off."

Picturing Tyler watching me at all makes me want to puke. "Ugh, that doesn't make me feel better. And umm . . . that's not exactly true," I admit, remembering my most recent video with Jack. "I may have done something . . ." I hesitate, unable to finish the sentence. Sloane's eyes widen.

"What?" she whispers. "What did you do?"

I take a deep breath. "I . . . I made a video. With Jack. On Christmas Eve."

Sloane's jaw drops. "You made a sex tape? With Jack! The fireman? And posted it on Dark Secrets?"

I nod, feeling my cheeks burn with embarrassment. "It was stupid, I know. We got caught up in the moment, and it seemed exciting at the time. I never thought . . ." I release a deep breath that comes out as a groan. "I never thought Tyler would be watching. Fuck my life."

"Oh god," Sloane groans, putting her head in her hands. "This is worse than I thought. If Tyler saw that . . ."

"I know," I say, my voice barely audible. "I'm so screwed."

We sit in silence for a moment, the gravity of the situation sinking in. Finally, Sloane asks, "Wait. What happened to that online watcher dude you were talking to? The one that you hooked up with at Naughty and Nice?"

"WinterWatcher and Jack are the same person," I answer. "I know, I know. Crazy. And that's what I came here to tell you about."

Sloane's eyes widen in disbelief. "Wait, what? Jack is Winter-Watcher? How did that happen?"

I take a deep breath, trying to focus on the positive memory amidst all this chaos. "It's a long story, but basically Jack figured out that BlackAsChlo was me due to my sloppy antics and showing my face. And he reached out, and well . . . yeah, he's the mystery man and has been all along. I discovered WinterWatcher was Jack as we were having sex and he pulled off my blindfold. It was shocking, confusing as hell, but also hot as hell. Part of me knew I should be mad, but my body exploded in happiness it was him. I always wanted Jack deep down. I wanted him to make a move. And well . . . he did. In his own way."

Sloane shakes her head, a small smile playing on her lips despite the gravity of our situation. "That's . . . actually kind of romantic. In a very modern, kinky way."

I can't suppress a little smile too, remembering that moment. "It was. It really was. And then we spent Christmas together, and it was just . . . perfect." My smile fades as I remember our current predicament. "And now this."

Sloane nods, her expression turning serious again. "Maybe I can convince him it's in his best interest to drop this altogether. If he tries to accuse you, he'll have to admit he was looking at the site too. And making an untrue accusation about you is grounds for a lawsuit. I'll try to scare him."

"True," I say, feeling a glimmer of hope. "And if he accessed it from work, just like you did. That could get him in trouble too."

Sloane nods enthusiastically. "Exactly. We could use that as our own leverage."

I take a sip of my drink, my mind racing as I notice that the snow is starting to fall. "I really should get back before it gets too ugly out there."

"Yeah, I think we should."

"Okay, you meet with Tyler tomorrow," I suggest, feeling a mix of hope and determination to make this right. "Make it clear that if he exposes you, he'll be exposing himself too."

She reaches out and squeezes my hand. "I got us into this mess, and I'll do whatever it takes to get us out of it."

I shake my head. "No, I am the one who took the risk by setting up the account. This is on me. But I do appreciate your help in this."

We step out into the snowy night, the cold air biting at my cheeks. As we say our goodbyes, I can't shake the feeling that everything is about to change. For better or worse, tomorrow will be a turning point.

On the cab ride home, my mind races with possible scenarios. What if Tyler has already told someone? What if he demands something in exchange for his silence? Should I tell Jack about this mess? He deserves to know what's happening, especially since he's involved now too . . . well sort of. He and I were extra careful to keep our faces darkened in the shadows. No way could anyone make out that my mystery man was Jack. But still . . . my life could explode and maybe he should be aware in case he's not up to flying shrapnel.

CHAPTER THIRTY-FOUR

CHLOE

As the cab drops me off at the house, and I tip the guy extra for braving the icy roads, I see Mr. Haven in the front of his house, a bag of salt in his gloved hands as he sprinkles it over the slick walkway. He looks up at the sound of the cab door slamming and gives me a wave.

"Evening, Chloe," he calls out, his breath visible in the frigid air. "Looks like we may get snowed in tonight. The forecast is calling for a couple of inches at least."

I notice that my walkway is shoveled, and I chastise him. "Mr. Haven, you shouldn't have done my walkway. What if you slipped again?"

"Oh, it wasn't me. I'm just out adding to the salt that was already laid. Your man, Jack, must have done this for us again."

A warmth spreads through my chest, despite the biting cold. Jack's thoughtfulness never fails to surprise me. He must have done this after he got off shift. I make a mental note to thank him later.

"That was kind of him," I say to Mr. Haven, trying to keep the smile from my voice. I don't want to make it too obvious how smitten I am over this man. It's still early and I don't want to go into this too fast and furious, although my heart already has her racing shoes on.

Mr. Haven smiles. "He's a great guy. It was also kind how he fixed your fire alarms."

I start to nod, then freeze. "What?"

Mr. Haven's eyes widen, and he shifts from one boot to the other. Is he realizing he's said something he shouldn't have? He fumbles with the salt bag, spilling some on his boots. "Your fire alarms. They were beeping and . . . I just assumed you wanted them fixed so I gave him a key and—"

I force a laugh, trying to keep my voice steady. "Right, of course. I'd just beaten them into silence with a broom. But Jack is . . . Jack."

Mr. Haven nods, clearly relieved I'm not upset. "Exactly. He's a good one to keep around. Well, you'd better get inside before this storm really hits. Good night, Chloe."

I hurry inside, my mind racing. As I close the door behind me, I lean against it, trying to calm my nerves. Jack's attentiveness had always seemed sweet, but now a seed of doubt has been planted. He was inside without me knowing . . . I shake my head, trying to dismiss the warning bells going off in my head.

Is it a coincidence that he happened to be dog sitting in my neighborhood? Coincidence that he happens to frequent my favorite coffee shop? Coincidence that he happened to be on Dark Secrets and discovered my secret account? Coincidence, right? Coincidence . . .

I hang up my coat and make my way to the kitchen, desperate for a hot cup of tea to warm me up. As I fill the kettle, I notice a note on the counter. Jack's handwriting.

HOPE YOU DON'T MIND, I STOCKED YOUR FRIDGE FOR THE STORM.
STAY WARM, BEAUTIFUL. —J

I didn't leave the house unlocked? Did I? But clearly Jack has a way of getting inside.

I open the refrigerator, and sure enough, it's filled with groceries I didn't buy. My hands shake as I close the refrigerator door. The thoughtful gesture that would have warmed my heart just hours ago now fills me with a sense of dread. I lean against the counter, trying to steady my breathing.

I'm just spooked by the news Sloane gave me. This doesn't have anything to do with Jack. Nothing to do with Jack, I mentally chant to myself again. I'm just on edge about Tyler.

The kettle whistles, making me jump. I quickly shut it off, suddenly aware of every sound in the house. The wind howls outside, rattling the windows. Is it the storm, or do I hear footsteps on the porch?

Maybe it's Tyler. Maybe it's Jack.

Maybe I'm losing my damn mind.

A text notification pops up on my screen. It's from Jack. **Hope you're staying warm. I'm worried about you in this storm. Mind if I stop by to check on you?**

The thought of spending the evening with Jack, having sex as the snow falls, sounds amazing. Or it would have if I wasn't such a hot mess of emotions right now. I blame Sloane and her news.

Trying to shake off my nerves, I text, **I'm home safe, having tea. Thank you for the food and the shoveling. But don't risk driving over here. I'd hate if something were to happen to you.**

I don't mind, he texts.

I'm fine. Truly. I have some work to catch up on anyway.

Okay, if you're sure.

I set my phone down, my hands tensing. I try to focus on making my tea, but my mind keeps racing. The silence of the house feels oppressive now, broken only by the bellowing wind outside.

Suddenly, I hear a faint scratching sound coming from the front door. My heart leaps into my throat. I freeze, straining to listen. There it is again—a soft scraping, like someone trying to pick a lock.

Panic floods through me. Is it Tyler? Jack? Or am I imagining things?

I grab my phone, ready to call 911, when I hear a familiar meow. Relief washes over me as I realize it's just my neighbor's cat, Miss Patches, probably seeking shelter from the storm. I laugh shakily at my own paranoia.

As I open the door to let the cat in, a gust of icy wind hits me. Snow swirls into the kitchen, and I shiver, quickly ushering the cat inside and shutting the door.

I'm about to turn back to my tea when something catches my eye. There, in the fresh snow on the porch, are footprints. Large, masculine footprints, leading to the side of the house. Leading to the Christmas light–covered hedge that conceals my bedroom window.

My heart races as I stare at the footprints, my mind reeling. I slam the door shut and lock it, my hands shaking so badly I can barely manage the dead bolt. The cat meows plaintively, sensing my distress, but I barely notice as I stumble back into the kitchen.

I grab my phone, ready to call the police, but hesitate. What if I'm overreacting? What if it's Mr. Haven checking on his salt job, or some other innocent explanation? I don't want to look foolish.

But those footprints . . . they looked fresh. And they led directly to my bedroom window.

I take a deep breath, trying to calm myself. Maybe I should call Jack after all. He'd come over in a heartbeat, I know he would. But the seed of doubt planted earlier grows, spreading tendrils of suspicion through my mind. What if . . . ?

No. I shake my head, angry at myself for even considering it. Jack has been nothing but kind and supportive. He doesn't deserve my suspicion just because of a few coincidences and some badly chosen words from others.

Still, I can't bring myself to call him. Instead, I grab a kitchen knife and make my way through the house, checking every lock, every window. The wind howls outside, tree branches scraping against the siding like skeletal fingers. Every sound makes me jump, my nerves frayed to the breaking point.

As I approach my bedroom, knife clutched tightly in my sweaty hand, I hear a soft thud from outside. I freeze, my breath catching in my throat. Slowly, I edge toward the window, my heart thrashing so hard it hurts.

I peer through the frosted glass, squinting against the snow swirling in the multicolored glow of the holiday lights. At first, I see nothing but the hedge, its branches laden with snow. Then, a shadow moves. A dark figure straightens up from behind the bushes, and for a moment, I catch a glimpse of a familiar profile.

My blood runs cold as recognition dawns. It can't be. It just can't be.

But as the figure turns, I know without a doubt who it is. The knife clatters to the floor as my world tilts on its axis.

"Jack," I choke out.

As if hearing my voice, he looks directly at my window. Our eyes meet through the glass, and I gasp and stumble backward. Jack's eyes widen in surprise, then narrow with determination. He takes a step toward the window, his hand reaching out as if to open it.

My mind races, trying to make sense of what I've just seen. Jack, outside my window in the middle of a snowstorm. Jack, who I thought was safely at home. Jack, who now seems like a stranger.

I fumble for my phone, my fingers shaking so badly I can barely unlock it. Who do I call? The police? But what would I say? My boyfriend—or whatever he is—is standing outside my window? It sounds ridiculous, even to my own ears.

A soft tapping on the glass makes me jump. "Chloe?" Jack's muffled voice comes through the window. "Chloe, I can explain. Please, let me in."

His tone is gentle, pleading, so like the Jack I thought I knew. For a moment, I'm tempted to open the window, to let him explain. But the warning bells banging in my head are deafening.

"Go away, Jack," I call out, hating how my voice quavers. "Go home!"

There's a pause, then a heavy sigh. "Chloe, please. I wanted to make sure you were safe in the storm. I didn't mean to scare you."

I back away from the window, my mind whirling. How long has this been going on? How many times has he been out there, watching me without my knowledge?

Suddenly, my phone buzzes in my hand, making me yelp. It's a text from Jack. I'm sorry. I'll go. But please, can we talk first? There's so much I need to tell you.

I stare at the message, torn between fear and a desperate desire to understand. Part of me wants to believe there's a reasonable explanation for all of this. But another part, a part that's growing stronger by the minute, knows that something is very, very wrong.

I hear the crunch of snow as Jack moves away from the window. Relief floods through me, quickly followed by a wave of exhaustion. I sink onto the edge of my bed, my legs suddenly too weak to support me.

There's a knock on the door. "Chloe. Please. Open up. Just for five minutes and then I'll go."

The rational part of my brain screams at me not to open it, but a small voice inside whispers that maybe, just maybe, there's an explanation for all of this.

"Jack," I call out, my voice trembling, "I need you to leave. Now. Or I'm calling the police."

There's a pause, then a soft thud against the door. Is he leaning his forehead against it? I can almost picture his pained expression.

"Chloe, please." His voice is low, desperate sounding. "I know how this looks. But it's not what you think. There's so much you don't know, so much I need to tell you."

I stand there, frozen, torn between curiosity and fear. The silence stretches, broken only by the whistling wind outside.

"Five minutes," I finally say, hating myself for giving in. "You have five minutes to explain, and then you leave. I mean it, Jack."

I approach the door cautiously, my hand hovering over the lock. Taking a deep breath, I turn it and open the door just a crack, keeping the chain on.

Jack stands there, snow dusting his dark hair and shoulders. His face is a mix of relief and anxiety. "Thank you," he breathes.

"Start talking," I say, trying to keep my voice steady.

He runs a hand through his hair, dislodging snowflakes. "God, where do I even begin?"

CHAPTER THIRTY-FIVE

JACK

It's cold. Can you at least let me inside?" I ask, but Chloe doesn't remove the chain. I can't say I blame her. I sigh, realizing I'll have to do this through the crack in the door. "Okay, look. I know this seems bad. Me outside your window, the groceries, all of it."

"Tell me the truth. How long? How long have you been doing this?"

I consider lying, but I can't. It's time. It's long overdue. "Two years. Ever since your parents' deaths."

She grips the doorframe, and her face goes white. "Two years? Two years what?"

"I've been here . . . watching."

"For two years!"

"Yes, I . . ." I swallow hard. "Yes."

"What! Standing outside my window? For two years?"

"Yes."

"Why? Why would you do this? None of this is making any sense."

I take a deep breath, knowing that what I'm about to say will change everything. "I was one of the firefighters that attended to you and your family the night of the car accident. I was the one who pulled you from the wreckage," I begin. "I held your hand as you slipped in and out of consciousness, promising you'd be okay. And when I found out later that your parents didn't make it . . . I couldn't get you out of my mind. It was Christmas, and I knew you'd be alone without them. I didn't want you to have to be alone and sad and—"

Chloe's eyes widen, a mix of shock and disbelief crossing her face. "What? No, that's . . . that's not possible. I don't remember . . ."

"You were in shock," I explain gently. "It's common for accident victims to have memory gaps. But I remember every detail of that night. Your blue coat, soaked with rain. The way you kept asking about your parents. The fear in your eyes."

I see tears welling up in Chloe's eyes, and I ache to comfort her, but I know I can't. Not yet.

"After that night, I . . . I felt responsible for you somehow. I wanted to make sure you were okay. So I started checking up on you. At first, it was just driving by your house occasionally. Then I found out where you worked, where you liked to get coffee. I told myself I was just being protective, but . . ."

"But you became obsessed," Chloe finishes, her voice barely above a whisper.

I nod, shame washing over me. "Yes. I know it was wrong. I know I should have told you the truth from the beginning. But I was afraid. Afraid you'd reject me, afraid you'd think I was crazy. And then when we actually met, when we started talking . . . I couldn't bear the thought of losing you."

"Stalking?" she asks. "Is that what you've been doing?"

I wince at the word, but I can't deny it. "I . . . yes. I suppose that's what it was, even if I didn't want to see it that way. I told myself I was protecting you, looking out for you. But I know now that I was violating your privacy and your trust."

She shakes her head, tears now flowing freely. "This is insane. You've been standing outside my house for *two years*? Is that what you're telling me? Two fucking years?"

I shake my head, feeling the weight of my actions crushing down on me. "Not . . . not every night. But yes, I've been checking on you regularly for two years. Just to make sure that you were safe. But then . . ."

"But then what?" Chloe demands, her voice rising. "Have you been jacking off outside my window?"

I recoil at her words. "Chloe, *no*. It wasn't like that at all. I just . . . I know it sounds crazy, but after pulling you from that wreck, after seeing how close you came to dying . . . I couldn't bear the thought of anything happening to you."

Chloe's face is a mix of emotions—anger, fear, confusion. "So what, you appointed yourself my guardian angel? My personal stalker? Do you have any idea how messed up this is?"

I nod, hanging my head. "I do. I know it's wrong. I've known for a long time, but I couldn't stop myself. Every time I tried to walk away, I'd remember that night, remember how fragile and scared you looked. And then when we actually met, when we started talking . . . I fell in love with you, Chloe. The real you, not just the idea of you I'd built up in my head."

"Love?" Chloe scoffs, but there's a hint of uncertainty in her voice. "Are you insane? One, we just met! Two, you are a fucking stalker! How can you claim to love me when everything between us has been based on a lie?"

"Not everything," I insist, desperate for her to understand. "My feelings for you are real. The connection we have, the way we talk, the way we understand each other—that's all real. I just . . . I should have told you the truth from the beginning. I know that now."

Chloe is quiet for a long moment, her eyes searching my face. I can see the conflict in her expression, the battle between her feelings for me and the shock of what she's learned. Then her eyes widen, and her hand covers her mouth.

"Oh my god. WinterWatcher. You knew about Dark Secrets and my account because you've been standing right outside my window the entire time. You knew! It wasn't by coincidence you found me. You always knew."

I close my eyes, feeling the full weight of my deception crashing down on me. "Yes," I admit, my voice barely above a whisper. "And because"—I take a deep breath—"because I also installed a camera in your place. In your fire alarm."

It was time to come clean. I can no longer hold back.

She looks over her shoulder at her fire alarm and then back at me with eyes wider than I've ever seen before. "What the fuck?"

"I saw you break your alarm, when I was standing outside your window, and the fireman in me *needed* to fix it. So I came here when I knew you'd be away. And well . . . I added a secret nanny camera while I fixed the alarm."

"You did *what?*"

"I never meant to invade your privacy like that, but once I started, I couldn't stop myself."

Chloe stumbles back from the door, her face a mask of horror and betrayal. "You're sick! Something is seriously wrong with you! Get away from my house, get off my property, and don't you ever come near me again."

I take a step back, feeling my heart shatter. "Chloe, please—"

"No!" she shouts, her voice cracking. "You don't get to explain anymore. You've been lying to me this entire time. You've violated my privacy, my trust, everything. Jesus Christ! You even broke into my house and installed a camera to spy on me! How could you think this was okay?"

I open my mouth to respond, but no words come out. What can I possibly say to make this right?

I back away, knowing it's over. Everything I've done, every lie I've told, it's all crashing down around me. As I turn to leave, I catch one last glimpse of Chloe's face—tears streaming down her cheeks, her expression a mix of fear and fury.

The snow is falling harder now as I stumble down the walkway, the Christmas lights blurring through my rage. Rage and fury at myself. I tried to protect her, to love her, and I've only ended up hurting her more. The irony of it all hits me as I trudge through the deepening snow, my heart as heavy as my footsteps.

I make it to my truck, parked around the corner, and slump into the driver's seat. The engine sputters to life, the heater slowly warming my frozen fingers. I sit there, staring at the falling snow, replaying Chloe's words in my head.

"Get away from my house, get off my property, and don't you ever come near me again."

The finality in her voice, the disgust in her eyes—it's all burned into my memory now. I've lost her. I've lost everything.

As I drive away, the snow pelting my windshield, I can't shake the image of Chloe's face—the hurt, the betrayal, the fear. What have I done? For two years, I've been living a lie. But now, faced with the consequences, I see the truth. I'm not her guardian angel.

I'm her nightmare.

My phone buzzes in my pocket. For a moment, my heart leaps— could it be Chloe? But when I check, it's a weather alert. Severe snowstorm warning. Stay indoors if possible.

I laugh bitterly. Stay indoors. If only I had done that in the first place, none of this would have happened. I wouldn't have seen Chloe through her window, wouldn't have been caught, wouldn't have had to reveal my twisted obsession.

Maybe I should turn around and be near her house.

Maybe I should park close enough where I can still see her front door.

Maybe I should—

What the fuck is wrong with me? This is how I got here.

I grip the steering wheel tighter, forcing myself to keep driving away from Chloe's house. Those thoughts, those impulses—they're what got me into this mess in the first place. I can't keep justifying my actions, can't keep pretending that what I'm doing is okay.

The snow is coming down harder now, reducing visibility to almost nothing. I should pull over, wait out the storm, but I can't bring myself to stop. I need to put as much distance between myself and Chloe as possible. For her sake, and for mine.

As I drive, memories of the past two years flash through my mind. The first time I saw Chloe after the accident, walking down the street, her face a mask of grief. The nights I spent parked outside her house, telling myself I was keeping her safe. The way my heart raced when we finally met *by chance*.

It was all a lie. Every moment, every interaction, tainted by my deception.

I slam my fists against the steering wheel, letting out a primal scream of frustration and self-loathing. How could I have let things go this far? How could I have convinced myself that what I was doing was right?

I somehow, luckily, make it back to my place, stumbling into my dark apartment, not bothering to turn on the lights. The silence is deafening after the howling wind outside. I shed my snow-covered coat and boots, leaving them in a soggy heap by the door.

I collapse onto my couch, burying my face in my hands, but then pull away and look toward my laptop. I could log on to the nanny cam and check on her. Make sure I didn't completely freak her out. Just for a second . . .

I shake my head violently, horrified at the thought that just crossed my mind. The realization of how far I've gone, how deeply my obsession has warped my sense of right and wrong, hits me like a physical blow.

Grabbing my laptop, I do the first right thing I've done in years. Taking a deep breath, I delete the app that is connected to the nanny cam.

I stare at the blank screen, feeling a mix of relief and emptiness. The app is gone, severing my last connection to Chloe's private life. It's the right thing to do, I know that, but it doesn't make the ache in my chest any less painful.

I then log on to Dark Secrets, determined to continue my purge. I can't be a subscriber any longer to her account. No doubt, she'll kick me off herself, but the least I can do is save her the time and energy. But as I try to find her name, I notice that she's no longer active. There is no BlackAsChlo to be found.

I stare at the screen, a mix of emotions washing over me. Of course she's gone from Dark Secrets. I've ruined that for her too. Another safe space I've violated and destroyed. The full weight of what I've done crashes down on me. I've not only lost Chloe, but I've taken away her outlets, her privacy, her sense of security. All because I couldn't control my obsession.

I close the laptop, unable to look at it anymore. The silence in my apartment is oppressive now, broken only by the raging wind outside. It reminds me of Chloe, alone in her house, probably terrified because of me.

I grab my phone, my finger hovering over Chloe's number. I should call her, apologize again, make sure she's okay. But I know that would only make things worse. I've done enough damage.

My phone buzzes and I see it's a text from my captain at the fire station. All hands on deck. This storm's causing havoc. Report ASAP.

For a moment, I consider ignoring it. I'm in no state to help anyone right now. But then I think of Chloe, of how I failed her, of how I've betrayed everything I once stood for as a firefighter. Maybe this is my chance to start making things right. At least I can try to do something.

CHAPTER THIRTY-SIX
CHLOE

Jack. Stalker. Jack. Jack!

How is this possible?

I slam the door shut, my hands shaking as I fumble with the locks. The sound of Jack's footsteps tromping through the snow fades away, but I can't shake the feeling of being watched. I lean against the door, sliding down to the floor as sobs rack my body.

How could I have been so blind? The signs were there all along, but I'd chosen to ignore them, to see only what I wanted to see. Now, the truth is laid bare, and it's uglier than I could have imagined.

Did I think I had a stalker? Maybe . . . if I'm being honest with myself. Yeah, maybe. But I thought it was Tyler. Not Jack! Never Jack. Even when he ended up being WinterWatcher, which was an unrealistic coincidence now that I think back . . . but even then, I didn't connect the dots.

I wrap my arms around myself, trying to stop shaking. The house feels different now, tainted by the knowledge that Jack has been watching me for years. Every window, every corner suddenly seems sinister.

He was watching. Has always been watching.

Oh Jesus . . . why in the fuck did my pussy contract at the thought? I'm sick. Yes, that's the only explanation. I shake my head, disgusted with myself. How can I feel anything but revulsion after what Jack's done?

This isn't sexy, Chloe! This isn't the sexy, consensual kind of watching my subscribers do.

My subscribers! Fuck. I run to my laptop and open it up to Dark Secrets. Between Tyler discovering my secret account and my job being on the line, and now Jack—I can't delete my account fast enough. I frantically log in to Dark Secrets, my fingers feeling as if they are pieces of lead as I navigate to my account settings. My safe space, my outlet for the thoughts and feelings I couldn't share anywhere else. Except it wasn't safe at all. Jack had been there too, watching, reading my most intimate confessions. The familiar interface that once brought me such excitement now fills me with dread.

My mind races back through our interactions, analyzing every word, every touch. Was any of it real? Or was it all part of his obsession, his invented idea of me?

I glance up at the fire alarm, feeling as if I'm going to be sick. Finding the broom as fast as I can, I quickly bash the living shit out of the alarm, breaking it and whatever camera is hidden inside it into a million pieces. I then run to the second alarm and do the same thing.

I pace the house, checking and rechecking the locks. The cat I let in earlier watches me with wary eyes, sensing my distress. I wish I could be as oblivious as it is, curled up on the couch without a care in the world.

As the night wears on, exhaustion begins to set in, but I can't bring myself to sleep. Every time I close my eyes, I see Jack's face, hear his voice explaining how he's been watching me since the night of the accident.

The accident. My parents. A fresh wave of grief stabs at my heart as I remember that night. How could I have forgotten the firefighter who pulled me from the wreckage? Was the trauma so severe that it blocked out that memory, or was Jack lying about that too?

I curl up on the couch, pulling a blanket tightly around me. The Christmas lights outside cast eerie shadows on the walls, and I consider unplugging them. But the thought of going outside, even for a moment, terrifies me.

My phone buzzes, and I flinch. Reluctantly, I retrieve it from where I threw it. I prepare myself for a long apology text from Jack but instead it's a text from Tyler.

Fuck.

I stare at Tyler's name on my phone screen, my stomach churning. With everything that's happened with Jack, I'd almost forgotten about the other crisis looming over me. I take a deep breath and open the message.

> **TYLER:** Chloe, we need to talk. Meet me at the office in an hour. This is not a request.

I might pass out. My ears ring in warning. Tyler knows. He really knows. And now he wants to meet. Is this it? Am I about to lose my job on top of everything else?

I type out a response with fumbling fingers. It's late and snowing really hard here. Any way this can wait until tomorrow?

I wait anxiously for Tyler's reply, hoping against hope that he'll agree to postpone this dreaded meeting. But my phone buzzes almost immediately with his response:

> **TYLER:** This can't wait. I'll send a car for you. Be ready in thirty minutes.

My heart sinks. There's no escaping this confrontation. I glance out the window at the swirling snow, then back at my phone. The thought of leaving the safety of my house terrifies me, but the prospect of losing my job is equally frightening. I try to call Sloane but don't get an answer, so I text her as well. Nothing. She wasn't planning on dealing with this until tomorrow. But clearly Tyler doesn't want to wait until then. And who knows what he'll do if I don't show?

With shaking hands, I start to get ready. I change into more professional attire, trying to project an air of confidence I certainly don't feel. As I apply a touch of makeup, I catch sight of my reflection in the mirror. The woman staring back at me looks haunted, her eyes wide with what appears to be fear and uncertainty.

The sound of a car horn outside makes me jump. I peer through the curtains to see a sleek black town car idling in my driveway, its headlights cutting through the falling snow.

Taking a deep breath, I grab my coat and purse. I hesitate at the door, my hand on the knob. Part of me wants to barricade myself inside, to hide from the world and all its complications. But I know I can't. I have to face this. Stick with the plan that I made with Sloane. It's my only shot.

As I step outside, the icy wind whips at my face. I hurry to the car, my feet crunching through the fresh snow. The driver, a stoic-faced man in a dark suit, opens the door for me without a word.

Once inside the warm interior of the car, I lean back against the leather seat, trying to calm my racing heart. The city lights blur past the window as we make our way through the storm-swept streets. With each passing minute, we draw closer to the office—and to whatever consequences await me there.

I close my eyes, trying to prepare myself for what's to come. But all I can see is Jack's face, his eyes full of desperation as he tried to explain his actions. I shake my head, pushing the image away. I can't think about Jack now. I need to focus on saving my career.

As the car pulls up to the office building, I see a lone figure standing in the lobby, silhouetted against the bright interior lights. Tyler. Waiting for me.

The driver opens my door, and I step out into the swirling snow. Each step toward the building feels like I'm walking to my own execution. But I straighten my spine, lift my chin, and push forward. Whatever happens in there, I'll face it head-on.

The glass doors slide open, and I step inside. Tyler's eyes lock on to mine, his expression unreadable.

"Chloe," he says, his voice cold and professional. "Let's talk in my office."

I follow Tyler to the elevator, my nerves silently screaming for me to stop. The ride up to his office feels interminable, the silence between us thick with tension. When we finally reach his floor, he leads me down the darkened hallway, our footsteps echoing in the empty building.

Tyler unlocks his office door and gestures for me to enter. As I step inside, I notice he's left the overhead lights off, with only his desk lamp illuminating the room. The city lights twinkle beyond the floor-to-ceiling windows, the snowstorm creating a surreal, muffled atmosphere.

"Sit," Tyler commands, pointing to the chair in front of his desk.

I lower myself into the seat, trying to keep my composure. Tyler remains standing, looming over me, his face half in shadow.

"So," he begins, his voice low and controlled. "Dark Secrets. Quite an interesting hobby you have there, Chloe."

I swallow hard, my mouth suddenly dry. "Sloane told me about your wild accusation about me. And I want you to know that if you drop this now I won't go to Jasmine and—"

He holds up a hand, silencing me. "Stop. I've seen it all. Every post, every video, every . . . interaction." He spits out the last word like it's poison.

"To assume it's me is—"

"It's you. I'm not an idiot. So stop with your innocent act." He smirks. "But if you want to go to Jasmine, fine by me. I'm sure she'll love seeing those videos of you."

"You don't have proof, and your accusations are—"

He rolls his eyes. "How long are we going to play this game? Bored yet? It's you. Anyone—including Jasmine—will see that. Not to mention you were wearing a necklace that was signed out by you and only you while you were rubbing your fingers all over your bare breasts. Sloane should have thought about deleting your name from the portal when she made up that pathetic lie."

My cheeks burn with shame and embarrassment. I want to defend myself, to explain that it's merely fantasy, just role-play. Frankly, I also want to tell him it's none of his business and what I do on my own time is up to me. But the words stick in my throat.

Tyler moves around his desk, his fingers trailing along the polished wood. "You know, when I first discovered your account, I was shocked. Angry, even. I thought about terminating your contract on the spot."

My heart sinks. This is it. I'm about to lose everything.

"But then," he continues, his voice taking on a strange tone, "I kept watching. Reading. And I realized something."

He turns to face me fully, and I'm struck by the intensity in his eyes. It's not anger I see there. It's . . . something else. Something that makes my skin prickle with a mix of fear and an emotion I don't want to name.

"You're incredibly talented, Chloe, or should I call you BlackAs-Chlo now?" Tyler says. "The way you captivate your audience. It's even more interesting than when you do your jewelry influencing as just boring ol' Chloe."

I shift uncomfortably in my seat, unsure where this is going.

Tyler leans against his desk, crossing his arms over his chest. "I have a proposition for you. One that could take your career—both of them—to new heights."

My mind reels. Is he suggesting what I think he's suggesting? "I don't understand," I say cautiously.

A slow smile spreads across Tyler's face, and in that moment, I realize I'm in deeper trouble than I ever imagined.

"Oh, I think you do," he says in a voice more sinister than I thought could come from this man. "I may not have been a subscriber at first. But I am now. A subscriber with expectations."

My blood runs cold at Tyler's words. The implications of what he's saying sink in, and I feel a wave of nausea strike.

"Tyler," I start, my voice shaking, "I don't think—"

"Don't think, Chloe," he interrupts, his eyes glinting in the dim light. "Just listen. I'm offering you a chance to keep your job and expand your extracurricular activities. All you have to do is follow my lead. Besides, I saw the video of you fucking one of your subscribers. I'm only asking for the same treatment."

I stand up abruptly, my chair scraping loudly against the floor. "No. Absolutely not. What I do in my private life is none of your business, and I won't be blackmailed."

Tyler's smile fades, replaced by a cold, hard look. "Are you sure about that? Because I'm certain Jasmine would be very interested to know what one of our top influencers does in her spare time. Not to mention your followers. How do you think they'd react if they knew their favorite jewelry expert is a fucking whore?"

I can't catch a full breath.

"There's a price for my silence and an even bigger one for cleaning up the mess so no one else at Moth to the Flame finds out," he says, his voice dripping with malice.

My mind races, searching for a way out of this nightmare. First Jack, now Tyler—it seems like my whole world is crumbling around me.

"What exactly are you proposing?" I ask, trying to buy time.

Tyler's eyes gleam with a predatory light as he steps toward me. "It's simple, really. You continue your work for Moth to the Flame during the day. But at night, you'll perform for me. Private shows, tailored to my . . . specific interests."

Bile rises in my throat.

"Starting with right now," he adds as he moves closer.

"No," I say firmly, gathering every ounce of courage I have. "I won't do it. Fire me if you want, tell anyone who'll believe you, but I won't be doing that."

Tyler's eyes narrow dangerously. He laughs. "You think that's really an option?" He closes the distance between us.

I back away from Tyler. "Don't come near me," I warn, but my voice cracks.

Tyler smirks, continuing to advance. "Come now, Chloe. We both know you enjoy this kind of thing. I've seen your videos, remember? The thrill of being watched, being controlled . . ."

"Fuck you. That's consensual role-play, not actual blackmail and assault!" I glance over my shoulder at the hallways, searching the corners for cameras.

"Of course I turned them off," Tyler says with a chuckle, reading my desperate mind.

My back hits the wall. I'm trapped. Tyler looms over me, his breath hot on my face.

"Last chance, Chloe. Play along, or lose everything. It'll be fun."

In that moment, something inside me snaps. All the fear and anger from the night's events comes rushing to the surface. Without thinking, I bring my knee up hard between Tyler's legs.

He doubles over with a pained grunt. I shove him aside and make a dash for the door.

"You bitch!" Tyler wheezes behind me.

I don't look back as I run down the hallway to the elevator. My hands shake as I frantically push the button. Come on, come on!

I scream as Tyler's weight crashes down on me, pinning me to the cold floor. His hands grope roughly at my clothes as I thrash and kick, desperately trying to break free.

"Stop fighting," he snarls, his face contorted with rage. "You know this is what you want. All your dark fantasies come to life."

Panic surges through me as his fingers work at my zipper. This can't be happening. In desperation, I slam my head back, feeling a satisfying crunch as my skull connects with his nose.

Tyler reels back with a howl of pain, blood streaming down his face. I scramble to my feet and run for the stairwell, but he takes hold of my ankle, pulling me back toward him.

The elevator dings and the doors slide open. I'm not sure if insanity has truly taken hold or not, because for a moment I wonder if I'm seeing things.

Jack.

Jack bursts out of the elevator, taking in the scene in an instant. His eyes lock on to mine, filled with a mix of concern and rage.

"Get away from her!" he roars, launching himself at Tyler.

The two men collide in a tangle of limbs. I scramble away, my heart thumping as I watch them grapple on the floor. Jack lands a solid punch to Tyler's already bloodied face, sending him reeling back.

Tyler scrambles to his feet and backs off, hands up in defeat. "I'm sorry! I'm sorry!" He's reverted to the whiney coward I always knew him to be.

Jack stands over Tyler, fists clenched, chest heaving. "You're sorry? You try to assault her and you think 'sorry' cuts it?"

Tyler flinches, blood still streaming from his nose. "It was a misunderstanding. I didn't mean—"

"Shut the fuck up," Jack snarls. He turns to me, his eyes softening. "Chloe, are you okay?"

I nod shakily, pulling myself to my feet. "I'm . . . I'm okay," I manage to say though my voice trembles.

Jack takes a step toward me, fear etched on his face. "Are you sure? Did he hurt you?"

I shake my head, wrapping my arms around myself. "No, I . . . I'm fine. Just shaken up." I glance at Tyler, who's still cowering.

"Listen," Tyler begins. "Why don't we pretend tonight didn't happen. Everything didn't happen. I'll keep your secret and you both leave and we can all go home."

Jack's eyes narrow dangerously as he turns back to Tyler. "You think you can just walk away from this? After what you tried to do?"

Tyler holds up his hands placatingly. "Look, I made a mistake. I let things get out of hand. But no real harm done, right? Let's forget this ever happened."

"Forget?" I ask. "You tried to rape me. You threatened my job, my reputation. And you want us to just forget?"

"What are you talking about?" Jack asks. "What did he threaten you about?"

I hesitate, unsure how much to reveal. But after everything that's happened, I realize there's no point in hiding anymore.

"He . . . he found out about my account. On Dark Secrets," I admit, my voice barely above a whisper. "He was trying to blackmail me into . . . performing for him."

Jack's face darkens with fury. He turns back to Tyler, his fists clenching at his sides. "You piece of shit," he growls.

Tyler scrambles backward, his eyes wide. "Now, let's not do anything rash," he pleads. "I said I was sorry. We can work this out."

"Work this out?" Jack scoffs. "The only thing we're working out is how long you'll be in prison."

"Prison?" Tyler scoffs. "You have no proof—"

"I don't need proof to beat your ass," Jack snarls.

I step forward, placing a hand on Jack's arm. "Jack, wait," I say softly.

He looks at me, surprise and confusion in his eyes. "Chloe, we can't let him get away with this."

I take a deep breath, steeling myself. "I know. But if we go to the police, everything will come out. About Dark Secrets, about . . . everything."

Jack's expression softens. "Chloe, none of that matters. What he did—"

"I know," I interrupt. "But I can't lose my job. I'd lose the house that once belonged to my parents. It means too much to me. I can't."

Jack's eyes search my face, understanding dawning in them. He nods slowly. "Okay. So what do you want to do?"

I turn to Tyler, who's still cowering on the floor. "Here's what's going to happen," I say, my voice steadier than I feel. "You're going to forget everything you saw on Dark Secrets. You're going to make sure no one else at Moth to the Flame ever finds out about it. And you're going to leave me alone. Completely."

Tyler nods frantically. "Yes, yes, of course. Whatever you say."

"And," I continue, "if I even suspect you're trying anything like this with anyone else, I'll go straight to the police. Do you understand?"

"I understand," Tyler whimpers. "It won't happen again. I swear."

I look at Jack, who's watching me with a mix of admiration and concern. "Let's go," I say softly.

Jack hesitates, clearly torn between his desire for justice and his concern for me. Finally, he nods. "Okay. But he doesn't just get to walk away from this. I understand what you want, but no way can we trust this fucker."

I turn to Tyler, who's watching us with a mix of fear and hope. "Jack . . . I want this awful night to end."

"Here's what's going to happen," he says, his voice steadier than I feel. "You're going to resign. Effective immediately. You'll cite personal reasons, health concerns, whatever. But you're done at Moth to the Flame."

Tyler opens his mouth to protest, but Jack takes a menacing step forward, and he quickly shuts it again.

"And if I ever hear that you've so much as looked at another woman the wrong way," he continues, "everything comes out. The blackmail, the assault, all of it. I gurantee we have it on security cameras if we press them to look. Do you understand? I have close friends on the force, and I'll have you locked up so fast."

Tyler nods frantically. "Yes, yes, I understand. I'll resign first thing in the morning, I swear."

He scrambles to his feet, wincing as he touches his bloodied nose. He gives us one last fearful look before hurrying down the hallway, disappearing into the stairwell.

As soon as he's gone, my legs give out from under me. Jack catches me before I hit the floor, his strong arms wrapping around me.

"I've got you," he reassures, holding me close. "You're safe now."

I lean into him, letting out a shaky breath. For a moment, I forget everything that's happened between us, all the lies and betrayal. In this moment, he's just Jack—the man who came to my rescue when I needed him most.

But as the adrenaline fades, reality comes crashing back. I pull away from him, wrapping my arms around myself. "Stay away. I told you to stop stalking me!"

I know this is hard to believe, but I wasn't stalking," I counter.

Chloe's eyes narrow, a mix of anger and confusion on her face. "So you just happened to stroll into my office building? Come on, Jack. Stop treating me like an idiot."

"I know how it looks, but I wasn't following you. When you left your house in the middle of a snowstorm, Mr. Haven called me worried about you. He didn't think you should be out in the weather. I was already in it, working at the station due to high calls. And well . . ." I take a deep breath, knowing I need to explain everything. "I had no idea where you'd go this late and in a storm. So I was just going to start checking off your usual places. Coming here was just one of the spots."

Chloe's expression softens slightly, but I can still see the doubt in her eyes. "And you just happened to arrive at the exact moment I needed help?"

"Thank god I did."

"I don't know what to believe anymore," she admits, her voice barely above a whisper. "Everything I thought I knew has been turned upside down."

"I know. And I'll regret that for the rest of my life. But, Chloe, you have to believe me when I say that my feelings for you are real. Everything between us—our conversations, our connection—that was all genuine."

"How can I trust that? How can I trust anything you say?"

"Because I'm telling you the whole truth now," I insist, taking a step toward her. "No more secrets, no more lies. Ask me anything, and I'll answer honestly."

"Why didn't you just talk to me? After the accident, why didn't you reach out normally instead of . . . watching from afar?"

"I tried, at first. I visited you in the hospital, but you were still in and out of consciousness. By the time you were lucid, I . . . I didn't know how to explain why I felt so connected to you. I was afraid you'd think I was crazy, or worse, that you'd reject me."

"So instead of talking to me like a normal person, you decided that watching me from afar for two years was the better option?" she asks, unable to keep the bitterness from her voice.

I wince at her words. "I know it sounds crazy. It was crazy. I just . . . I couldn't get you out of my head. I know what it feels like to be alone. Really alone. Knowing you were going to have to feel that way, the same way I had, well . . . I couldn't let that happen. The memory of that night, of pulling you from the wreckage . . . it haunted me. I told myself I was checking up on you, making sure you were okay. But it spiraled into something I couldn't control."

"Jack," she starts, her voice breaking slightly, "I appreciate that you're being honest now. And I'm grateful you showed up when you did tonight. But you have to understand how messed up this all is."

I nod, making eye contact with her that she doesn't break. "I wish I could go back and do things differently. From this moment on, I swear to you, I'll respect your boundaries completely."

Chloe studies my face, searching for any sign of deception. "And if I tell you to leave me alone? To never contact me again?"

The thought of never seeing her again feels like a physical blow, but I force myself to nod. "Then that's what I'll do."

She's quiet for a long moment, her eyes never leaving mine. Finally, she speaks, her voice soft but firm. "I need time, Jack. Time to process everything that's happened tonight. With you, with Tyler, all of it. I can't make any decisions right now."

"Of course," I say quickly. "Take all the time you need. I'll be here if and when you want to talk. And if you don't . . . I'll understand."

Chloe nods, then glances around the empty office. "I should go. It's late, and I—"

"Let me drive you home," I offer. "It's still storming out there, and after everything that's happened . . ."

She hesitates, clearly torn between her desire for solitude and the practicality of a safe ride home. Finally, she nods. "Okay. But just a ride home. Nothing else."

"Absolutely," I agree. "Just a ride home."

As we make our way to my truck, the silence between us is heavy with unspoken words and emotions. The snow is still falling heavily, blanketing the city in white. I open the passenger door for Chloe, then circle around to the driver's side.

The drive to her house is quiet, the only sound the soft swish of windshield wipers clearing away the snow. I can feel Chloe's eyes on me occasionally, but I keep my gaze fixed on the road, giving her the space she needs.

When we pull up to her house, I put the truck in Park but leave the engine running. Chloe turns to me, her expression unreadable in the dim light.

"Thank you," she says softly. "For the ride. And . . . for earlier."

I nod, gripping the steering wheel tightly to keep from reaching out to her. "You're welcome. I'm glad you're safe."

She hesitates, her hand on the door handle. "Jack, I . . ."

"It's okay," I interrupt gently. "You don't have to say anything. Take all the time you need."

Chloe nods, then opens the door. The cold air rushes in, carrying with it swirling snowflakes. She pauses halfway out of the truck, turning back to me.

"Good night, Jack," she says, her voice barely above a whisper.

"Good night, Chloe," I reply, watching as she makes her way up the snow-covered walkway to her front door.

I'm watching her still. Watching her walk away from me.

CHAPTER THIRTY-EIGHT

CHLOE

I can't believe he actually resigned," Sloane says from across her desk.

"He didn't have much of a choice," I say. "He was a fucking creep."

Sloane leans back in her chair, a wry smile playing on her lips.

"What? Why are you smiling like that?"

She shrugs. "Nothing."

I narrow my eyes at her. "Sloane, what?"

"I know you're pissed at Jack, but—"

"We aren't discussing Jack," I interrupt.

Her friend raises an eyebrow. "Aren't we though? I mean, he saved the day. He saved you."

My jaw clenches. "He didn't save me. I didn't need saving."

Sloane sighs, her smile fading. "Come on, Chloe. From what you just told me, you know that's not true. If Jack hadn't arrived when he did—"

"I had it under control," I snap, more harshly than I intended. I take a deep breath, trying to calm the sudden surge of anger. "Look, I appreciate what Jack did, okay? But that doesn't change anything. It doesn't erase all the other crap he's pulled. You don't find it sick as hell that the man has stalked me for years?"

"I think it's kind of romantic. Sexy even," she admits. "Sorry, but I don't think I'd be throwing away the man because he's obsessed with you."

I scoff, shaking my head. "You're unbelievable. Since when are you Team Stalker?"

"I haven't met the man, but he sounds like a catch."

"A catch! He's been standing outside my window without my knowledge. How in the hell is that considered a catch?"

Sloane holds up her hands in mock surrender. "Okay, okay. I get it. You're not ready to see it from another perspective yet."

I glare at her, my frustration building. "There is no other perspective. It's creepy, end of story."

She leans forward, her expression turning serious. "Look, Chloe, I'm not trying to invalidate your feelings. I know you've been through a lot. But maybe . . . maybe there's more to Jack than you're willing to see right now."

"Oh, please," I sneer. "Like what?"

"Like the fact that this man has only had your best interests in the forefront of his mind."

"He let us meet, connect, and made me believe it was all . . . He's been lying this entire time."

"People do crazy things when they're in love, Chloe."

A flush creeps up my neck. "He's not in love with me. He's obsessed. There's a difference."

"I want the insane asylum kind of love."

I stare at Sloane incredulously. "The *insane asylum* kind of love? Are you serious right now?"

She shrugs, a mischievous curve to her smile. "What can I say? I'm a romantic at heart."

"You're certifiable is what you are," I mutter, shaking my

head. "Look, can we drop this? I don't want to talk about Jack anymore."

Sloane holds my gaze for a moment, then nods. "All right, consider it dropped. For now." She shuffles some rings on her desk, clearly changing the subject. "So since you insisted on working on our day off today instead of going out for pancakes and mimosas like I suggested—"

"I need the distraction."

She rolls her eyes but smiles. "Then let's talk about these new ring designs . . ."

I try to focus on work, but my mind keeps drifting back to Jack. Despite my anger, I can't shake the memory of his face when he stepped in to save me. The fierce determination in his eyes, the way he put himself between me and danger without hesitation.

No, I tell myself firmly. Don't go down that road. He's a stalker, plain and simple.

But as I leave Moth to the Flame to return home, I find myself wondering: *What if Sloane is right? What if there is more to Jack than I'm willing to see?*

What is he doing right now?

Is he working?

Is he having coffee at our favorite spot?

Is he—

Stop! Stop obsessing over the man. I'm no better than he is.

I shake my head, trying to clear my thoughts as I walk down the bustling city street. The morning air is cool against my skin, a welcome relief from the stuffy office. I pull my jacket tighter around me, more for comfort than warmth.

I turn the corner and see his fire station. Could I have avoided it? Yes. The truth of the matter is I didn't need to come near it and yet, here I am. I pause for a moment, my feet rooted to the spot. The redbrick building looms before me, its large bay doors closed. A faint light glows from one of the upper windows, and I wonder if Jack is up there, perhaps filling out paperwork or chatting with his fellow firefighters.

Before I can stop myself, I'm walking toward the station. My heart races as I approach, half hoping and half dreading that I might catch a glimpse of him. I tell myself I'm just curious, that I'm just double-checking that he isn't outside my window again, but at work, a safe distance from me.

As I near the station, I hear the sound of laughter drifting from an open door. My steps falter, and I find myself ducking into the shadows of a nearby alley. What am I doing here? This is ridiculous. I'm acting like . . . like Jack.

I'm about to turn and leave when I hear a familiar voice. Jack's voice. My breath catches in my throat as I peer around the corner.

He's standing outside the station, chatting with a couple of his coworkers. The sight of him sends a jolt through my system—a mixture of anger, fear, and something else I don't want to name.

"You heading out, Jack?" one of the other firefighters asks.

Jack nods, running a hand through his hair. "Yeah, I've got some stuff to take care of."

My heart rate picks up. Is he going to my house? The thought both thrills and terrifies me.

"All right, man. Take care," his coworker says, clapping him on the shoulder.

As Jack turns to leave, his eyes sweep across the street. For a heart-stopping moment, I think he's seen me. But his gaze passes over my hiding spot without pausing.

I watch as he walks away, his broad shoulders beckoning me like a goddamn beacon. Without thinking, I step out of the alley and begin to follow him.

What am I doing? This is insane. I'm stalking my stalker.

But I can't seem to stop myself. I keep a safe distance, ducking behind cars and into doorways whenever he looks back.

I follow Jack for several blocks, my feet feeling as if they are trudging through thick mud. He seems oblivious to my presence, walking with purpose toward an unknown destination. Part of me hopes he's heading to his own apartment, while another part dreads the possibility that he might be going to my place. Or do I? My traitorous heart quickens at the thought of him watching me, his obsession, his need to be outside my window all those nights. I should be sickened by the idea, and yet I'm not. I'm actually . . . excited.

I try to push the feeling away but it strangles me like a vine, wrapping around my chest and squeezing tighter with each breath.

What's wrong with me? He's a stalker, a predator. I should be calling the police, not fantasizing about him in my bedroom.

But I can't help imagining his eyes on me as I undress, his ragged breathing fogging up the glass. Would he press his palm against the window, aching to touch me? Or would he remain perfectly still, drinking in every detail?

I shake my head, trying to clear these twisted thoughts. This isn't me. I'm not the type of person who gets turned on by danger. Am I?

Fuck me . . . maybe I am.

As we turn onto a quieter street, I nearly lose sight of him. I quicken my pace, rounding the corner in time to see him enter a small coffee shop. Relief washes over me, followed quickly by a pang of disappointment. I'm not sure what I expected, but this feels oddly anticlimactic.

And this coffee shop isn't our coffee shop. It's an imposter coffee shop.

I hesitate outside the shop, peering through the window. Jack is at the counter, ordering something. Before I can talk myself out of it, I push open the door and step inside.

The bell above the door chimes, and Jack turns. Our eyes meet, and for a moment, time seems to stand still. His expression shifts from surprise to confusion to something I can't quite read.

"Chloe?" he says, his voice a mixture of hope and uncertainty.

I open my mouth, but no words come out. What am I doing here? What could I possibly say?

"I . . . I was just . . ." I stammer, feeling my face grow hot.

Jack takes a step toward me, his brow furrowed with concern. "Are you okay?"

The genuine worry in his voice catches me off guard.

"I'm fine," I manage to say. "I was just . . . passing by."

It's a weak excuse, and we both know it. Jack's lips quirk into a small, sad smile.

"Passing by, huh?" he says softly.

The words hang in the air between us, heavy with implication. I should be angry, should turn and walk out right now. But something keeps me rooted to the spot.

"Jack, I . . ." I start, then hesitate, unsure of what I want to say.

"I'm trying a new place," he says, looking around the imposter coffee shop. "I gave you custody of Pete's." He smirks, and I appreciate he's trying to cut the tension between us.

I feel a mix of emotions at his words—gratitude for his consideration, frustration at his charm, and a strange sense of loss at the idea of him no longer frequenting our usual spot.

"Well, since you are here . . . can I buy you a coffee? No strings attached, I promise. Just two people who used to know each other, having a drink."

I hesitate, every instinct telling me to run. But something keeps me rooted to the spot. Maybe it's curiosity, maybe it's the sincerity in his eyes, or maybe it's something else entirely.

"Okay," I hear myself say. "One coffee. But this doesn't change anything."

He turns to the barista and orders me a latte, then gestures to a small table in the corner. I follow him, my heart beating so aggressively, I'm sure he can hear it or even see it expanding and contracting against my flesh.

We sit across from each other, an awkward silence settling between us. I fidget with my napkin, avoiding his gaze.

"So," Jack says finally, "in the neighborhood?"

I let out a nervous laugh, my eyes darting to meet his before quickly looking away. "Something like that," I mutter, knowing how ridiculous I sound.

Jack leans back in his chair, studying me with those intense eyes of his. "Chloe," he says softly, "what's really going on?"

I take a deep breath, trying to gather my thoughts. How can I explain something I don't even understand myself?

"I don't know," I admit finally. "I saw you at the station and I just . . . I followed you. I don't know why."

Jack's eyebrows shoot up in surprise. "You followed me?"

"I know, I know," I say quickly, feeling my cheeks flush with embarrassment. "It's crazy and hypocritical and—"

"And a little bit flattering," Jack interrupts, a small smile playing on his lips.

I glare at him. "This isn't funny, Jack."

He reaches across the table, his hand stopping short of mine. "I'm going to do something I've never been good at," he says. "I'm handing over control to you. You call the shots on this."

I stare at his hand, so close to mine. It would be so easy to reach out, to bridge that gap. But I can't. Not yet.

We sit in silence for a moment, the weight of his words hanging between us. I take a sip of my latte, buying myself time to think.

"So what now?" I ask finally.

"That's up to you. I meant what I said about giving you space. If you want me to walk away right now and never contact you again, I will."

I feel a pang in my chest at the thought. As angry as I am, the idea of never seeing Jack again hurts more than I want to admit.

"And if I don't want that?" I ask, surprising myself with the words. "If I don't want you to give up control." I swallow hard, even more surprised I'm about to reveal this. "What if I want you to take control?"

Jack's eyes widen, a mix of shock and something darker casting across his face. He leans forward, his voice low and intense. "I need you to be certain. If we do this, there's no turning back. No more running away, no more hiding in the shadows watching from afar. It's all or nothing, Chloe."

I close my eyes for a moment, trying to quiet the storm of thoughts in my head. When I open them again, I meet Jack's gaze with newfound resolve.

"I'm certain," I say, my voice barely above a whisper. "I don't want you on the outside looking in. I want you to come inside."

CHAPTER THIRTY-NINE
CHLOE

It's New Year's Eve, and Jack and I are going to ring in the New Year with a bang. Literally.

We're back at Naughty and Nice where we *met*. Tonight's theme is Midnight Masquerade. The club is decked out in glittering black and gold decorations, with mysterious masked figures mingling throughout the dimly lit rooms.

Jack squeezes my hand as we make our way through the entrance, handing over our coats and donning ornate Venetian masks. The pulsing music and heady scent of perfume and desire wash over us. Writhing bodies cover every surface—the dance floor, the plush velvet couches, even suspended from intricate rope harnesses hanging from the ceiling.

We weave our way deeper into the club, past couples and groups engaged in various stages of debauchery. In one corner, a woman in a feathered mask writhes in ecstasy as two men pleasure her. On a nearby chaise lounge, a group of masked figures form a tangle of limbs and flesh.

We pause at the bar, where a bartender in nothing but a bow tie and mask serves up champagne in gleaming flutes. Jack orders two, handing me a glass with a wicked grin.

"To new adventures. To new fantasies," he seductively says, clinking his glass against mine.

"To experiencing each and every one," I add.

As we sip our champagne, Jack's hand slides down my back, coming to rest on the curve of my ass. His touch ignites a familiar heat in my core. I brush my lips against his ear.

"What's your fantasy for tonight?" I ask.

Jack's eyes darken behind his mask. "I want to watch you." He leans in and kisses my neck. "From outside your window."

My pulse quickens at his words. Tonight feels different—charged with possibility.

"What's *your* fantasy for tonight?" he asks.

"To be watched."

We make our way across the room, weaving between gyrating bodies.

"It's almost midnight," I say with a smile. "Shall we toast to the New Year?"

"To watching," both Jack and I cheer at the same time.

The party has reached a fevered pitch. Bodies writhe on every surface, a tangle of flesh and desire. The air is thick with the scent of sex and champagne.

Jack presses against my back, his hands roaming my body. As the crowd begins to chant the countdown, we lose ourselves in a blur of hands and mouths and skin.

"Ten! Nine! Eight!"

His fingers find their way under my dress, teasing along my inner thigh.

"Seven! Six! Five!"

Jack's lips trace a path down my neck, nipping at my collarbone.

"Four! Three! Two!"

I'm overwhelmed by sensation.

"One! Happy New Year!"

As cheers erupt around us, Jack spins me to face him, claiming my mouth in a searing kiss.

As the crowd erupts in cheers and confetti rains down, Jack and I remain locked in our passionate embrace. His hands roam my body possessively, igniting sparks of desire everywhere he touches. The music swells to a deafening volume, matching the pulsing of my heart.

When we finally break apart, breathless, I see a glint of mischief in Jack's eyes behind his mask. He leans in close, his lips brushing my ear as he speaks. "I'm obsessed."

"Good," I say as I pull him closer, pressing my body against his. "Because I'm obsessed too. I want you," I say in his ear. "Right here. Right now."

He groans, his grip tightening. "Here? In front of everyone?"

I nod, feeling daring and uninhibited. "Let them see how much I want you."

Without another word, Jack spins me around so my back is to his chest. His hand snakes under my dress, pushing my thong aside. I gasp as he slides two fingers inside me, finding me already wet and ready.

"So eager," he growls, nipping at my earlobe. "Such a naughty girl."

I brace myself against a nearby pillar as Jack works his fingers in and out of me. To anyone watching, it might look like we're just dancing closely. But I know several pairs of eyes have turned our way, intrigued by our not-so-subtle activities.

Jack's other hand comes up to cup my breast through my dress, pinching my nipple. The dual stimulation has me panting, my hips rocking back against him.

"Please," I whimper. "I need more."

In one swift motion, Jack withdraws his fingers and spins me to face him again. He lifts me easily, pressing me against the pillar as I wrap my legs around his waist. He fumbles effortlessly with his zipper, and then he's pushing inside me in one long, delicious thrust.

I cry out, not caring who hears. Jack sets a punishing pace, driving into me again and again. The music and the crowd fade away until all I can focus on is the exquisite friction where our bodies join.

Through half-lidded eyes, I see we've drawn quite an audience. Masked figures watch us openly, some touching themselves or their partners as they observe our passionate display.

The knowledge that we're being watched, that we're the center of attention, pushes me closer to the edge. I cling to Jack's shoulders, meeting him thrust for thrust.

My sweet fireman. My WinterWatcher. My stalker. My man— the one man who is willing to give me every fantasy and every dark secret I desire.

"That's it," he urges. "Let them see how beautiful you are when you come. Show them you're mine. Let them watch."

I'm on the cusp, but suddenly I know that I want something different tonight. Something that's just for us. "Jack, wait," I gasp. He slows his thrusts. "I only want you to see me. Just you."

He spins me around and kisses me with a level of hunger I haven't felt from him before. When I pull away I see Jack's eyes blaze with intensity behind his mask. "Home. Now."

We hastily disentangle ourselves, adjusting our clothing as best we can. Jack grabs my hand and practically drags me through the pulsating crowd toward the exit. The winter night air hits us like a shock as we burst out of the club.

"Taxi!" Jack yells, flagging down a passing cab. We tumble into the back seat, a tangle of limbs and lingering desire.

As soon as he gives the address, his mouth is on mine again, hot and demanding. His hands roam my body, reigniting the fire that had barely begun to cool. I moan into the kiss, my fingers threading through his hair.

"God, I want you," he growls against my neck. "I can't wait to get you home and watch you come undone."

The ride seems interminable, but finally we screech to a halt outside my house. Jack throws some bills at the driver and we stumble out, feverish and touching like we can't get enough.

When we get to my front door, he presses me against the wall, his thigh wedged between my legs. I grind shamelessly against him, desperate for friction.

"Patience," he murmurs, nipping at my earlobe. "I want you to go inside, get naked, and spread out on your bed."

I fumble with my keys, my hands shaking with anticipation. As soon as I get the door open, Jack gives me a searing kiss before gently pushing me inside.

"Don't keep me waiting," he says with a devilish grin, closing the door between us.

My heart races as I make my way to the bedroom, shedding clothes as I go. By the time I reach the bed, I'm completely naked. I sprawl out on the sheets, my skin tingling with excitement.

Minutes tick by. I squirm restlessly, wondering what Jack has planned. Just as I'm about to call out for him, I hear a faint tapping sound. My eyes dart to the window, where I see Jack's figure outside lit up by the string of Christmas lights.

He's made good on his promise to watch me from outside. I

rise slowly, making my way to the window with deliberate, sensual movements. When I reach it, I press my palm against the glass, meeting Jack's hungry gaze.

Without breaking eye contact, I trail my other hand down my body, cupping my breast and rolling my nipple between my fingers. Jack's eyes darken with desire, his breath fogging the glass.

My deepest, darkest fantasy come to life.

He's outside. I'm inside, and yet somehow we are closer together than I thought we could be.

I continue my show, sliding my hand lower, dipping between my thighs. Jack's gaze follows every movement, his expression a mix of lust and awe. I circle my clit slowly, putting on a performance just for him.

As I pleasure myself, I imagine Jack's hands on me, his mouth, his cock. My movements become more frantic, my breath coming in short gasps. Jack presses closer to the window. This time, there's no need for secrecy or stealth. I want him here, want him desperately.

The knowledge that he's watching me pushes me over the edge. I come with a cry, my body shuddering against the cool glass. Through half-lidded eyes, I see Jack's face, open and ravenous.

For a moment, we stay frozen like that, separated by a thin pane of glass yet intimately connected.

My stalker. My watcher. Now my lover.

As I catch my breath, I see Jack motion for me to open the window. With trembling hands, I unlatch it and slide it up. The cold night air rushes in, raising goose bumps on my flushed skin.

Jack climbs through gracefully, his eyes never leaving mine. Once inside, he cups my face in his hands and kisses me deeply. I melt into him, savoring the taste of champagne and desire on his lips.

In one swift motion, Jack lifts me and carries me to the bed. He lays me down gently, then steps back to remove his clothes. I watch hungrily as each new expanse of skin is revealed.

Once naked, he joins me on the bed, hovering over me. He presses his forehead to mine. "This time, and every time from now on," he says, his voice husky with desire, "I want to do more than just *watch*."

Keep Reading for a Sneak Peek of

He Knows When You're Awake

CHAPTER ONE
COLE

Three months of watching her every move, and she still manages to surprise me.

I leave my scotch untouched on top of quarterly reports, watching the security feed from Moth to the Flame instead. The image quality is shit, but it's enough.

From my penthouse office, it's possible to see half of Manhattan. But I'm focused on the wall of screens, their glow reflecting off the mahogany panels and marble floor. I built this room to keep tabs on my investments. Now I spend most of my time watching one jewelry designer work.

"Another female entrepreneur gets screwed by the banking system." Knox drops an iPad on my desk, helping himself to my scotch. The Chase Bank rejection letter glows on the screen—standard corporate bullshit about risk factors and lack of collateral. "That's the third one this week. Though I gotta say, this one's different from our usual finds."

He's right. I started monitoring loan rejections from major banks after noticing a pattern—brilliant women with innovative ideas getting shut down by old, outdated men too stupid to see

past their own biases. It became almost a hobby, finding these diamonds in the rough, proving the banks wrong.

But Sloane . . . Sloane Whitmore was something else entirely.

"Run her numbers again."

Knox snorts. "You've got them memorized."

"Humor me."

He flicks through the file on his iPad. The security feed shows
Sloane at her desk, lost in her work. Even with Moth to the Flame's
garbage cameras, I can see the moment inspiration hits.

"All right," Knox says. "Graduated top of her class at Parsons.
Sells more than anyone else at her level but keeps getting passed
over. Went to Moth to the Flame thinking a female boss would get
it." He looks up from the iPad. "But they've got her making the
same cookie-cutter crap as everyone else." A pause. "You know, this
is usually where you tell me how you're going to prove the bank
wrong. But that's not what this is, is it?"

I pull up her latest design. "Take a look."

"Jesus." Knox leans in. The necklace on screen is all sharp angles
and fractured metal. "It's not your average necklace. I'll give you
that."

"This is what they're too stupid to understand." I zoom in on
the detail work. "Everything else this company makes belongs on
a grandmother."

"And Chase won't touch it." Knox tops off our drinks. He's been
with me through enough deals to know where this is going. "Bet
that just makes you want it more."

I just raise an eyebrow. Knox knows me too well for lies.

"Their loss." I turn back to the screens. "Banks keep making the
same mistakes. Makes my job easier."

"Sure." Knox's voice is dry. "That's why you hacked every camera in the building, the camera in her apartment building, and her computer. Because it makes your job easier."

On screen, Sloane runs her hands through her hair in frustration, destroying her usually neat bun. She does this when her boss shoots down her ideas, which happens with infuriating frequency. I've cataloged all her tells by now. The way she talks to herself while working, how she sketches on cocktail napkins at bars when she thinks no one's watching, her secret stash of peppermint tea hidden in her desk drawer.

"The arrangements at Tonic tonight?" I ask, changing the subject.

"Everything's set. Though I still think staging a collision is overthinking it. You could just approach her like a normal person." Knox's tone suggests he knows exactly how likely that is. "But since you're determined to be extra about this, the bartender will direct her to the right spot, your scotch will be perfectly positioned, and your ridiculously expensive suit is ready to be sacrificed to the cause."

I check my watch. Through the cameras, I see Sloane pack up for the day, carefully storing her latest designs in that battered portfolio she carries everywhere. The same portfolio that will soon hold the collection she'll create for me.

She just doesn't know it yet.

She also reaches for a sweater she had delivered to her office a couple of days ago.

"So she's still wearing that sweater tonight? Christ, it's got actual antlers."

"Battery-powered lights too." I don't mention how I know this. That I watched her open the package, saw her face light up like the ridiculous sweater itself. "Cost her nearly a day's pay."

"How would you even know—" Knox stops himself.

"Annual tradition with her friend Chloe." I tap the screen where Sloane's grinning at the sweater. "They hit Tonic every December. Ugly sweaters, expensive drinks they can barely afford. Been doing it since college."

"You could've just followed her Instagram and saved all this stalking time." Knox scrolls through his phone. "Look, there they are last year. Same bar, same ridiculous sweaters."

"That's the cleaned-up version." I turn back to the feed where Sloane's now shoving prototypes into her bottom drawer. The ones her boss would hate. "People show what they think others want to see. She's guilty of that."

"And you prefer the unfiltered version." It's not a question. Knox has watched me build and break enough empires to know how I operate.

He sighs, the sound of a man who's seen me go down obsessive rabbit holes before, but never on one person. Never like this.

"There's something about her that's already getting under your skin."

He's right, though I'm not ready to examine why. I've built my empire on finding undervalued assets, on seeing potential others miss. But Sloane . . .

"Time to go," I say instead of answering, standing to adjust my cuffs in the window's reflection. The Manhattan skyline spreads out behind me, a glittering empire of steel and glass. "The scotch needs to hit my suit at precisely the right moment."

"You know normal people just ask women out for coffee, right?" Knox follows me through my office, past walls of awards and acquisitions that suddenly seem meaningless compared to the port-folio Sloane carries everywhere. "They don't orchestrate elaborate meet-cutes involving property damage."

"Since when have I ever been normal?"

The elevator doors slide open silently to my private garage, where a sleek black Bentley waits. The car's interior smells of leather and power, everything as I like it. Everything controlled.

I check my watch one last time as Knox slides behind the wheel. In exactly thirty-seven minutes, Sloane Whitmore will walk into Tonic wearing that ridiculous sweater, looking out of place among the suits and cocktail dresses. My guess is she'll try to make herself smaller, less noticeable.

But I'll notice.

Through the tinted windows, I watch my tower recede into the Manhattan skyline. I can imagine on the screens we're leaving behind, Sloane stepping into a taxi. She'll be trying to figure out her next move after another rejection, another setback. What she doesn't realize is every closed door has been leading her exactly where I want her.

To me.

CHAPTER TWO

SLOANE

I'm already regretting this sweater.

The reindeer's nose blinks accusingly as I squeeze through Tonic's crowded entryway, feeling like a walking Christmas tree in a sea of sleek cocktail attire. A guy in an impeccable suit gives me a look of barely concealed disdain as I accidentally jostle his martini. I mumble an apology, not that he hears or would care.

The bartender catches my eye and nods toward an open spot at the far end of the bar. I silently thank whatever Christmas spirit guided me here as I make my way over, the blinking reindeer nose on my sweater creating a small red beacon in the dim light.

I'm early, and I know Chloe won't be here for another ten minutes at least. I scan the room, searching for a familiar face, but find only strangers. The contrast between their polished appearances and my garish sweater makes me want to sink into the floor.

Which frankly is unlike me. I'm normally confident in who I am and what I do, but ever since I began this process of starting my own jewelry line, I've felt like a fish out of water. Every rejection letter, every condescending meeting with potential investors. It's all chipped away at the certainty I once had in my self-worth.

I flag down the bartender, desperately in need of liquid courage. "Peppermint martini, please."

As he nods and turns to make my drink, I pull out my phone, needing something to do with my hands. No new emails. No missed calls. Just the same deafening silence that's followed every pitch and proposal I've sent out.

I'm so focused on my screen that I don't notice the man approaching until it's too late. I take a step back, right as he's moving forward with a glass of amber liquid. There's a moment of suspended time where I see it all happening but can't stop it—my elbow connecting with his arm, the arc of expensive scotch as it flies through the air, the look of surprise on his face.

Then time catches up, and I feel the splash of liquid against my chest, soaking through the ridiculous sweater.

"Oh my god, I'm so sorry!" I exclaim, mortified. I grab for the cocktail napkins on the bar, dabbing ineffectually at his perfectly tailored suit jacket. "I wasn't looking where I was going, I—"

I look up, and the words die in my throat.

He's gorgeous. Tall, with dark hair and eyes that seem to look right through me. But it's not just his looks. There's an aura of power around him, like he's used to commanding every room he enters. And right now, those penetrating brown eyes are fixed solely on me.

"No harm done," he says, his voice a low rumble that I feel in my chest. "Though I think your reindeer might need resuscitation."

I glance down to see that the scotch has shorted out the battery pack for my sweater's lights. The nose blinks weakly a few times before going dark.

"Rudolph, nooo," I deadpan. "He was so young."

The man's lips quirk up in a half-smile that shouldn't make my heart skip a beat but does. "A tragic loss. I feel partially responsible. Maybe I can make it up to you with a drink?"

I should say no. I'm here to meet Chloe, to commiserate over peppermint martinis about the state of my life and career. I don't have time for distractions, no matter how devastatingly handsome they might be.

But something in his gaze holds me there, makes me want to say yes to whatever he's offering.

"I suppose it's the least you can do, considering you've ruined my favorite holiday attire," I find myself saying.

He signals to the bartender, who appears with two glasses of scotch—instead of my peppermint martini, but who am I to criticize—before I can even blink. I raise an eyebrow at the efficiency, wondering if this man has the entire bar staff at his beck and call.

"To new beginnings," he says, raising his glass. "And sweaters that die heroically in the line of duty."

I smile as I clink my glass against his. The scotch burns pleasantly as it goes down, warming me from the inside out. It's easily the most expensive thing I've tasted in months.

"I'm Cole," he says, those intense eyes never leaving mine. "And you are?"

"Sloane," I reply, suddenly very aware of how ridiculous I must look in this damp, no longer light-up sweater. "Sloane Whitmore."

Something flashes in his eyes at my name, gone so quickly I wonder if I imagined it.

"Sloane Whitmore," Cole repeats, as if savoring the sound of my name. "A pleasure to meet you, despite the circumstances."

It's then that I notice that it's not just my sweater that has the drink on it. Cole's expensive suit jacket is also stained with scotch, a dark patch spreading across his chest.

"Oh god, your suit," I say, mortified all over again. "I'm so sorry. I'll pay for the dry cleaning, of course."

Cole waves off my concern with a dismissive gesture. "It's just a suit. Easily replaced." His eyes lock onto mine again, intense and searching. "I'm curious about the woman brave enough to wear a light-up reindeer sweater to Tonic on a Friday night."

A blush creeps up my neck at his scrutiny. "It's a tradition," I explain, fiddling with my now-dark reindeer nose. "My best friend and I do this every year. Ugly sweaters and peppermint martinis to kick off the holiday season."

"Ah, so there's more to the story," Cole says, leaning in slightly. The scent of his cologne, something woodsy and expensive, makes my head spin. Or maybe that's the scotch. "Tell me, what does Sloane Whitmore do when she's not electrocuting reindeer?"

I hesitate, unsure how to answer. My job at Moth to the Flame feels increasingly like a cage, while my dreams of starting my own line seem further away than ever. But something in Cole's gaze makes me want to be honest.

"I'm a jewelry designer," I say finally. "Or at least, I'm trying to be. Right now I mostly design what other people tell me to create."

Cole's eyes light up with interest. "A creator, then. What kind of jewelry do you design when left to your own devices?"

The question catches me off guard. It's been so long since anyone asked about my personal vision rather than what will sell or what fits the brand.

"I . . . I create pieces that tell stories," I say, surprising myself with my candor. "Not the pretty, delicate things most people expect.

My designs are about contrast. Beauty with an edge. The interplay of light and shadow, strength and vulnerability."

I pause, realizing I'm rambling. But Cole is watching me intently, genuinely interested. It emboldens me to continue.

"My latest collection, the one I'm trying to launch, it's called Midnight Frost. It's inspired by those moments just before dawn in the dead of winter, when everything is still and silent and dangerous. One slip on the ice can break everything. The way ice can be both breathtakingly beautiful and lethal. To be frank, my designs have a BDSM vibe, but I can't exactly tell possible investors that."

What. The. Fuck?!?

Why did I just include that last part? What the hell is wrong with me?

Cole's eyes seem to darken as I speak, a hint of something hungry in his gaze.

Needing to recover fast, I add, "I actually have some sketches on my phone," I reach for my purse. "I always have them handy, just in case I run into someone who—"

"Sloane!" Chloe's voice cuts through the moment. I turn to see her weaving through the crowd, her own ugly sweater a riot of tinsel and blinking lights.

I glance back at Cole. This man is clearly out of my league, probably just being polite to the clumsy woman who ruined his expensive suit. But there's something in his eyes that makes me hesitate to dismiss our encounter so easily.

"I should go," I say reluctantly. "My friend . . ."

Cole nods, understanding. "I won't keep you from your tradition."

But as I start to turn away, he catches my hand. The touch of Cole's fingertips sends an electric current up my arm. His skin is warm, his grip firm but gentle.

Our eyes lock for a moment, and I feel like I'm standing on ice, about to slip and fall. Then Chloe's hand is on my arm, tugging me away, and the spell is broken.

"Oh my god, what happened to Rudolph?" she asks as we make our way to a table.

I glance back over my shoulder, but Cole has already melted into the crowd with a grace that seems impossible for someone of his size.

"It's a long story," I say, unable to keep the wistfulness out of my voice. "Involving a very expensive scotch and a very handsome stranger."

Chloe's eyes widen with interest. "Ooh, do tell! Was he hot? Rich? Both?"

I laugh, settling into our usual booth. "Definitely both. But it doesn't matter. He was just being nice after I ruined his suit."

"Sure, sure," Chloe says, clearly not buying it. "That's why you look like you've been hit by a truck. A very sexy truck."

I roll my eyes, but I can feel heat rising up to my cheeks. "Can we just order our drinks and pretend I'm not a walking disaster?"

The waitress arrives, and we place our usual order of peppermint martinis. As she walks away, Chloe leans in, her expression turning serious.

"So, how did it go today? Any word from the banks?"

I sigh, the brief spark of excitement from my encounter with Cole fading. "Another rejection. Apparently, my 'lack of collateral' and 'unproven market potential' make me too risky."

Chloe reaches across the table to squeeze my hand. "Their loss. Your designs are amazing, Sloane. Someone's going to see that eventually."

"Maybe," I say, not entirely convinced. "But right now, it feels like I'm screaming into the void. No one wants to take a chance on something different."

Our drinks arrive, and I take a long sip, letting the cool peppermint wash away the taste of disappointment. The familiar flavors remind me of past Christmases, of the excitement and hope I used to feel at this time of year. Now, it just feels like one more reminder of dreams deferred.

"I've been thinking," I say slowly, tracing patterns in the condensation on my glass. "Maybe it's time for a change. A big one."

Chloe leans forward, intrigued. "What kind of change are we talking about here?"

I take a deep breath, finally voicing the idea that's been growing in my mind for weeks. "I'm thinking of leaving Moth to the Flame. Diving off the cliff with no safety net. I need to do something drastic to make this dream of mine happen."

"Wow," Chloe breathes. "That's . . . that's huge. Are you sure?"

I nod, feeling a mix of terror and exhilaration at the thought. "I'm suffocating there, Chlo. Every day, I'm forced to create things that don't represent me, that don't challenge anyone or anything. If I stay, I'll lose myself completely."

Chloe studies me, her brow furrowed in concern. "I get it, I do. But how will you support yourself? You said the banks won't give you a loan."

I take another sip of my martini, steeling myself. "I've been saving every penny I can. It's not much, but it's enough to get started. I figure I have about three months of runway before I'd have to start waiting tables or something."

"Three months isn't a lot of time," Chloe points out gently.

"I know," I admit. "But I have to try. If I don't do this now, I never will."

Chloe nods slowly, a smile spreading across her face. "You know what? You're right. It's time for Sloane Whitmore to take over the world with her badass jewelry."

I laugh, feeling some of the tension leave my shoulders. "I don't know about taking over the world. I'd settle for making enough to pay rent and keep designing."

"Oh please," Chloe scoffs. "Your stuff is incredible. Once people see it, you'll be the next big thing. I can see it now—'Sloane Whitmore: The Dark Rose of Manhattan Jewelry Scene.'"

I nearly choke on my drink. "The Dark Rose? Really?"

Chloe grins. "Hey, every designer needs a dramatic nickname. Might as well claim yours early."

"I think the nickname needs work." I laugh, shaking my head at Chloe's enthusiasm.

But beneath the amusement, I feel a spark of something I haven't felt in months—hope. Maybe she's right. Maybe this is my moment to finally show the world what I can do.

As we finish our drinks, I can't resist the urge to scan the bar, wondering if I'll catch another glimpse of Cole. But the crowd has thinned, and there's no sign of his commanding presence.

"Earth to Sloane," Chloe says, waving a hand in front of my face. "You're thinking about Mr. Expensive Scotch, aren't you?"

I feel my face heat. "No, I was just . . . okay, maybe a little."

Chloe grins. "I knew it. Spill. What exactly happened before I got here?"

I recount the collision, the ruined sweater, and our brief conversation. As I describe Cole's interest in my designs, I find myself wishing I'd had the courage to show him my sketches.

"Sounds like you made quite an impression," Chloe says, wiggling her eyebrows suggestively.

I roll my eyes. "Please. He was just being polite after I ruined his suit. Besides, men like that don't go for women who wear light-up reindeer sweaters and can't afford their own scotch."

"Don't sell yourself short," Chloe insists. "You're brilliant, talented, and gorgeous. Any man would be lucky to have you spill drinks on him."

"Thanks, Chlo. But right now, I need to focus on my career, not some random encounter with a handsome stranger."

"Fair enough," she concedes. "So, what's the plan? How are we launching the Sloane Whitmore collection?"

I take a deep breath, suddenly feeling the weight of my decision. "First, I need to give notice at Moth to the Flame. Then I'll need to find a small studio space, maybe sublet something in the Garment District. I've got some contacts from fashion week who might be interested in featuring a piece or two . . ."

As I outline my fledgling plans, I feel a mix of excitement and terror. This is really happening. I'm really doing this.

"You've got this," Chloe says, squeezing my hand. "And I'll be here every step of the way. Even if that means modeling your pieces in my pajamas at three a.m."

I laugh, picturing Chloe draped in my edgy designs while wearing her favorite fuzzy cat pajamas. "I might take you up on that." Changing the subject, I ask, "Do you and Jack have any big holiday plans this year?" I love that my friend is in a happy relationship, but a small part of me is envious. Jack is exactly the kind of supportive partner I've always dreamed of having.

"Staying put since he'll have to work. But I'm actually looking forward to another Christmas at the fire station this year. What about you? Are you going to Montauk?"

I shake my head, feeling a familiar pang of loneliness. "Not this year. I really need to focus on my line."

Chloe's brow furrows again. "Sloane, you can't work through Christmas. Your family will be devastated."

I shrug, trying to seem nonchalant. "They'll understand. This is important."

"So is family," Chloe counters gently. "Promise me you'll at least take some time off on Christmas Day?"

"Of course," I assure her, though the thought of explaining my decision to my parents over the phone fills me with dread. They've never quite understood my passion for jewelry design, always pushing me toward more "practical" career paths.

"One more for the road?" Chloe asks, signaling the waitress.

I hesitate, glancing at my watch. It's getting late, and I should probably head home to start working on my resignation letter. But the warmth of the bar and Chloe's company are comforting, a buffer against the uncertainty that awaits me.

"Sure," I say, smiling. "One more."

As the waitress brings our final round, I scan the bar one last time. No sign of Cole. I try to push away the disappointment, reminding myself that I have bigger things to focus on.

"To new beginnings," Chloe says, raising her glass. "And to the soon-to-be-famous Sloane Whitmore, the Dark Rose of Manhattan."

I laugh, clinking my glass against hers. "Oh god, that nickname is going to stick."

We finish our drinks, chatting about Chloe's latest freelance gig and her plans with Jack for the holidays. As we gather our things to leave, I'm both relaxed from the booze and energized by the possibilities of what's ahead.

Outside, the cold December air hits me like a slap, making me acutely aware of my still-damp sweater. I pull my coat tighter around me as Chloe hails a cab.

"Text me when you get home," she says, hugging me tight. "And let me know if you need anything, okay? I mean it. Anything at all."

I nod, grateful for her unwavering support. "I will. Thanks, Chlo. For everything."

As her cab pulls away, I decide to walk for a bit, needing to clear my head before heading home. The streets of Manhattan are alive with holiday spirit—twinkling lights, the scent of roasted chestnuts, the faint sound of carols drifting from storefronts. The city is bustling with early holiday shoppers and tourists, and I weave my way through the crowds, my mind still preoccupied with thoughts of my resignation.

It all feels surreal, like I'm watching someone else's life unfold.

But as I walk, something shifts inside me. Maybe it's the festive atmosphere or the sight of families bundled up and laughing together. Or maybe it's just a moment of clarity brought on by Chloe's words at the bar.

Either way, I find myself questioning my decision to leave my job without a backup plan.

Am I insane . . .

Yes, my boss is difficult to work for and the company culture stifling, but it's a steady paycheck and steady clients. My heart sinks as I realize that this may all be coming to an end. My dream of becoming a successful independent jeweler may not be as realistic as I had hoped.

I find myself stopping in front of a jewelry store window, drawn in by the glittering display. The pieces are beautiful, but safe.

Predictable. Nothing like the edgy, boundary-pushing designs I dream of creating.

"Is this really what you want?" I whisper to my reflection in the glass. The woman staring back at me looks uncertain, her ridiculous sweater a stark contrast to the polished luxury behind the glass.

But then I see something else in my reflection. A spark of determination in my eyes. I straighten my shoulders, lifting my chin. Yes, this is what I want. More than anything.

ABOUT THE AUTHOR

ALTA HENSLEY is a *USA Today* bestselling author of hot, dark and dirty romance. She lives in Astoria, Oregon, with her husband, two daughters, and an Australian shepherd. When she isn't walking the coastline and drinking beer in her favorite breweries, she is writing about villains who always get their love story and happily ever after.